By Kimberla Lawson Roby

KIMBERLA LAWSON ROBY

The Best-Kept Secret

HARPER

An Imprint of HarperCollins*Publishers*

This is a work of fiction. Names, characters, places, and incidents are products of the author's imagination or are used fictitiously and are not to be construed as real. Any resemblance to actual events, locales, organizations, or persons, living or dead, is entirely coincidental.

HARPER

An Imprint of HarperCollins*Publishers*
10 East 53rd Street
New York, New York 10022-5299

Copyright © 2005 by Kimberla Lawson Roby
ISBN 978-0-06-226845-7

First Harper special mass market printing: February 2013
First Avon Books paperback printing: January 2006
First William Morrow hardcover printing: February 2005

Visit Harper paperbacks on the World Wide Web at
www.harpercollins.com

10 9 8 7 6 5 4 3 2 1

For Lori Whitaker Thurman

For Kelli Tunson Bullard

Two women who epitomize the essence of true friendship.
Two women who always remember to be there for me.
Two women who I will always be there for also.

The Best-Kept Secret

Chapter 1

THE REVEREND CURTIS BLACK PROOFED THE LAST LINE OF HIS NEWS column and e-mailed it to his editor. His deadline was noon tomorrow, and that meant he was cutting it rather close. Not purposely, of course, but primarily because he'd taken on a large number of commitments over the past month. Last week, he'd preached at a revival in Dallas five days straight, prepared his sermon for Sunday worship, and handled a ton of other pastoral responsibilities as soon as he returned to Mitchell, a city ninety miles northwest of Chicago.

Once upon a time, he would have thrived on traveling long distance, just to escape his home environment or whatever wife he was married to, but to his surprise, he no longer felt that way. Now he wanted nothing more than to spend as much time as possible with his wife and seven-year-old son. Charlotte and Matthew were his life, and he was proud of the fact that he'd been faithful to her the entire two years of their marriage. Which was quite an accomplishment on his part, since he hadn't been true to either of his first two wives. He'd finally mastered the ability to resist temptation, and his world was better because of it. Still, he had to admit, it wasn't always easy, not with two noticeably attractive women at the church constantly trying to come on to him. The forty-year-old was quiet and discreet with her advances, but the younger one was almost blatant. It didn't matter one way or the other, though, because Curtis basically ignored them. He'd learned the hard way that sleeping with outside women just wasn't worth it.

He flipped the light switch of his newly renovated study, engaged the security system, and walked out to the well-lit parking lot. After sitting inside his Cadillac SUV, the same one he'd driven for three years, he turned the ignition and drove away from the church. Life was a lot different, now that they were living in Mitchell, but Curtis couldn't be happier. True, he was no longer earning five thousand per week, residing in a six-thousand-square-foot house, or preaching to a three-thousand-plus congregation, but based on Mitchell's cost of living, he wasn't doing badly, especially since he and Charlotte had founded Deliverance Outreach the first month of their relocation. They'd started out with maybe fifty members during the first six months, increased to just over a hundred the first year, and now they were easily five hundred strong. Curtis had built a well-known ministry that drew people in, but it certainly hadn't hurt when another local pastor had retired and some of those members had sought a new church home. It also hadn't hurt when he approached the local newspaper about doing a weekly column.

Before arriving in Mitchell, he'd written a church business plan, and when he'd realized he needed something that would get people stirred up and taking notice of him, he'd decided to submit a column to the *Mitchell Post*. The features editor was clearly interested but, after deciding that the material was a bit controversial, she asked Curtis to rethink some of his subject matter. He wasn't happy about the request but decided to do whatever he needed to in order to get his work published.

In the beginning, he'd centered his column on polite topics such as the importance of going to church on Sunday, the reason families needed to pray together, what couples should do when their marriages were falling apart. But three months later, his editor left for vacation, and Curtis snatched his golden opportunity. His interim editor was much more liberal and quickly approved a piece that Curtis had written on atheism, its effect on society and how nonbelievers were going straight to hell. And as Curtis suspected, letters to the editor poured in at an unusual rate. Days later, the editor in chief called a meeting with Curtis and offered him more control over his topics, which ranged from teenage sex to gang violence to adultery, the latter being something Curtis knew a lot about. But once a month, he crafted inspirational messages, hoping to motivate his readers, and he was almost finished writing his first book, *How to Have Almost Everything You Want.* His editor in chief was also talking possible syndication for his column.

When Curtis arrived home, Matthew rushed toward him with a piece of paper.

"Dad, look what I have," he said, beaming and hugging his father around his waist.

Curtis took the sheet of paper from his son and playfully grabbed him in a headlock. "What's this?"

"It's a permission slip for the Milwaukee zoo!"

"Wow. So you're going to the zoo, huh?"

"Yep. And my teacher said that they need something called chaperones, too."

"Really? And what exactly is a chaperone?"

"I'm not sure. But I think you could be one if you wanted, because she told us to ask our parents."

"Is that so? Well, just so you know, a chaperone is an adult who escorts young children. They sort of watch over them."

"Oh. Well, I really want you to go, okay?"

Curtis smiled at his son with all the love any child could stand.

"You know I wouldn't miss it for the world."

"Wait 'til I tell Jonathan and Elijah," he announced. "We're gonna have so much fun."

Matthew brushed past his mother and ran back upstairs.

Charlotte smiled at her little boy, then strutted into the kitchen and over to Curtis.

"Hi, baby," she said.

"Hey, beautiful." Curtis pulled her into his arms and kissed her.

"What was that all about?"

"Field trip. His class is going to the zoo, and I told him I'd be a chaperone."

"That little booger. He never said one word to *me* about any trip."

"What can I say? Maybe he prefers spending time with his father," Curtis teased, still holding his wife closely.

"That he does. Matthew is definitely a daddy's boy."

"That doesn't bother you, does it?"

"Not at all. Nothing makes me happier than when I see the two of you together. Even with all your church obligations, you spend a lot of time with Matthew, and I'm really thankful for that."

"And baby, I'm thankful for you. Very few women would have stuck by me. Not with everything I did and went through. But you still loved me no matter what. You've been the best wife, and I can't thank you enough for being so supportive and so dedicated to the church. I love you so much," he said and kissed her again. Curtis didn't want to let her go. He wished he could hold her in his arms for the rest of his days, because for the first time ever, he felt content. He felt as though God had forgiven him for all his transgressions and was allowing him another chance to do the right thing.

Charlotte loosened her embrace. "I hate to end this, sweetheart, but duty calls."

"Baby, not tonight?" Curtis protested.

"Unfortunately, yes. I hate going back in, but the partners are working double time on this wrongful death case. And as their paralegal, I have to do the same. But after this week, I won't have to put in so many hours because it looks like the trial will be over in a few days. We've finally got them cornered. And there's a chance that the company we're suing will be offering our client a huge settlement."

Curtis tried to be excited for Charlotte, especially since her eyes always lit up whenever she spoke about her work, but in reality, he wanted her to quit and work full-time at the church. They'd discussed it a few times before, but Charlotte was clear on her disapproval. She worked for a top law firm in Mitchell, which was a privilege since she only had two years of work experience, but Curtis still wanted her by his side. He wanted them to concentrate on building their ministry.

Charlotte pecked Curtis on the lips, apologized again for having to leave, and went upstairs to throw on a jogging suit. Curtis walked down into the sunken family room, shed his blazer, and collapsed on the plush, oversized sofa. He scanned his surroundings and realized how satisfied he was with the way Charlotte had decorated their home. Every room had a distinct color scheme, and this was the red room. The living room was adorned in black and white, the dining room in off-white, and the kitchen displayed hues of browns, tans, and various shades of orange. Their master suite was graced with rich purples and greens, Matthew's room was consumed with masculine blues, and the guest bedroom with dark and light teals.

Curtis turned on the television and then glanced at the fireplace mantel lined with photos. At first, he smiled, but when he saw the picture of Alicia, his sixteen-year-old daughter, his spirit dropped instantly. It was hard to forget about all the pain he'd caused for so many people. Seven years ago, he was ousted from a large Baptist church in Chicago due to his obsession with money, power, and women and, as a result, lost his first wife, Tanya, to her current husband. He'd also lost part of his daughter's love. Alicia had even witnessed one of the deacons telling the entire congregation that Curtis had been sleeping with Adrienne, the deacon's wife, and that Curtis had paid for Adrienne to have an abortion. Alicia had only been nine at the time and was devastated. Then, after leaving the ministry for five years, Curtis was offered another pastoral position at an even larger church and then married his second wife, Mariah. He could still kick himself for not being faithful to her. If he had, things surely would have turned out differently. He never would have started seeing Adrienne again, and she never would have shot him down from his own pulpit and then turned the gun on herself. It had been an absolute nightmare and the reason Curtis had made the decision to relocate. He'd wanted to move to a city like Mitchell where there were only one hundred fifty thousand residents. That way, he and Charlotte could found their own church and start their lives afresh. He'd wanted to give Matthew a normal, decent life, and thus far, they'd been able to do that. But the worst of all was that horrid incident Alicia had experienced at fourteen. She'd been begging Curtis to spend more time with her and acting out in obvious ways to gain his attention, but he hadn't taken her seriously. Not because he didn't want to, but because he'd had so many other responsibilities on his plate, and because he just didn't think she'd resort to anything dangerous. But to his regret, she had. She'd formed an online relationship with a seemingly nice young boy who, in person, turned out to be a twenty-one-year-old drug dealer. She'd allowed him to pick her up from school and take her to his apartment, but when she refused to give him what he wanted, he took it anyway.

Charlotte and Matthew entered the family room, and Matthew dropped down next to Curtis, playing his Game Boy.

"Dad, let's order a pizza."

"Pizza? Don't you ever get tired of that?"

"Nope. I could eat it over and over and over, every single day."

"Apparently, so. But I was thinking more along the lines of Thai."

"What's that?"

"It's similar to Chinese. And I know you like Chinese."

"Yeah, but I *want* pizza."

Charlotte smiled at Curtis. "Sorry."

"So what time will you be finished?" Curtis asked.

"I don't know, but I promise I'll be home as soon as I can. I'm hoping I won't have to be there more than a couple of hours."

"We'll miss you," Curtis said.

Charlotte kissed Curtis on the lips and their son on his cheek.

"I'll miss you guys, too. Oh, and Matthew has some homework that needs to be checked. Right, Matthew?"

"Uh-huh."

"Don't worry, we'll take care of it. You just go so you can get back here."

"I love you, too," Charlotte said and headed toward the garage.

When she left, Curtis double-tapped the back of Matthew's head, provoking a father-and-son wrestling match.

Chapter 2

CHARLOTTE COULDN'T REMEMBER EVER FEELING THE WAY SHE FELT right now.

"Oh my God, Aaron. Baby . . . you . . . are . . . driving . . . me . . . crazy," she said between breaths. She was lying facedown across the king-size bed, savoring every moment of what she was getting: a very intense tongue-lashing.

Aaron Malone was six foot two and, ironically enough, reminded her of Curtis. Most people assumed they were brothers since they had the same muscular build and deep-mocha complexion. In a word, they were both gorgeous. The only difference was, Curtis had recently turned forty, and Aaron was five years his junior. Charlotte was ten years younger than that. But at twenty-five, she felt much older and wanted nothing to do with any man she was close in age to.

Aaron slid his tongue in and out of Charlotte's ear, slowly and gently maneuvering across her neck. He mimicked the same exercise again and again and then rolled his tongue down the center of her back. He outlined her entire backbone. He worked his way toward her buttocks, licking back and forth and then returning to the starting position. Charlotte moaned deeply and wondered if she had died and gone to heaven.

Aaron suddenly raised his body from her. "Turn over for me."

Charlotte gracefully obeyed and rested her head on two pillows.

Aaron locked his fingers inside hers and kissed her forcefully. She felt him growing harder and wanted to explode. They kissed wildly, and Aaron swerved his lower body, torturing but not entering her. Then, he moved his tongue inside her ear again, across the front of her neck, and devoured her breasts one at a time. Charlotte didn't know how much more of this man she could take. She needed him inside her right now. But she knew he loved extended foreplay. He loved pleasuring her, so she never argued with him. She never tried stopping him from doing what he did best.

Aaron slid his body closer to the foot of the bed and flicked his tongue across her stomach with featherlike strokes. Charlotte closed her eyes, waiting for his grand performance.

"Hey," he said. "You know I love you, right?"

"Yes, baby."

"And that I would do anything for you?"

"Yes."

"Then promise you won't ever try to end what we have."

"You know I would *never* do that, Aaron."

Charlotte pulled him toward her and kissed him ravenously. Aaron pulled away, stared at her for a few seconds, and then nestled his head between her legs. Charlotte arched her back, caressing the sides of his face with her thighs, groaning and twisting her body with excitement. She was unquestionably on fire. Aaron loved her in perfect rhythm, and in seconds, Charlotte released one hot flame after another.

Then, like a reflex, Aaron eased inside her. He moaned loudly, working his groove fast and furiously. Sweat beaded on his skin, and Charlotte labored right along with him. They loved each other to an extreme, their hearts beating accordingly. The climax was as satisfying as always.

Aaron lay there, wordless and spent. Charlotte tried to rid herself of the guilt she was feeling. She knew what they were doing was flat-out wrong, but she just couldn't get enough of Aaron. She couldn't stop thinking about this man who, for the last two years, had been Curtis's closest friend in Mitchell— and still was. Aaron was also a member of the church's governing committee and the one person at Deliverance, besides Charlotte, who Curtis trusted completely. He trusted Aaron, because to Curtis's knowledge, there was no reason not to. The mere thought of that made Charlotte feel worse. She'd even tried to break things off with Aaron, but it never worked. She tried, but she always ended up back in bed with him.

At first, she'd only been attracted to Aaron and never planned on taking things further. But eventually, they became close friends, and she found herself sharing secret information about her past and also her discontent with Curtis. Soon they were checking into hotel rooms on a regular basis. They'd had sex in every way possible, including ways that were probably illegal in certain states. They literally craved each other, and Charlotte didn't know how she was ever going to end these trysts of theirs. She didn't love Aaron, but she needed him.

If only Curtis had delivered the great and wonderful life he'd promised her, this might not be happening. While married to his first two wives he'd earned three and five thousand per week, respectively, was given a housing allowance and luxury vehicle, and received upward of fifty thousand dollars per year from love offerings and anniversary gifts. Now, though, he barely earned two thousand dollars a week and it wasn't enough for her. It wasn't even close. She expected and needed so much more than that, but Curtis kept insisting that she look at the bigger picture. He reminded her that if they stuck to the plan, she'd have everything she'd ever dreamed of. But two long years of mediocrity had caused her to lose a certain amount of respect for Curtis and was one of the reasons she slept with Aaron every chance she got. She was starting to feel as though she'd signed some get-rich-quick contract that hadn't paid what it was supposed to. Curtis, on the other hand, had gotten everything he wanted—that church, which she couldn't care less about, and the son he wanted to raise so badly. Actually, if it hadn't been for Matthew, she would probably leave Curtis. It wasn't like she couldn't live without him, and she was tired of all the pretending she did on Sunday mornings, anyway. Curtis didn't know it, but she hated being first lady of their church. Hated the label and all the expectations that went along with it. So Curtis could forget about her ever leaving her job, because it just wasn't happening.

Then there were these flashes from the past that she tried hard not to think about; namely, Curtis taking advantage of her when she was only seventeen and his getting her pregnant. He'd been much too old to be having sex with her, and though it hadn't mattered to her back then or in recent years, it was now starting to anger her.

But she knew she was mainly searching for reasons that would justify what she was doing. She and Aaron were definitely betraying Curtis, and there was simply no denying it. He would kill both of them if he ever found out. She was sure of it.

"So." Aaron exhaled. "Curtis was making a big deal about you working overtime, huh?"

"Yeah, he was."

"Oh well. I mean, I do feel for my boy and all, but I'm not about to give you up under any circumstances. Not the best thing that has ever happened to me. So Curtis might as well get used to you spending time away from home."

"I just wish we didn't have to sneak around like this, and I wish the two of you weren't friends. It makes all of this so uncomfortable."

"Maybe. But it is what it is. And if we hadn't become friends, and I hadn't joined the church, you and I never would have met."

"True, but I still think we're playing with fire."

"Well, if you'd take my advice, we wouldn't have to hide any part of our relationship."

"No. I've already told you. I can't leave Curtis, because I would never take Matthew away from his father. Curtis may not be what I want him to be, but he is definitely a good father to his son."

"He's not what you want him to be because he doesn't make the big bucks anymore."

Aaron laughed, but Charlotte turned her back to him. She knew he was telling the truth.

"I'm just kidding," he said.

"I don't see anything funny."

"I'm sure you don't, but how many times have you told me that you expected to have so much more by marrying Curtis?"

"Well, if he'd stop trying to be the perfect minister and perfect family man, he just might earn some real money. The Curtis I used to know would stop at nothing to get what he wanted. He'd have schemes going on all the time, but now he's focused on this newspaper column, and, of all things, he's writing a book. I mean, what kind of pipe dream is that?"

"I don't know, but he believes in what he's doing, and you have to admit, that column is the reason some people even buy a paper now."

"Yeah, but he's not making any real money from it," Charlotte added.

"He will if it goes into syndication."

"Maybe, but I'm concerned with the here and now. I love my job, but if Curtis earned a lot more than what he does, I could at least have the option to quit if I wanted to."

"Then you'd be free to work at the church full-time," Aaron said, smirking.

"Yeah, right. I think you and I both know that that's out of the question."

"Well, that's what Curtis wants." Aaron caressed Charlotte's back. "He talks about it all the time."

"Well, it's not happening. Not now, not ever."

"I hear you. But hey, on a different note, what was up with Sister Hamilton last Sunday? She must have walked in and out of the sanctuary at least three times."

"Please. That woman was just tryin' to be seen. She had on a new outfit and whenever that happens, she does all that parading. But then, next Sunday, when she wears something we've already seen, she'll be shouting across the entire church. It's so ridiculous."

"Actually, there's a ton of fakers at Deliverance if you ask me," Aaron added. "And what cracks me up is that the same people do the same things like clockwork. Sister Simmons passes out as soon as the choir finishes singing, Sister Thompson speaks in tongues as soon as Curtis finishes his sermon, and Sister Amos screams at the top of her lungs during altar prayer."

"Hmmph. As far as I'm concerned, *all* those women are touched. And I don't mean by the Holy Ghost either."

Aaron laughed at Charlotte. "You might be right about that."

"And if I'm not, then they're basically just putting on a show. Trying to make everyone believe they're so righteous."

"Well, we all know that actions don't mean a thing when it comes to church folks."

"Isn't that the truth," Charlotte said, laughing. "Sister Norris went around every single day, talking about God and what he was doing for her. Did it the whole first year she was a member. And every time you asked her how she was doing, the answer was 'just blessed.' I mean, my goodness."

"Well, you know that's the answer a lot of people give these days. It's almost like some sort of fad statement. You can tell that some people are sincere with it, but others are just saying it because it sounds good."

"Maybe, but Sister Norris shouldn't ever fix her lips to say much of anything after coming up pregnant the way she did. Knowing she didn't have husband the first. What a joke."

"I didn't even know she had a boyfriend. Because whenever you heard her talk, she made it seem like sex was something dirty. Let her tell it, people shouldn't even be kissing in certain ways."

"Now you know why I don't like playing this first lady role. I'm not feeling a lot of those members, and to be honest, I have no desire to sit in church every Wednesday night or Sunday morning. And don't get me started on all those extra services and meetings."

"Well, what did you expect? You married a minister."

"Yeah, but I want things to run on my terms. I want the

power and the money, but that's pretty much where it ends with me. It may be wrong, but that's the way I feel."

Aaron moved his body onto Charlotte's. "Well, you could leave Curtis and marry me. Right?"

"You know I can't do that."

"Why? Because regular people don't have the same money or prestige as big-time ministers?"

"You know that's not it," she lied. "I've already told you why."

Aaron smiled and then turned serious. "Well, regardless, I'm never giving you up. Curtis might have the marriage license, but I'll always have you. And I do mean always."

Charlotte didn't like his tone. She'd never heard him speak so strongly, and it made her nervous. And she wondered why he kept mentioning the idea of her leaving Curtis. Because while she wasn't thrilled about Curtis's low six figures, she would never leave him for an insurance rep, claims adjuster, or whatever the hell Aaron said he was. She didn't mean to be cruel, but that was the reality. She cared about Aaron a great deal and needed him sexually, but she hoped this wasn't turning into some sort of an obsession. She hoped he understood that they had an arrangement and that their relationship could never be any more than what it was.

"Did you hear what I said?" he asked.

"Yeah, I heard you. But you need to keep in mind that Curtis is not someone to be played with. Not when it comes to Matthew and me."

"Really? Well, baby, I'm not someone to be played with either."

Chapter 3

CHARLOTTE DROVE HER PLATINUM CONVERTIBLE T-BIRD ONTO Bypass 30 and headed west to the other side of town. She and Matthew were on their way to Aunt Emma's. Charlotte and Curtis were holding a monthly elder board meeting at the church, and Aunt Emma had quickly agreed to watch Matthew for them. As always, Matthew was ecstatic about it. The reason: Aunt Emma spoiled him as much or more than Curtis did. She treated him like the grandson she didn't have, and her daughter, Anise, bought him more Game Boy cartridges than he had time to play with.

But to be honest, Charlotte actually didn't mind and was thankful to have her aunt and cousin living right there in the city with them. Aunt Emma was her mother's oldest sister, and though her aunt and mother had never been that close, thanks to her mother sleeping with Aunt Emma's fiancé right after college, Charlotte had grown to love her aunt like a second mother.

Charlotte flipped on the CD player and cruised into the left lane. Beyoncé's voice resonated throughout the car. Curtis never listened to R&B music, believing it was inappropriate for a minister, but Charlotte didn't see a thing wrong with it. Granted, she didn't listen to music that focused on vulgarity, violence, and sex, but she loved artists such as Beyoncé, Ashanti, Mary J., Montel, and a list of others. She was only twenty-five and couldn't imagine *not* listening to something other than gospel, so maybe that was the reason Curtis never complained about it.

Charlotte glanced over at her son. "Now, as soon as we get to Aunt Emma's, I want you to start doing your homework, okay?"

"Yes. But I really don't have that much, and I could probably do it in the morning."

"Absolutely not. Because you know you never want to get up, and we practically have to drag you out of bed."

"But whenever I go over on a school night, Aunt Emma and I always watch *The Proud Family*."

"And that's fine as long as you finish your homework first."

"Okay," he said, moaning.

"I also want you to look over your spelling words again for the quiz tomorrow."

"But I already know all of those."

"Maybe, but I want you to look them over a couple of more times just to be safe."

Matthew didn't say anything, but Charlotte looked straight ahead and smiled. Matthew truly was an intelligent child, but she never wanted him taking his education for granted. Not for one second. She wanted him to take every subject seriously, so that he would always score better than average. She wanted him to continue getting straight A's all the way through high school and score in the top percentile on the SATs or whatever tests he'd have to take ten years from now to enter college. She wanted him to surpass what both she and Curtis had been able to accomplish; she wanted him to graduate from Harvard, Princeton, or Yale. She wanted the very best for her little boy and wasn't willing to accept anything less. Which was why she resented Curtis for not doing everything he could to give them a better lifestyle. They weren't living like paupers, she had to admit, but they weren't living like the rich and famous either. She wanted everything for Matthew. She'd even dreamed about the day Matthew would turn sixteen and how she and Curtis would surprise him at his party with a baby Mercedes or BMW. Even now, she wanted to give him lavish birthday parties like those that some of the celebrities gave their children, but Curtis thought she was way over the top with her thinking. He couldn't understand why she wanted so much status and so much money, when they basically had everything they needed and also a lot of the things they wanted. But Charlotte always reminded him of the way he used to live and how, once upon a time, he, too, wanted only the best for himself. Sure, his values had lessened when it came to material possessions, but that wasn't her fault. It wasn't her problem to worry about either. All she knew was that she and Matthew were supposed to be living a lot better than they were.

Charlotte pulled into her aunt's driveway and turned off the ignition.

"Look, Mom, Cousin Anise is here."

"Yep, she sure is. She's going with me to the meeting at the church."

Charlotte and Matthew got out of the car and walked up to the front door. Anise opened it right after they rang the doorbell.

"Hey, sweetie," Anise said, hugging Matthew.

"Hi." He smiled.

"How are you, girl?" Charlotte said, embracing her cousin.

"Can't complain. What about you?"

"I'm fine."

Anise closed the door and they walked into the den where Aunt Emma was sitting.

"Hi, baby," Emma said, reaching out to Matthew.

"Hi," he said and took a seat right next to her on the sofa.

"So, how was school today?"

"It was good. I have a spelling test tomorrow, though, and Mom wants me to do my homework before I watch TV, so I'm going into the dining room and do it now before the *The Proud Family* comes on," he said without taking a breath.

"Now, that was a mouthful," Emma said, and they all laughed.

Matthew left the room as promised, and Charlotte and Emma shared a hug.

"Well, I guess we should get going," Anise said.

"Yeah, because the quicker we can get started, the quicker it'll be over with," Charlotte said.

"Now that doesn't sound like the right attitude for the pastor's wife to be having," Emma teased. Charlotte couldn't help but smile because she knew she'd stressed her discontent many times before with her aunt about all the church meetings and services she had to attend.

"I know, but I can't help it."

"Well, not everything is going to be perfect in any marriage, and as time goes on and you grow more spiritually, I think you'll feel a lot differently. Some of your feelings will also change with age."

"Hopefully" was all Charlotte could think to say, but she couldn't disagree with her aunt more. As far as she was concerned, she would still feel the same way when she was fifty.

"You'll be fine. And if you don't do anything else, just stay prayerful."

"I will. And thanks again, Aunt Emma, for keeping Matthew."

"Don't say another word, because you know I've told you a thousand times how much I love having him around. He keeps me company, and he and I have the best time together."

"Still," Charlotte continued. "I just want you to know how much I appreciate everything you and Anise do for us. I don't know what we would do without you."

Charlotte and Anise chitchatted with Emma for a few more minutes and then grabbed their purses and left for the church.

"You know, you might be thankful to have us, but I'm just as thankful to have you," Anise said to Charlotte. "Ever since you and Curtis moved here, you and I have been like sisters. I mean, I've always had my best friend, Monica, but I feel just as close to you."

"Yeah, but that's also the reason Monica doesn't care for me."

Anise laughed. "I won't even deny it. It's not that she doesn't like you, it's just that she feels a little envious when you and I do things together. But I'm sure I would feel the same way, because nobody likes to feel replaced."

"I just hate that she sees me that way, because I really do like Monica, and I would never try to damage your friendship with her."

"I know, and deep down, Monica knows that, too. And regardless of how she sometimes feels, she would never expect me to ignore my own family. Plus, I always invite her to do things with us."

"I know, but every time we go shopping or to the spa or wherever, she never wants to go with us. She always has an excuse, and I know it's because she wants to do things with you on her own."

"And I do. I mean, she and I do stuff all the time, and I talk to her every single day, so don't even worry about it."

Charlotte really did feel bad about Monica, but she was still glad that she and Anise had bonded so quickly and so completely. She could still remember how diligently Anise had worked toward helping her and Curtis find their new house and with starting their church and how she never complained.

"But I will admit," Anise added. "I do wish I had someone other than you and Monica to spend all my time with."

Charlotte laughed. "I can only imagine."

"Sometimes I really wonder if I made the right decision about Frank. Because I really did love that man."

"Maybe you should give him another chance. I mean, it has been two years since you broke up. And it's not like he dated his ex-wife that long anyway."

"But I would never be able to trust him again. I mean, when Frank and I first started seeing each other, he treated me like a queen, and it seemed like we were so in love with each other. And then he dropped that bomb about his ex-wife. I was so devastated. And I was also going through the divorce thing with David at the same time."

"Let's not even talk about that jerk. No matter how many times we discuss him, I still can't believe the way he felt about other black people—especially since he was black himself. And I get even angrier when I think about some of the names you said he called you."

"He's definitely one person I don't miss. For a while, I missed having someone in the house, but I've never missed being married to him."

"You deserved a lot better, that's for sure."

"That might be true, but I'm still basically alone. And that's no fun when you get to be thirty-eight."

"You'll find someone. Just wait."

"I don't have much longer, girl. Pretty soon I'll be eligible for senior citizen discounts."

"Yeah, right."

"I'm serious. Because to be honest, I really thought I would have met the perfect guy by now."

"I hear you, but I still think it will happen. Probably when you least expect it."

More than anything, Charlotte wanted to tell Anise how lucky she was that she didn't have a marriage like hers. She wanted to tell her just how miserable she was with Curtis and how sometimes she didn't know if having a husband made much of a difference if he couldn't give you everything you wanted. She hadn't shared her feelings with anyone except Aaron, though, and decided it was probably best to keep it that way. Anise thought the world of Curtis, anyhow, so it wasn't like she'd really understand where Charlotte was coming from.

"So tell me," Charlotte said. "What was it like dating Frank?"

"What you really mean is, what was it like dating a white man."

"Well . . . yeah. I've been wanting to ask you that for the longest, but I was trying to mind my own business," Charlotte said, slowing for a stoplight.

"It was the best feeling in the world. But I'm not sure that the way he treated me was based on the fact that he was white. I just think it was because he was such a wonderful person and the fact that we fell in love with each other. He was extremely romantic and he gave me so much attention. He would do things for me that I didn't even know I wanted to have done."

"Did he have money?"

"You're a trip."

"I know. But did he?"

"As a matter of fact, he did. His parents own the Lexus dealership out near the mall, and his grandparents left him a large trust fund."

"What? You never told me that."

"Because it wasn't important."

"Hmmph. Maybe not to you."

Anise looked over at Charlotte.

"What? I'm just sayin'. There's no way I would have let someone like Frank get away. Not someone who loved me and who had money."

"Well, for me, it's about trust and being happy with a person."

Charlotte didn't respond because at this point, it was better to agree at disagreeing. Still, it was funny how she and Anise were so different when it came to men and what they needed from them. They were as different as Goodman, Mississippi, and Times Square. Charlotte, of course, symbolized the latter.

Chapter 4

CURTIS REVIEWED THE AGENDA AND WAITED FOR LANA, HIS FIFTY-
year-old administrative assistant to pass out copies to
everyone else. The elder board consisted of twelve
members: Curtis; Charlotte; her cousin, Anise; his good friend,
Aaron; and eight others whom the four of them had chosen very
carefully. The elder board was something new for Curtis and not
at all like the deacon boards he'd been forced to deal with at his
other churches. This board was more or less a governing committee, similar to a board of directors at certain corporations and
nonprofit agencies. But the noticeable difference was that Curtis
could not be vetoed on any issue. The members were free to discuss and vote on various topics, but in the end, Curtis had the
final say. He and Charlotte had made sure to include that particular stipulation in the bylaws when they'd founded the church.

When Lana took her seat adjacent to Curtis, Curtis asked
Brother Bailey, the newest member, to say a word of prayer.
Then, Curtis called the meeting to order.

"So, how is everyone this evening?" Curtis asked.

Everyone was "fine," "well," or "just blessed."

"Good. Now, for the most part, we're going to stick right with the agenda that you have in front of you," he continued. "So, Sister Mason, if you would, please give us an update on the day-care program."

"So far, everything is running pretty smoothly. The state is currently doing a license study, but I don't foresee us having any problems. Our permit is good for six months, and I definitely think we'll have our license before it expires. And once we have it, it'll be in effect for three years."

"Are you okay with the number of employees you have?" Anise asked. "Because I remember you saying you might need to add another worker."

"Right now we're fine with the five we've hired, but if we want to take on any more than twenty children, we'll need to bring in a sixth person."

"But I thought I read somewhere that you could have one worker for every eight children," Brother Dixon commented.

"Yes, but that's only if all eight children are two years old," Sister Mason explained. "It drops to five if the children are toddlers and four when they are infants. Then, if you have a mixed-age group like we do, you have to use the ratio standard for the youngest child in the group, which is why we have to have one worker for every four children we take in."

"Sister Mason went over that at one of our other meetings, Brother Dixon, but I think you were out recovering from your knee surgery," Curtis added.

"Oh, okay. I was just wondering."

"Not a problem," Sister Mason said, smiling. It was common knowledge that Brother Dixon and Sister Mason had a thing for each other. They would never admit it to anyone, but the chemistry between them was as warm as Miami.

"If that's all regarding the day-care program, the next order of business is the expansion project. Sister Miller," Curtis said, referring to Anise, "Brother Malone and I met with another architect last week, and this one had even better ideas than the last two. He's very excited about what we want to do, and I have to say, we were pretty happy with his personality and reputation as a whole. What we want is for him to attend the next elder board meeting so that he can present his plans to all of us. But I think you'll be pretty satisfied."

"Yes, I think so, too," Anise said. "He's very good at what he does, and he seems extremely knowledgeable. He's also very well organized and that's another major benefit. And he's worked with a number of top builders in the area, too. I also did some reference checking and found nothing but favorable news about him. He comes highly, highly recommended."

Curtis was always so impressed with Anise, and while he loved Charlotte from the bottom of his heart, he wished Charlotte could be more like her cousin when it came to church business. He wished she would find the same sort of enthusiasm and spend more time working with them on their various projects. There was something to be said about women who were intelligent—but there was much more to be said about women who were smart, beautiful, and well educated, which is why he couldn't fathom Anise not being in a serious relationship. From where he was sitting, she should have been able to get just about any man she wanted. But according to her, it wasn't that easy.

"I agree," Aaron said. "I liked this one, too. He really had his stuff together, and I think we'll get everything we expect from him and then some. He had some great contemporary designs. Not like any others I've seen."

"So does it look like we'll still be able to break ground next year?" Brother Dixon wanted to know.

"Lord willing," Curtis answered. "Anise has been working with our accountant to finish up the financial plan, and we'll be presenting it to the bank fairly soon. We shouldn't have a problem with getting the bank loan, though, and by next year, we'll have a nice down payment in our own account that we can add to it."

"The entire congregation has been giving pretty generously toward the expansion project, and that's all while they're still paying their regular tithes and offerings," Charlotte said, and Curtis was glad she finally had something to say. It always looked bad when the first lady of the church acted as though she didn't care or didn't want to be there.

"We truly do have some dedicated members," Sister Mason said.

"Amen," another female member agreed.

"To be honest, it can't happen soon enough with all the new members we keep getting every week," Curtis said. "Our ministry is growing faster and stronger every day."

"What if we outgrow this church before the new one is complete?" Brother Bailey asked.

"Anise?" Curtis said.

"Actually, we've already been speaking with the school district about possibly renting one of their high school auditoriums. Specifically, Mitchell High, since it can accommodate the most people," Anise said, glancing at the agenda and looking at Curtis. "Which sort of brings us to our new business for the month."

Curtis motioned his hand, giving her the okay to continue.

"We were thinking that maybe it might be a good idea to

draw up a contract with the district now, because the last thing we want is for someone else to rent out the space right when we need it. But, of course, that would probably mean paying at least a portion of the normal rent before we actually start utilizing the facility."

"Hmmm," Brother Bailey stressed his concern. "I don't know if that's a good idea or not, because basically we'd be paying for something we're not using and that money could go toward the new building."

"But we don't want to take the chance of it being leased to someone else either," Brother Dixon argued.

"I agree with Brother Dixon and Sister Miller," Sister Mason said. "I don't think we should take any chances. Because if we can't get the high school when we need it, where will we go?"

"There must be other places besides Mitchell High School, so maybe we need to take a vote," Brother Bailey said.

Anise and Charlotte looked at each other. Curtis wondered why Brother Bailey always had to have an opinion. In the beginning, he'd been nice and quiet like everyone else, but over the last six months, Curtis had noticed how much more vocal he'd become and how he tended to make comments about everything. It was to the point where he thrived on disagreeing with anything the majority wanted to do.

"You're right, Brother Bailey," Curtis finally said. "There are other places, but Mitchell High School is where we want to be. It's practically brand-new, and it has comfortable seating."

"I understand that, but I still think we need to take a vote."

"Fine," Curtis said, since voting ultimately wouldn't matter one way or the other. "How many are in favor of entering in a contract with the school district as soon as possible?"

Everyone raised their hand except Brother Bailey and two

other members, one male and one female. Curtis was somewhat shocked because the latter two never said very much and mostly went along with everyone else. He wondered if Brother Bailey had privately influenced them to do otherwise.

"That's nine to three, so I guess we'll be going forward with securing the auditorium," Curtis announced.

Brother Bailey laughed out loud. "It's not like it would have mattered anyway, even if eleven of us had voted not to."

Suddenly, one could hear a pin drop onto the floor if there had been one rolling from the table. And the floor was carpeted. Within seconds, Curtis thought some of his old thoughts and felt some of his ugly ways rearing inside of him. He prayed silently, begging God to keep him from saying something he would regret or have to apologize for.

"Look, Brother Bailey. I'm sorry that you don't agree with our decision, but we voted, just like you wanted, and this is the outcome."

"Whatever."

Curtis prayed some more. He asked God to suppress the words he knew he had no business saying. He knew this whole scenario was something Satan had concocted, testing him the same as always. Curtis was faithfully living his life right, and Satan wasn't happy about it. Curtis would never let him win, though.

"And since we're on the subject of money, there's something else I want us to discuss," Brother Bailey said. "We're collecting an average of fourteen thousand dollars every Sunday, but a nice chunk of it seems to be going toward salaries for the clerical staff, the musicians, and the pastor. So what I want to know is how those salaries were determined?"

"Those salaries were decided when the church was founded

and until now, not one member of this board has had a problem with it," Charlotte told him. Curtis knew his wife would have something to say about this. It was the one subject she did in fact care about.

"Really?" Brother Bailey said. "Well, who decided that the pastor should receive fifteen percent of whatever is collected? I mean, I've been asking around, and no other churches seem to be operating like that. Every other church I know of pays the pastor a set sala—"

"Well, in case you hadn't noticed, we're *not* every other church," Curtis interrupted. "This is Deliverance Outreach, and *we* do things here the way *we* choose to."

"No, we do things the way *you* and *your wife* want them to be done."

"Brother Bailey, what has gotten into you?" Brother Dixon asked. "Because this ain't nothin' but a bunch of foolishness you talkin' in here tonight."

"Ya'll are just mad because I'm not a yes-man like the rest of you."

"You know what," Aaron said, "I think you should step outside and cool off before this goes too far."

"Uh-uh. I'm a member of this board just like everyone else, and I'm not leaving until I get ready."

"Whether you realize this or not," Anise said, "Pastor and Sister Black started this church with hardly any members at all and now we have over five hundred. So I don't need to tell you how much of their own money they sacrificed or how much money they borrowed, which I might add is all paid back. And let's not talk about this great ministry and how many souls have been saved because of it."

Curtis was proud to have Anise defending him and Charlotte, but he didn't like the way she was making him feel. He'd known her for two whole years, but suddenly he felt a certain attraction for her. The wrong kind of attraction. The kind he didn't want to feel for anyone other than his wife and especially not his wife's first cousin. He wondered why Satan was trying to trip him up like this. He felt nervous, and it wasn't because of what the board was discussing.

"Please!" Brother Bailey spat at Anise. "You're part of Sister Black's family, so of course you're going to say whatever will make them look good."

"Okay, that's enough," Aaron said. "Pastor, if it's okay with you, I'd like to move that we adjourn."

"Dismissed," Curtis said and was beside himself. He was so angry he could burst wide open. Who did Bailey think he was anyway, questioning Curtis's authority and, of all things, his money? Curtis didn't know what this Negro's problem was, but the one thing he did know was that Bailey had to be removed from the board. Not in a few days and not next week, but immediately.

Curtis pulled Aaron aside. "We need to take care of this right now, so that we won't ever have to deal with this madness again."

"I agree. Brother Bailey, can Pastor and I speak to you for a few minutes?" Aaron asked.

"About what?" Bailey spoke loudly. Everyone stopped in their tracks, ceasing their conversations.

"If you'll just walk with us up to Pastor's study, we can discuss everything in private," Aaron told him.

"No. Just say whatever you have to say to me right now—in front of everybody."

"Okay, fine; we're removing you from the board, effective immediately."

"Why? Because I called you crooks on your mess?" he said, moving toward Aaron.

"Look, I think you'd better step back and then get your behind out of here," Aaron said, and the other men in the room walked toward them. "We don't want you here and that's that."

Bailey laughed, his tone sarcastic. "I don't want to be here anyway, and the rest of you are fools if you keep going along with this money show Pastor Black has everyone caught up in. He's so slick that all of you are too blind to see it. Or maybe everyone in here has forgotten about all those women he slept with over in Chicago. You've heard him talk about them during his own sermons. Yeah, he claims to be a changed man and all that, but where I come from, once a whoremonger, always a whoremonger."

Bailey turned and walked toward the doorway and sang, "Suckers!"

Everyone was speechless.

Chapter 5

WELL, WE CERTAINLY CHOSE THE WRONG PERSON TO BE ON THE board, didn't we?" Curtis said to Charlotte, while unbuttoning his shirt.

"I guess we did. Which is strange because Brother Bailey would have been the last person I would have expected something like this from. All of it seems so out of character for him."

"Yeah, I have to agree, but it just goes to show that you really can't trust anyone, and I'm just glad we have the right to remove anyone we're not happy with."

"This is true." Charlotte removed her suit and blouse and strolled inside the closet.

Curtis sat on the edge of the king-size bed and slipped off his socks. "It's so amazing how quickly people will betray you, which makes me feel even worse about all the terrible things I did to people for so many years."

"But *did* is the key word," Charlotte yelled out to the bedroom. "You are a completely changed man now and that's all that matters. The past is exactly that. And what Brother Bailey pulled tonight was totally uncalled for."

Curtis met Charlotte as she walked out of the closet and pulled her into his arms. "I love you so much, you know that?"

"I do, Curtis, and I love you, too."

"Having you and Matthew in my life is the reason days like today basically don't mean a thing. The two of you give me so many reasons to be thankful about life in general."

Curtis kissed Charlotte, but she pulled away and said, "It's getting pretty late, so you should probably go read Matthew his story before he falls off to sleep. And I need to jump in the shower."

Curtis didn't like what he was sensing. She was so distant and unaffectionate. He'd been slowly but surely noticing a change in their relationship, but he'd told himself that it simply was his imagination. Charlotte had been working a lot of hours, and he'd been doing the same thing, so he'd decided that this was the reason things weren't exactly the same between them. Maybe he wasn't spending enough time with her. Tanya had complained about that very thing, and Mariah had constantly complained about all the time he spent away from her. So maybe that was what the problem was.

He walked into Matthew's room and Matthew smiled at him. He was already tucked under his covers.

"Which book are you going to read from tonight, Dad?" he asked.

Curtis sat down on Matthew's bed. "Actually, I think I'm going to tell you a real story instead."

Ever since the day he and Matthew began living under the same roof, Curtis had started this nightly ritual of reading a story to him at bedtime. It was the one thing he'd envied about the children he saw on television back in the seventies. He'd wished a thousand times that his father could be as wonderful as the fathers on each of his favorite sitcoms, and even now, it was still a dream he'd never fulfilled. It was a dream that no one would have ever suspected from a strong, take-charge sort of man like him. But he'd promised himself that Matthew would get everything he hadn't as a child, including a bedtime story.

"What kind of real story?" Matthew asked, locking his fingers together and resting them on top of his stomach.

"A story about you and me."

Matthew raised his eyebrows.

"When I was a small boy just like you are now, I wasn't very happy. I didn't have any of the things you have right here in your room or in this house, and sometimes I didn't even have food to eat. We were very poor, and I never knew what it was like to spend time with my father. My mother tried to be there for us when she wasn't working, but my father was never home until late at night, and there were some days when he didn't come home at all. But no matter how many months and years passed by, I still wished for things to change. I always believed that, one day, my father would change and that he would rush home as fast as he could to tell me how much he loved me. But he never did," Curtis said, blinking back tears. "He never took me in his arms, he never did anything."

"Dad, why are you crying?"

"Because, son, after all these years, it still hurts me sometimes." Curtis wiped his face with both hands. Matthew's eyes filled with water, and Curtis placed his hands on top of his son's.

"I didn't mean to upset you, but it's important for you to know that not everyone has had the best life and not everyone is perfect. Not even me."

"But you are. You're the best person in the whole world and

you can do anything," Matthew said proudly. "I always tell Jonathan and Elijah that, and even when they say that nobody can do everything, I still tell them you can."

"Well, I appreciate that, but unfortunately, they're right. I can't do everything. But there are two things I can do and the two things you will always be able to count on no matter what. I'll always love you, and I'll always be here for you."

Matthew smiled.

"And there's something else I need to say while it's on my heart. I know you look up to me, and I'm very happy about that, but there was a time, before I met you, when I wasn't such a good person. I did some things that God wasn't happy with, and I had to pay some major consequences for them."

"You mean like when you got shot back in Chicago?"

"Yes, like that."

"Well, if God made you all better, then that means he's not mad at you anymore."

Curtis couldn't help chuckling. "I guess maybe it does, doesn't it?"

"Yep," Matthew said, smiling.

"God does forgive us, but it's so much easier if we do what he expects from us from the start. So, no matter how old you get or how successful you become, son, always try to do the right thing. Always try to treat people the way you want to be treated. Always keep God first in your life from now on."

Curtis grabbed his son in a bear hug and held him for longer than usual. Shortly after, Matthew slid out of bed, onto the floor, to recite his prayers. When he finished, Curtis tucked him in again, kissed his forehead, and left the room.

When he went back into his own bedroom, Curtis heard the shower still running. Maybe Charlotte was a lot more relaxed now, so he removed the rest of his clothing and cracked open the pewter-trimmed shower door. "Want some company?"

Charlotte jerked her head around.

"I didn't mean to scare you."

"You didn't," she said. "I guess my mind was somewhere else."

"Well, do you?" Curtis said, taking one step inside the shower.

"What?"

"Want some company?"

"Baby, not tonight. I'm really, really exhausted, and all I want to do now is get some sleep."

"If not tonight, then when?" he yelled without planning to. He'd just told his son about doing the right thing and about treating people the way he wanted to be treated, and now here he was totally irritated with his own wife.

"Tomorrow," she said, turning off the water and reaching for her towel.

Curtis stepped away, leaned against his vanity, and crossed his arms. "You were tired last night and the night before that, too. And as a matter of fact, last night, you didn't even get home until after eleven. So, what's going on, Charlotte?"

"Nothing. You know how many hours I've been working, and then we have church every Sunday and, of course, meetings like we did tonight. I'm just tired. That's all."

"Well, where exactly do I come in? And when do you plan on spending some real time with your son for that matter?" Curtis couldn't believe he was sounding like his former wives. He was repeating some of the same words they had spoken to him only a few years ago.

"When this trial is over. I already told you that. And if it wasn't for all this church business, I *could* spend more time with Matthew."

"No, if you quit that job of yours, you'd have time to be a good wife and a good mother."

"Well, I've already told you. That's never going to happen. Not as long as you continue earning what you do from the church."

"It's always about money with you, isn't it?"

"As a matter of fact it is. And if I remember correctly, money used to be important to you, too."

"Well, it's not anymore. You and Matthew are."

"Please. If that were true, you'd find a way to give us a lot more. You talked a real good game before I married you, and now two years later, we're basically still living a middle-class lifestyle."

"What is it you want me to do? I mean, every dime of your paycheck is yours. I pay all the bills, and I even give you money for groceries. And sometimes I give you money just because."

"And that's fine, but all I'm saying is, you don't earn enough for me to quit my job. And I can't help the fact that my firm needs me to work late from time to time."

"No, lately, it's *all* the time, and something has got to change."

"Well, I've already told you. I'm not quitting my job."

Charlotte dried her back, threw the towel across a hook, and walked out of the bathroom. She never even looked back at Curtis.

What in the world was wrong with her? Why was she being so cruel and cold-natured toward him? Every couple had problems, but Charlotte was acting as if she couldn't stand to be naked in front of him. She acted as though she didn't want him touching her.

She was making him feel unsure about himself and about their marriage. He hoped this wasn't all he could expect, not with him being 100 percent faithful to her.

He prayed that God would end these sudden marital issues.

Charlotte climbed into bed and turned her back to Curtis. She hated arguing with him, and, she had to admit, this was their worst disagreement ever. He was becoming more and more impatient in regard to their lovemaking, but she couldn't help herself. It wasn't that she didn't desire him, it was just that she wanted Aaron more. He was so much more interesting and daring and the reason she could barely contain herself during the meeting. For months, she'd begged him not to sit directly across from her, but he never listened. And while she knew it was horribly wrong, it turned her on. The fact that she and Aaron were sneaking off together multiple times per week without anyone at the church realizing it was sort of fascinating. It was almost like the whole secrecy of their sexcapades made them that much more mesmerizing. And mesmerized she was. Twice this evening, she'd had to stop herself from staring at Aaron, hoping that no one had seen her. Hoping that Curtis hadn't paid any attention to what she was doing. But of course he probably hadn't since he'd been so consumed with his meeting agenda.

She heard Curtis breathing a lot deeper than when she'd first laid down and was glad he hadn't started another argument or tried to touch her.

More than that, she was glad he didn't know the real reason she couldn't make love to him.

God forgive her.

Only hours ago, during her lunch break, Aaron had sucked the upper inside of her right thigh so intensely, she now had a purple bruise plastered across it.

She'd begged him to stop, but he'd ignored her. She'd told him that Curtis would kill her if he ever discovered it. But Aaron never broke his rhythm.

Finally, Charlotte had given in and enjoyed what he was doing to her.

She begged him to do whatever he wanted.

Chapter 6

CHARLOTTE GLANCED AT HER WATCH AND SAW THAT IT WAS ALMOST ten o'clock. She was sitting in her office, meeting with a client who had hired her firm to handle all of her estate matters. The woman was seventy-two, recently widowed, and filthy rich. Meredith Connolly Christiansen was undeniably the classiest woman Charlotte had ever met. Over the last forty years, her husband had founded two manufacturing companies, purchased two hotels, and opened a very ritzy restaurant. But now everything had fallen to Meredith, and since she had never been too fond of her husband's longtime legal team, she'd contacted Schaefer, Williamson, and Goldberg to take over. Charlotte's bosses couldn't have been happier, and Charlotte was thrilled to be handling some of the smaller aspects of what Meredith had hired them to do. Right now, Charlotte was waiting for her to finish signing a couple of documents pertaining to her health-care power of attorney. She'd decided to name her oldest daughter as the person responsible for making these particular decisions.

"Well, I think that should do it," Meredith said, smiling.

"I think so, and we'll get copies made of everything and delivered over to you sometime next week."

"You know, it's been six months now since Harry passed away, and still, I have to remind myself that he's really gone."

"Mrs. Christiansen, I can only imagine."

Meredith gave Charlotte a stern, yet playful look.

"I mean, Meredith."

"Now, that's better. The one policy my husband enforced at all five of his businesses was that he wanted everyone on a first-name basis. Said it just wasn't necessary to make anyone feel as though they were beneath him or any other executive. And personally, I always loved that policy, because it makes people feel a lot more comfortable when they are trying to communicate with you."

"I agree. But sometimes I forget, because my parents taught me to use Mr. and Mrs. at a very young age. They always felt that a younger person should, as they put it, 'add some gravy' to someone's last name out of respect. Specifically, when speaking to elders."

"And there's nothing wrong with that. But with me, you don't have to add anything. I prefer everything to be straight, no chaser."

They both laughed and Charlotte thought about how spunky Meredith was. She'd lost her husband, yet she was so vibrant and full of conversation. Not to mention, she looked better than most women in their sixties. She'd definitely taken care of herself, and if Curtis would find the ambition he once had, there would be more than enough money for Charlotte to do the same. She'd be able to get weekly facials, body massages, body wraps, and anything else she needed. She'd be able to pay for anything she wanted—even cosmetic surgery when it became necessary.

"So enough about me," Meredith said. "Let's talk about you. When are you going to stop doing this paralegal thing and go back to school to get your law degree?"

"To be honest, I've never considered doing that."

"And why not? Because after meeting with you on three separate occasions, I can see that you are definitely capable. You'd make a fine attorney. There's no doubt about it."

"I don't know. My husband and I have a son to raise, and we have a church to run."

"I remember you mentioning that the last time I was here, but my question to you is, what do you want?"

"The truth?"

"I wouldn't want to hear anything else."

"I'd love to be like you."

"And how's that?"

"I'd love nothing more than to be married to a man like Mr. Christiansen."

"Really? You're sure about that?"

"Yes. Because what I want is not to want for anything. I know it sounds selfish, but that's what I truly want in life. I want the best for my son and myself for the rest of our lives."

Meredith laughed. "Then, young lady, you have a lot to learn."

"Why do you say that?"

"Because being rich and having the best of everything doesn't mean that you're going to be happy. As a matter of fact, if Harry hadn't been so *ambitious*, as you put it, he might have been in the country when our first daughter was born, and he might have spent more time trying to help our youngest daughter stop using drugs. I did the best I could as a mother and sent her to the best treatment facilities in this country, but it was her father's attention that she wanted. She begged him to spend more time with her, but his work was always more important. The man actually thought that giving an eighteen-year-old a brand-new Mercedes and a credit card with no limit was going to make everything better. Can you believe he thought *everything* would be fine after that? That he actually thought he could fix our daughter's problems with money?"

Charlotte was speechless. She was shocked at what she was hearing about Mr. Christiansen and even more shocked that Meredith was telling her about any of this.

"But when it was all said and done, Harry finally fixed things all right. He fixed things real good, because shortly after Bethany got that car, she committed suicide."

"I'm so sorry," Charlotte said, covering her mouth.

"So, you see, ambition isn't always a good thing. It needs to be taken in moderation just like anything else. And don't get me started on all the women Harry slept with over the years. Secretaries, colleagues, you name it. But through it all, I pretended to be happy, and I told myself that I should just be thankful for all the *things* he'd given me. I told myself that at the end of the day, I was Mrs. Harry Christiansen, the richest wife in Mitchell."

Charlotte heard what Meredith was saying, but while she would never admit it, she wanted the whole package. She wanted Curtis to sleep with only her *and* make a ton of money. She wanted him to be the husband he'd said he was going to be before they'd left Chicago. Maybe it wasn't logical thinking, but that's what she wanted. She deserved to have all of that and then some, because Curtis had promised her the world right after he was shot. He'd promised her everything in exchange for her standing by him no matter what. Even after he'd been ousted from two different churches. Even when he'd said he wanted to move to a small town like this one. But if she couldn't have everything and had to choose between a happy marriage and a lot of money, the money was her choice by far.

"I had no idea," Charlotte said.

"Most people see what they want to see. Don't you think?"

"To a certain extent, but usually when you speak of your husband, you talk about how much you miss him."

"Because I do. I miss him more than you could possibly ever know. Harry and I had fifty years of history together. And regardless of how many unhappy times there were, we did have many that were enjoyable. But what I regret is that I didn't do something I wanted to do career-wise. I regret that I didn't focus on something that was just about me for at least a few hours of every day. Because after all these years, all I can say is that I was Harry Christiansen's wife, I sat on a few boards, I ran a few charities, and I went to the country club on a regular basis. So, you tell me, how great was all of that?"

"Maybe you didn't get to have your own career, but I still think you've had a wonderful life."

"Then, it's like I said, you've got a lot more to learn and a lot more to experience. As time goes on, you'll begin to see what's really important and what doesn't matter at all."

"Well, I do agree with you about one thing."

"Which is?"

"That I should have something that I do just for me, and that's why I won't quit working here at the firm the way my husband wants me to. He keeps asking me to come work at the church full-time, and it's his belief that I would be able to spend more time with him and our son if I did."

"It seems that nowadays, there are many pastors' wives that

play a major role in their church's leadership, but, and this is just my opinion, I think it can only work if the wife truly wants to do that. It should not be a forced situation. But I will say this, if your job is taking you away from your son and your husband more than you know it should be, you shouldn't overlook that either. I'm not saying you should stop working altogether, but maybe you need to reevaluate your workload. Okay?"

"I will."

"I'm not trying to tell you what to do, but spending or not spending enough time with your family can make it or break it. And please don't ever forget that."

"I won't."

"Well, I guess I should get off my soapbox and let you get back to work." Meredith stood up and smoothed her hands across the tan-colored tailored suit she was wearing. Charlotte would give anything to dress like her.

"Thanks for coming in, Meredith, and as always it's been a pleasure chatting with you."

"I like you a lot, Charlotte, and if you ever need anything, anything at all, you have my number."

"You're too kind, and I really appreciate hearing that." Charlotte shook Meredith's hand and escorted her toward the door.

"And when school is out next month, maybe you can bring your son out to see the horses. I'm sure he'd love that."

"I'm sure he would."

"You take care."

"You, too," Charlotte said and closed her door.

Women like Meredith didn't come along every day. Wealthy, yet noticeably down-to-earth. And Charlotte admired her. She was sorry that Meredith's marriage hadn't been as wonderful as she'd wanted, but from where Charlotte was sitting, life had still been exceptional for her. As a matter of fact, Charlotte was starting to believe that the word *happiness* could only be defined on a case-by-case basis. It basically depended on the wants and desires of any given individual.

As Charlotte gathered the signed documents and placed them in a folder, the phone rang.

"This is Charlotte speaking."

"Hey, beautiful," Curtis said.

"How are you?"

"Not so good."

"And why is that?"

"Because things aren't right between us."

"I know. And I'm sorry that we had that disagreement last night."

"I'm sorry, too. Yes, I wanted to make love to you, but it was wrong of me to get upset just because you said you were tired. I know it's not easy leaving a full-time job and then going to meetings at the church."

Charlotte didn't say anything. Mainly because of all the guilt she was feeling.

"But this is a new day, it's the end of the workweek, and I've got plans for you and me."

"Really?"

"Yep. I've already asked your aunt Emma to keep Matthew overnight, so that I can take you out to dinner this evening. I started thinking this morning how it's been a very long time since you and I spent any quality time together."

"Sounds good to me," she said but wondered what she was going to tell Aaron. He'd phoned her first thing this morning, right after she'd arrived at her office, and they'd made plans to meet this evening. But with the way things were going between her and Curtis, she knew she couldn't say no to her husband. She would just have to make Aaron understand her situation.

"What time do you think you'll be home?" Curtis asked.

"I'm leaving here a little early today, so probably no later than five."

"Then I'll make the reservations for seven-thirty, if that's okay."

"Works for me."

"I'll pick up Matthew from school and take him over to your aunt's before then."

"Good."

"Okay, baby, well, I'm gonna let you go, but I'll see you later."

"See ya."

"And, baby?"

"Yes?"

"I love you."

"I love you, too, Curtis."

"I hope so."

"I do."

"Talk to ya."

Charlotte hung up the phone and sighed. It was at times like this that she felt even worse about what she was doing to Curtis, but she couldn't help herself. She paused for a few minutes longer, deep in thought, and then dialed Aaron's phone number. She told him they'd have to meet for lunch instead of dinner.

"Girl, you make me crazy," Aaron said, lying on his back, panting.

"That's what I'm supposed to do," Charlotte teased him, caressing his chest and stomach. They were relaxing at the country home of one of Aaron's childhood friends.

Aaron took more deep breaths. "Maybe, but I don't know how long I can keep hearing about you and Curtis spending all this special time together. First, you call me saying that we can't meet tonight because Curtis wants to take you to dinner, and then he calls me and mentions that he's got plans to take you to some hotel after you finish eating."

"Well, he never said anything to me about going to a hotel."

"I know he didn't, because he said he wanted to surprise you. And I won't even go into how excited he was about it. He was sounding like some little kid at Christmas."

"I know you don't like hearing about Curtis and me being intimate, but what am I supposed to do?"

Aaron looked over at her. "Leave his ass. That's what."

Charlotte didn't respond, because Aaron seemed more angry than usual.

He sat up on the side of the bed. "Pack your things and come live with me. It's as simple as that."

"Baby, how many times do we have to go through this? Because you know I can't do that."

Charlotte slid across the bed and sat next to him.

"Well, regardless of what you feel you can and cannot do, I'm tired of playing second to the Reverend Curtis Black. When we first started seeing each other, your relationship with Curtis didn't bother me, but now I can't stand it. Just the thought of him kissing you and making love to you makes me cringe. And the bottom line is that I'm tired of sharing you with him. So you need to make a choice."

Only a few days ago, Aaron had said he would never give her up under any circumstances, but now he was trying to give her an ultimatum? It sounded as though he'd changed his mind about their arrangement and was now making it clear that she could be with him or Curtis, but not both. This turn of events wasn't working for her. Not at all.

"Aaron, baby, look. You knew from the very beginning that I was married and what my situation was, so why are you doing this?"

"Because I'm in love with you. I wasn't counting on falling in love with you, but now that it's happened, there's nothing I can do about it. Curtis doesn't deserve you anyway, not with his long history of women and the way he treated them. That Negro is nothing but a big joke, and you know it."

"What? Well, Aaron, I guess I'm a little shocked at what you're saying because I always assumed that you felt just as guilty about betraying Curtis as I did. Especially since he considers you to be one of his best friends. Actually, you're the closest friend he has in this city."

"Well, I can't help that. And now that we're on the subject, I also agree with everything Bailey said about him at that meeting. As a matter of fact, I'm the one who convinced Bailey to stand up to Curtis. Because the truth is, no pastor should be earning a flat percentage of what is collected, and as far as I'm concerned, Curtis is no different than any of those money-hoarding ministers on television."

"I don't get this."

"You don't get what? The fact that I sometimes despise Curtis? The fact that I hate the way people treat him like he's some god but pretty much ignore men like me? Men like me who earn a decent living but don't have any real power or money to throw around. And sometimes I get just as pissed off at you because you're always talking about the amount of money Curtis could be earning just because he's a well-known minister. That's all you seem to care about, and I'm sick of hearing about it."

"I'm sorry you feel that way."

"And I'm sorry you feel compelled to stay with him. But let me say this, I won't wait around on you forever, Charlotte. I won't."

Charlotte watched him leave the room and walk into the bathroom. Shortly after, she heard the shower running. She was so baffled by all of this and wondered why Aaron was acting so strangely. He'd asked her to leave Curtis a number of times before, but now he was acting as though his life depended on it. He was acting as though he hated everything about Curtis. Maybe he was merely having a bad day and would feel differently the next time she spoke to him. Maybe all they needed was some time apart, so that Aaron could rethink their relationship.

She hoped things between them would return to normal very soon, because she didn't want to lose him. She didn't want to lose the good thing they had going with each other. She didn't want to lose the pleasure he gave so naturally.

Chapter 7

CURTIS DROVE INTO THE HOTEL PARKING LOT, AND CHARLOTTE TRIED to act surprised about it. During dinner, she'd asked him what they were going to do afterward, but he'd told her that she would know soon enough. She could still see the grin on his face when he'd said it.

"Okay, Curtis, so what is this all about?" she asked, smiling.

"It's about you and me spending the night together without any interruption. It's about us spending quality time with each other the way we used to."

"And what are we supposed to wear when we get up tomorrow morning?"

Curtis parked and opened the car door. "If I were you, I wouldn't worry about that," he said, winking at her.

"Whatever you say."

He closed his door and walked around to open Charlotte's. Inside the building, Curtis strolled closer to the reception desk, but Charlotte wanted to run back outside. She could tell that the desk clerk recognized her immediately. Charlotte and Aaron had frequented this quaint little inn, situated on the outskirts of town, more times than she could remember, and now Charlotte wondered why they'd become so careless. Once upon a time, they would have driven no less than twenty miles outside the city limits, but they hadn't done that in a long while. It was almost as if they'd become much too lax for their own good.

"I just wanted to thank you again for all your help this afternoon," Curtis told the clerk while laying an envelope on the desk. "I really do appreciate it."

"I was happy to do it," the woman responded, smiling.

"Well, baby, are you ready?" Curtis took Charlotte's hand.

"Ready when you are." They headed toward the elevator, and Charlotte didn't have the nerve to look at the clerk, face-to-face, a second time. She was so ashamed of herself.

When they arrived at their room, Curtis swiped the plastic card and pushed the door open. Charlotte walked in first and couldn't believe what she was seeing. The room was filled with dozens of red roses, a bottle of nonalcoholic champagne, and two small boxes, which he picked up and gave to her. There were even two overnight bags sitting on the floor and jazz playing on a CD player. Curtis had planned their evening to the last detail.

"Oh, Curtis," she said, after opening her gifts. He'd gotten her the diamond necklace and matching bracelet she'd been admiring for over six months. She hugged him tightly.

"I'll bet you weren't expecting anything like this, were you?" he said.

"No. Not at all."

"I'm just sorry I haven't done it before now. Because, sweetheart," he said, slightly pushing her away from him and holding both of her hands, "you are everything to me. You and Matthew both. The whole reason I changed my life around was so that I could do right by you and our son. I wanted to change for God, too, no doubt, but you were the other reason I knew I had to give up my old ways. The women, the money schemes, the way I manipulated so many people. You are my life, girl," he said matter-of-factly. "You hear me?"

Tears streamed down Charlotte's face. Not because she was happy, but because of all the guilt she was feeling inside. She did love Curtis, but it was at this very moment that she realized she wasn't head over heels the way she used to be. Partly because she'd been splitting her time between him and Aaron. She hugged him tightly and cried even harder.

"Baby, what's the matter?" Curtis asked.

"I just can't believe you've done all of this for me."

Curtis laughed and stroked her hair. "I don't know why not. Because you deserve this and a whole lot more. I know you're not happy with my income, but I promise you, baby, this is only temporary. I guarantee it."

Charlotte wanted to believe him, and she wanted them to be as happy as they were in the beginning, but she was so confused. Here she'd just made love with Aaron only a few hours ago, and now she was embracing her own husband—and preparing to do the same thing with him. The thought of it all turned her stomach. Just thinking about the person she'd become made her sick. Her parents would be mortified if they knew what she was doing. Her father didn't like Curtis, but he would never approve of her messing around on him. Her mother would think the world had come to an end.

Curtis kissed Charlotte and then removed his blazer. "Why don't you undress for me, the way you used to," he said, sitting down on the bed and kicking off his shoes.

Charlotte smiled at him and turned around so he could unzip

her dress. Curtis removed the rest of his clothing and lay on his back with his hands behind his head, staring at her.

"You know, it's a shame that not every man has been blessed with a beautiful wife."

"Are you saying that I'm beautiful?" she said, removing her bra and tossing it at him.

"That's exactly what I'm saying."

She smiled and tossed over her pantyhose and panties. Curtis pushed both pieces of lingerie onto the floor and returned his right hand behind his head.

Charlotte stared at her husband and regardless of how she felt about him emotionally, she couldn't help noticing how gorgeous he still looked. His skin was nearly flawless, his hair soft and wavy, and his body was as muscular as any woman would want it to be. Which made Charlotte wonder how she ever got herself mixed up with Aaron. Not to mention the explosive sex she and Curtis always had whenever they made love to each other. But who was she kidding? Her feelings for Curtis had changed because of material possessions and material possessions only. She'd started resenting him without even realizing it. She'd become bored with him as a husband.

"Come here, you," he said.

Charlotte climbed on top of him, and Curtis held her closely, kissing her again. Charlotte could feel him swelling beneath her, and it turned her on. She moved her lower body against his, and he responded similarly. Curtis rested his hands on her shoulders and gently pushed her body downward. Charlotte knew what he wanted and had no problem giving it to him. For as long as she'd known Curtis, he'd always been happy with the way she satisfied him, and this was the least she could do, considering the way she was carrying on with Aaron behind his back.

Curtis moaned gratifyingly, begging her not to stop. So Charlotte picked up speed. She could tell she was driving him wild. She could feel him swelling even further.

"Okay, baby, that's enough," he said.

But Charlotte disregarded what he was saying.

"Baby, please," he begged. "I said that's enough."

Charlotte tuned him out completely and continued her tempo. She loved controlling Curtis sexually.

"Oh . . . baby . . . yes," he said, succumbing to her desire to keep going. "I love you so much," he said.

Charlotte sustained her pace until the very last minute and then stopped. Curtis quickly sat up, and Charlotte moved to the side of him. Curtis entered her, moving in and out of her, slowly at first and then much more rapidly. Charlotte closed her eyes, wishing that this feeling she had would last forever. She loved the way Curtis made her feel, the way they were together, at this very moment.

Curtis worked his body back and forth, with moisture building across his forehead, and Charlotte moaned with pleasure.

"Oh, Curtis. Oh, baby."

Curtis worked his body even faster and then moaned, breathlessly.

He breathed deeply for almost a minute and then pulled away from Charlotte.

But he frowned as soon as he did. "What is that?"

"What?" Charlotte played dumb but knew full well what he was talking about. The real reason she'd wanted to give him oral sex was to get him so heated up that by the time they had intercourse, he wouldn't pay any attention to what he was seeing now. But she hadn't taken the time to consider that he might see it when they finished.

Curtis just stared at her.

"What?" she repeated.

"You know exactly what I'm talking about. That bruise between your legs," he said, pointing right at it.

"Oh. That? I got that a couple of days ago when I was riding one of the bicycles at the health club. The seat was sort of loose, and I guess it was rubbing my thigh the wrong way. Actually, it was pretty sore, but it's a lot better today."

Curtis looked away from her and walked into the bathroom.

Charlotte felt her stomach churning. What was she going to do if Curtis didn't believe her? How could she have been so stupid? So consumed with Aaron that she'd allowed him to leave such glowing evidence on her body? She must have been out of her mind.

Curtis walked back into the room and sat on the bed with his back turned to her. She wanted to say something, plead her case, but was afraid to.

Curtis finally turned and looked at her. "Can I ask you something?"

"What?"

"How in the world would you even think you could con a con artist? I mean, I don't con people anymore, but I certainly know a con when I hear it. Especially since the lie you're telling me is no different from the lies I used to tell my ex-wives, and even you for that matter."

"But I'm not lying to you, baby. And how else would I get a bruise like this anyway?"

"How?" Curtis laughed. "By lettin' some other man suck on you. That's how."

"Baby, you know I would never do that," she said, stroking the side of his face.

"Don't touch me, Charlotte," he said, moving away again. "Don't you even think about it."

"But Curtis, baby, please, don't do this. I swear to you. I haven't been sleeping around. You know I would never do that."

"Right now, I don't know anything. And I feel like hurtin' somebody."

Charlotte opened her mouth to speak, but nothing came out. She didn't know how she was going to make him see that he was imagining all of this. Make him see that he was blowing this all out of proportion.

"You know what?" he said. "Let's get dressed and get out of here."

"Curtis, I'm begging you, please don't do this. Don't let your own paranoia about your own life jeopardize our marriage."

"Meaning what?"

"That I knew it was only a matter of time before you started accusing me of messing around, because you know how many times you did it to Tanya and Mariah."

Curtis cracked up laughing again. "Oh, so, now you think you can use head games with me? Girl, you'd better remember who you're dealing with."

"I do know who I'm dealing with," she said, standing her ground. "I'm dealing with a man who messed around with three women at the same time all while claiming he was called by God to preach. A man who knocked me up before I was eighteen and a man who was shot by another mistress just two years ago. So, yes, Curtis, I do know who I'm dealing with, but I still stood by you and took your hand in marriage."

"And that's supposed to justify you sleeping with another man?"

"No. It doesn't. And I keep telling you I haven't."

"Whatever. But like I said, let's get dressed and go. Because I don't want to be here with you anymore."

Curtis walked into the bathroom again, slammed the door, and started the shower.

What was she going to do? How was she going to make him see that he was so wrong about her? Yes, she was being unfaithful to him, but she'd never be able to stand him sleeping with another woman. She wasn't proud of it, but she was the essence of that old cliché: she wanted to have her cake and eat it, too. Regardless of what she was doing, she didn't want Curtis doing the same thing. Maybe it was time she ended her affair with Aaron altogether and time she made things right with her husband. Maybe Aaron's ultimatum this afternoon had been a blessing in disguise, a warning from God, if you will. Maybe her seeing that receptionist downstairs was another admonition she shouldn't ignore. Maybe it was time she stopped breaking that commandment that centered on adultery. Maybe it was time she thought about her little boy and how her infidelity just might hurt him in the long run.

Charlotte entered the bathroom in tears. She pulled the shower curtain back, stepped inside the tub, and grabbed Curtis from behind. Curtis turned toward her, and to her astonishment, he hugged her back.

"Baby, I am so sorry that you think I've been with someone else," she said. "But I haven't. That bruise really did come from that bike at Bally's. You have to believe me."

Curtis held her but didn't respond. She couldn't tell what he was thinking, but at least he wasn't pushing her away.

"All I'm going to say is this," he finally said. "Don't ever let this happen again."

"But——"

"Hey," he interrupted. "I mean it, Charlotte. Don't *ever* let this happen again while you're married to me."

She wanted to tell him again and again that she was innocent. She knew she was as guilty as a convicted felon, but she didn't want him thinking that about her. She didn't want him treating her any differently or feeling as though he couldn't trust her. But she could tell from his tone of voice that the subject was no longer open for discussion. That they would go on with their lives as if tonight never happened. She wanted to beg and plead with him, but instead, she stood there holding him and even loving him more than she had only hours before. Maybe this had all needed to happen, because right now, she felt very close to Curtis. She felt safe and secure the way she used to whenever he held her. She felt as though she could end this thing with Aaron without really missing him.

She prayed that Aaron would understand.

Chapter 8

I T WAS A BEAUTIFUL SUNDAY MORNING IN MAY, AND WHILE DEVOTION WAS
just about to begin, Curtis sat quietly in the pulpit, deep in
thought. He'd tried to forget about the bruise he'd discovered two nights ago on Charlotte's thigh, but he just couldn't
stop picturing it. She'd sworn multiple times throughout the
weekend that she hadn't slept around with anyone, but Curtis
still didn't believe her. Lord knows he wanted to and needed to,
but he didn't. His instinct told him that his wife had actually
been with someone else. Which is why there had been many
moments on Friday evening at the hotel, and then again at
home yesterday, that he'd wanted to hurt Charlotte. He'd
wanted to hurt her mentally and physically. He'd wanted to do
something even worse to the man she was having an affair
with—whoever it was. But as soon as she'd stepped inside the
shower at the hotel, he'd decided right then and there to forgive
her. He told himself that everyone made mistakes, and based
on all the pain and agony he'd caused Charlotte over the last
seven years, she deserved at least that much from him. And of
course, he did love her. But most important, he never wanted to

be separated from his son, and that was reason enough to stay with her.

Curtis watched the elders take their places across the front of the sanctuary.

"Good morning, church," Brother Dixon said, and members of the congregation responded.

"This is the day the Lord hath made, let us rejoice and be glad in it," Brother Dixon continued.

There were many resounding "Amens."

"We're going to follow the order of service as usual, but instead of singing a hymn right off, I'd like to share something important with you. Something that God lay on my heart this past week."

"All right now" came from the elder standing to the right of him.

"Speak today," said a woman from the audience.

"You know, every man or woman who claims to be a Christian is not a Christian," Brother Dixon began.

"True, true," someone commented. Other members of the congregation also voiced their words of agreement.

"You see," Brother Dixon said. "We have Christians, we have lukewarm Christians, and then we have just plain old church folks!"

The congregation applauded, with some members rising to their feet.

"And you see it's those *church folks* that we need to be careful of. Those people who I like to call Sunday morning churchgoers. Those who party to the wee hours on Saturday night, get all dolled up for church on Sunday morning, and then will curse you out like a sailor by Sunday evening."

The applause grew louder, and there were even more members standing and thanking God for the message they were hearing. Curtis stood up himself, smiling at Brother Dixon.

"Many years ago, my mother used to say, 'Watch out for certain people who are at the church every time the doors of the church are open. Those who can't miss morning or afternoon service because they're so holy. Those who can't miss anything going on at the church during the week. And those who are members of every choir or organization the church has to offer. Because the reason some of these people are at church all the time is so they can hide their true colors. They're trying to cover up all the devilment they've got going on on the outside of the church.'"

"Amen" came from all around.

"Now I'm not standing here saying that you shouldn't be in church all the time or that you shouldn't stay involved with church activities, because this is the best place for any of us to be. But what I am saying is that we need to keep our minds focused on Jesus. We need to come here with a mindful spirit, so that we can not only worship God but also do His work. What I'm saying is, we need to leave *mess* on the outside where it belongs. If you don't like the way things are run here at Deliverance, then maybe this isn't the place for you. If you have personal problems with Pastor Black, then, again, you need to find another church home. It's as simple as that. Because our great pastor here has done great things for this church, and it is our responsibility to support his efforts. It's our responsibility to stand by him unconditionally. And that's all I have to say about that," Brother Dixon said and passed the cordless microphone to Brother Thomas.

The congregation was in full agreement, and Curtis stood at the podium, clapping with them.

"Amen, Brother Dixon," Curtis said. "And thank you. Thank you for saying what needed to be said."

Brother Dixon hadn't told Curtis that he was going to speak to the congregation, but Curtis knew he was referring to that outburst from Brother Bailey at the meeting last week.

"I know we're supposed to move on to the scripture, song, and prayer, but isn't it amazing how God works?" Curtis said. "It's so amazing how he lays words and thoughts on our hearts the way he just did with Brother Dixon and how he works with each and every one of us when we need him to. I say this not from hearsay but from personal experience. A lot of you know the kind of life I used to live when I was a pastor in Chicago, but God turned me around completely. Some of us grow spiritually, but some of us need to be changed. Some of us need to change everything we are doing, thinking, and saying. Some of us are just that corrupt. But you see, even after we decide that we are going to live for God and only God, Satan works overtime, trying to win us back. The more good we do, the more temptation and trouble Satan is going to throw our way. The stronger you grow in the Lord, the more Satan will come at you with one thing or another." Curtis looked over at Charlotte who was sitting on the second pew.

"Just this week, Satan tested me with the act of forgiveness. He tried to make me believe that I didn't have to forgive anyone for anything and that if someone does me wrong, I should hurt them back. He tried to convince me that I should get revenge on them any way I can."

"Well, well," a man shouted.

"That old Satan is something else," a woman added.

"But he's no match for Jesus," another woman said.

"And I won't stand here and lie to you," Curtis continued. "I

wanted to hurt the person who hurt me like I'd never hurt anyone before. I wanted them to feel even more pain than what
they'd inflicted upon me. But thank God, it wasn't long before
I remembered all the times I've hurt people. All the times I've
schemed and scammed. All the times I've had to ask God to forgive me. And that's what brought me to my senses. I realized
that everyone deserves a second chance," he said and again
looked directly at Charlotte, who was staring at him with tears
flowing down her face.

"We have to remember the Golden Rule," Curtis said and
took his seat. The elder board resumed devotion, and the or-
ganist and pianist played the morning hymn. But soon after,
Curtis saw some of the members watching Charlotte, and he
knew this meant they were already making assumptions regarding what he'd said. But at this point, Curtis didn't care
about any of that, because sharing his message on forgiveness
was a good thing for everyone in attendance. He was also trying to convince himself that he and Charlotte could actually go
on as if nothing had happened. Because even with all the God
that Curtis had in him, he could tell it wasn't going to be easy.
He could tell that trying to forget about what Charlotte had
done was going to be difficult. He knew because for the last
half hour, he hadn't been able to keep his eyes off some woman
sitting in the fourth pew. She was sitting just two rows behind
his wife, but Curtis couldn't help it. She was as beautiful as
Charlotte and even more so. And it wasn't helping that the
woman was gazing right back at him—which meant Satan was
working his tricks again. He was trying to make Curtis see that
when Curtis worked for him, Curtis never got his feelings hurt.
At least not by women. And now that Curtis was faithful to his
wife and working for God, his life was falling apart. Satan was

trying to make Curtis believe that living his life right wasn't a good thing, but Curtis wasn't going to fall for it. He would try his best not to look at this woman again.

When devotion ended, the choir sang a couple of songs, one of the associate ministers led altar prayer, and Curtis preached his sermon. The topic was "Trying to Do Right in a Do Wrong World." Now, though, the doors of the church were open, which meant it was time for any visitors who were interested in joining Deliverance Outreach to come forward.

"Isn't it good when God moves through the church the way He has this afternoon?" Curtis said.

"Amen," most every member agreed.

"When we say that the doors of the church are open, we don't mean the actual doors that you walk through, we mean the doors of Jesus, His mercy and His grace. If you are currently looking for a church home or even if you just want to come to Jesus and accept Him as your personal savior, we invite you to come right now."

The church sang, "Come to Jesus, come to Jesus, come to Jesus just now," and four women, two men, and three children walked to the front of the church.

"Praise God, praise God," Curtis continued. "Bless His holy name. You know, sometimes those aisles can seem like a mile long, especially if you're sitting at the back of the church. That long walk can even frighten some people. But I'm here to tell you that God will take care of you. He'll walk with you. He will take care of your every need."

Curtis spoke to each person individually. Four of them were candidates for baptism, four others were joining the church on Christian experience, meaning they were already Christians but were leaving other churches, and one young woman, a cur-

rent member, rededicated her life to Christ and repented pub-
licly for having a child out of wedlock. Once they'd all stood up
and had a couple of words to say, Curtis asked them to follow
the church clerk so that she could advise them about the orien-
tation process and give the baptismal candidates the information they needed.

Right after tithes and offerings were given and general an-
nouncements were made, Charlotte stood and walked to the
podium. She and Curtis had discussed her making an appeal to
the congregation a few weeks ago regarding a few issues, and
she was always the one to appeal to them when it came to anything regarding money.

"Good afternoon," Charlotte began.

"Good afternoon," everyone spoke in unison.

"I know you all are ready to go home, so I'll be very brief. For
the last four weeks, I've been monitoring both the Sunday
school and Wednesday night Bible study attendance, and there
are not very many members participating. Coming to church on
Sunday is one thing, but studying the Word is what makes all
the difference. Reading the Word, discussing it, and asking
questions about it are what we all should be doing. Myself in-
cluded for that matter. So please, madam, and please, sir, let's try
to become more active with our Bible teaching programs. And
let's bring our children with us when we come because they
need to learn the Word also. They need to have something to fall
back on when they are older and are trying to make it in this
sinful world.

"The other thing I want to stress is how important it is for us
to pay our tithes and offerings. Not just occasionally or when we
feel like we have extra money, but we need to do it on a regular
and consistent basis. We need to do what God has told us to do

and we'll all be blessed for it. There was a time when I didn't believe in tithing, but what I came to realize was that God will collect His money one way or another. We can give the amount He has told us to give or we can experience unnecessary financial trouble. Our cars break down unexpectedly, major appliances go out in our homes, we get speeding tickets, we have accidents, and the list goes on. But either way, God will get His ten percent. So it's much better for us to give it on our own, because if we do, He'll give it back to us sometimes tenfold. And even when that doesn't happen, He always sets things up so that we never miss that ten percent at all. So, come on Deliverance, let's do what God has asked us to do. Okay? Thank you."

Curtis stood up, expressed final words of wisdom, and delivered the benediction.

As soon as he'd finished, his eyes locked with those of that mysterious woman. The woman stood inside the pew for a few seconds and then walked down the aisle toward the exit. Curtis tried to ignore her by turning his attention to some of his members and shaking their hands, but when he looked up, he saw the woman smiling at him. She smiled until she was completely out of sight.

And it was then that Curtis's body felt like it was on fire.

Chapter 9

EDORA'S, THE ONLY SOUL FOOD RESTAURANT IN TOWN, WASN'T AS packed as Charlotte had expected. Usually, it took forty-five minutes just to be seated, but today, the place was half-empty. Although, since this was Memorial Day weekend, most people were probably grilling at home with their families. Normally, she, Curtis, and Matthew would have been doing the same, but this year, they were heading to Chicago to spend the day with her parents. They were leaving first thing in the morning.

They waited at the entrance for only a couple of minutes and were seated toward the back of the restaurant near a window in a round booth. Curtis was acting as though their marriage was business as usual, but Charlotte could tell that he wasn't happy with her. He'd insisted he was fine on Friday night and again yesterday afternoon, but it was pretty obvious that he wasn't. He'd made it very clear that he still had a problem with her when he'd told the congregation that story about forgiveness. No one knew for sure who he was talking about, but when he'd looked directly at her more than once while he was speaking, Charlotte had wanted to crawl under the pew. She'd wanted to stand up and swear to everyone that she hadn't done anything. Of course, it would have been a lie, but she was prepared to lie until the end if she had to. She would die before ever admitting that she'd slept with Aaron or any other man.

"I'll give you all some time to look at the menus, and then I'll come back in a few minutes," the waiter said, smiling.

"Sounds good," Curtis said. "So, Mr. Matthew, what are you having?"

"Pizza."

Curtis laughed and so did Matthew because they both knew Ledora didn't serve anything like that.

"Sweetie, why don't you order the barbecued shoulder dinner," Charlotte suggested to him.

"Okay," Matthew answered. "And I want coleslaw and French fries to go with it."

"And, baby, what about you?" Charlotte asked Curtis.

"Haven't decided yet," he said but didn't take his eyes from the menu.

"Normally, you get the chicken and dressing special, so what about that?" she said, still trying to soften him.

"Maybe," he said, playfully punching Matthew in the arm. He acted as though she wasn't even sitting there.

"Stop it, Dad," Matthew said, punching him back.

"Mom, what are you going to get?" Matthew asked.

"I think I'll get the shoulder dinner just like you."

"Oh."

"So, Matthew, did you hear anything during service that you didn't understand?" Curtis asked.

"No. Well, yeah. You said we have to remember the Golden Rule, but I don't know what that is."

"It's a rule that means, 'Do unto others as you would have them do unto you.' Remember the other night when I told you to always treat people the way you want to be treated?"

"Yes."

"Well, it basically means the same thing as that. But unfortunately, not everyone lives by that rule," Curtis said, still ignoring Charlotte, but she knew he was referring to her.

"Oh," Matthew said, not too enthused about his current Bible lesson. "Dad, I have to go to the bathroom."

"Go. But don't forget to wash your hands when you finish."

"I won't."

"Why are you doing this?" Charlotte asked when Matthew left the table.

"Doing what?"

"Curtis, you know what I mean."

"Okay, you're right. I apologize."

"Baby, how are we ever going to get past this?"

"I don't know, you tell me."

"I've told you over and over what happened, but you just won't believe me. One minute you seem okay, and then the next thing I know, you're not speaking to me. It's been like this since Friday evening."

"Charlotte, I'm trying to deal with this the best way I can, so you're just going to have to be patient—" Curtis cut his sentence when he saw the waiter walking toward them, preparing to seat Aaron and some woman he was with.

"Hey, man," Curtis said. "I didn't know you were coming here for dinner."

"I didn't either at first, but I remembered you saying that you were bringing Charlotte and Matthew here, and I figured this would be a good time for you guys to meet Michelle.

Michelle, this is my good friend, Curtis, and his lovely wife, Charlotte."

"It's wonderful to meet you," Curtis said, shaking her hand.

"Good to meet you," Charlotte managed to say.

"It's a pleasure meeting you both," she said. "I've heard a lot about you."

"Really?" Curtis said. "Well, if I were you, I wouldn't believe any of it."

They all laughed. Everyone but Charlotte.

"Well, unless you two want to be alone, you're more than welcome to sit here with us," Curtis offered.

"You want to?" Aaron asked Michelle.

"Sure," she said, already sliding into the booth. Aaron sat next to his date. Charlotte couldn't believe this was happening.

She couldn't believe Aaron was flaunting this woman, a beautiful one at that, in front of her. She couldn't believe the envy she was feeling. She wondered if Aaron was sleeping with her.

"So how long has this been going on?" Curtis asked.

"Just since Friday really," Aaron said. "We've known each other for years, but when I saw her at the store on Friday, I asked her out to dinner. Then I asked her out again last night and now again this afternoon."

"Well, that's an awful lot of asking out if you ask me," Curtis teased. "Because for as long as I've known you, I don't think I've ever seen you this enthused about any woman. So, Michelle, you must be doing something right."

"I hope so."

Charlotte felt her blood pressure rising.

"Hi, Uncle Aaron," Matthew said, returning to the table and sliding in next to his dad.

"Hey, Matt. This is my friend, Michelle."

"Nice to meet you, Miss Michelle."

"Nice to meet you, too, Matthew. And I've heard all about you being *the* Game Boy champion."

Matthew smiled. "Yep. I can beat both my dad and my uncle Aaron at all the games I have."

"Well, good for you," she said.

It took everything in Charlotte not to ask Aaron why he'd been discussing her son with another woman. A woman she had never seen before and didn't know a thing about. But more than that, she *still* wanted to know if Aaron was sleeping with her. She knew she had no right, her being married and all, but she wanted to know. Just thinking about the possibility was starting to piss her off.

"That was a great sermon you preached today, Rev," Aaron said.

"Thanks, man. I try."

"Yes, it really was a wonderful sermon," Michelle agreed.

"Oh, you were at our service this morning?" The words left Charlotte's mouth before she realized it.

"Yes. But I had to leave before it was over because of a page I received. One of my patients has a bad case of pneumonia and wasn't responding to any of the meds I prescribed for her a couple of days ago. So, by the time I finished speaking to the nurse, Aaron was already coming out of the church."

"A doctor, huh?" Curtis said. "I'm impressed."

"Well, thank you," she said.

"What do you practice?"

"Internal medicine."

"I'll have to keep that in mind the next time one of our members is looking for a physician."

"I would really appreciate that."

"As a matter of fact, baby," Curtis said to Charlotte, "we should probably ask Michelle to come speak at the health fair we're planning for this fall."

"Yes, that would be nice," Charlotte said. But it would be over her dead body.

"I'd love to," Michelle said. "Anything you need."

The waiter returned and took everyone's order. Charlotte still wanted to know the answer to her question. The question that was eating at her little by little, minute by minute.

"So, Charlotte, how's everything going at the firm?" Aaron asked. "Curtis told me that you've been working a lot more hours than you used to."

"Actually, I have because of this big case we're working on."

"Well, just be glad you aren't one of the actual attorneys because then you'd really be working sunup to sundown," he said and then rested his arm on the back of the booth behind Michelle.

"Michelle works a ton of hours, too, don't you, baby?" he continued.

Baby. Charlotte didn't know how much more of this she could take.

"Unfortunately, I do," Michelle said.

"But at least they pay you the big bucks for doing it," Aaron boasted. Or at least that's how Charlotte took it. She knew he was trying to belittle her in front of both Michelle and Curtis, mentioning that she wasn't an actual attorney. He was doing a good job of it, too, but she would never let him know it. She would never give him that kind of satisfaction.

"So, what are you guys planning to do for the rest of the evening?" Curtis asked Aaron.

"Michelle has to stop by the hospital as soon as we leave here, so I guess I'll be sitting home for a couple of hours by my lonesome," Aaron said, smiling at Michelle.

"But a couple of hours is all it will be. I promise," she said.

"Then I'll probably stop by your place to discuss a little church business, if you don't mind," Curtis told Aaron.

"Don't mind at all. I'll be there."

Charlotte didn't believe for one second this thing about church business and wondered what Curtis really wanted to speak to Aaron about. All she could do was hope that Aaron wouldn't say anything against her. Of course, he would never tell Curtis anything derogatory, because it would also mean telling on himself.

After leaving the restaurant, Curtis drove them home, changed into something more casual, and left to go visit Aaron. Charlotte closed her bedroom door and dialed Aaron immediately.

"Hello?" he answered.

"What was that all about?" she asked.

"What was what all about?"

"You bringing that chick to the restaurant."

"Maybe I didn't make myself clear, Charlotte, but I told you on Friday that I wouldn't wait on you forever. And I meant it."

"What do you expect me to do?"

"I've already told you. I expect you to leave that fool you're married to."

"Are you sleeping with her?"

"If I am, I would be totally within my rights. Now, wouldn't I?"

"I can't believe you're doing this. First you say you don't ever want to be without me, then you give me this crazy ultimatum, and now you show up with some chick, acting like you're in love with her?"

"But it doesn't have to be this way. You could have me all to yourself if you wanted."

"You know my hands are tied."

"Well, then expect to see a lot more of Michelle, because I'm not about to keep playing these cancellation games with you."

"Aaron, what was I supposed to do? Tell Curtis that I couldn't go to dinner with him? That I couldn't go to a hotel with him? Knowing that he is my husband?"

"That's exactly what you should have done."

"You're unbelievable."

"Maybe to you, but I'm very real to Michelle. So real that she can't get enough of me."

"Why are you being so cruel?"

"I'm not. I'm just taking care of me for a change and not concerning myself with you."

"Okay, so what if I did decide to leave Curtis?"

"Then Michelle is history."

"Just like that?"

"Just like that. And you won't ever have to worry about me being with her again."

"Aaron, you really, really hurt me this afternoon."

"And you really hurt me on Friday when you canceled our evening together."

"But my situation is different. I have obligations to Curtis because of our marriage. But you don't have any responsibilities with Michelle."

"Look, Charlotte, just stop it, okay? Because the deal is this: as long as you are with Curtis, expect to see me with Michelle and any other woman I feel like being with. Like it or not, that's the way it's going to be."

"Fine, Aaron, you do what you have to."

"I already am," he said and slammed down the phone.

Charlotte felt like bawling. What was wrong with her? Why couldn't she just leave Aaron alone and concentrate on Curtis? Why couldn't she just be happy with Curtis and the life he was trying to give her? Maybe she could as time went on. If only she could get Aaron out of her system. Which she could easily do if the sex between them wasn't so incredible.

Curtis walked into Aaron's condo, and they both sat down in the living room.

"Man, I like your girl, Michelle. A doctor and beautiful. It doesn't get any better than that. You'd better keep her."

"Yeah, I know. She's been after me for a while, but you know me."

"Yeah, I do know you, and that's what I'm afraid of."

Aaron chuckled. "No, she's a good woman, and I like her. Actually, I like her a lot."

"This is good, and I'm happy for you, man. Every man needs a good woman in his life," Curtis said. "And until lately, I thought I had one myself."

"What does that mean?"

"Actually, I debated whether I was even going to tell you this, but I have to tell somebody."

"Man, what's up?"

"Do you know what I saw when I was making love to Charlotte Friday evening?"

"No. What?"

"A purple bruise, hickey, or whatever you want to call it."

"Man, get outta here. You must have been seeing things."

"I'm telling you, I know what I saw."

"Did you ask her about it?"

"Yeah, but of course she lied about it."

"What did she say?"

"That the seat on the bicycle she was riding at the health club was loose and it rubbed her the wrong way."

Aaron laughed. "Well, maybe it did."

"Yeah, right. Even you know that's a bunch of crap."

"Man, no. I'm only laughing because of the way you said it. But if Charlotte says that she got the bruise from working out, then I believe her."

"That's because you're not married to her."

"No, I'm not, but I still don't think she would do anything like that. She loves you far too much."

"Maybe she did once upon a time, but for the last few months, she's been acting very strangely. She's been distant and she hardly ever wants to make love to me anymore. And to be honest with you, I don't understand what brought on this sudden change of attitude. First she started working late, then she started being too exhausted, and now I find this spot on her thigh," Curtis said, leaning his head back on the sofa. For the first time in his life, he knew what it was like to be hurt by a woman. Satan had tried to make him see that earlier, and now he saw it as clear as day. The old Curtis wouldn't have cared one way or the other and would have simply moved on to the next prospect. This was definitely a different state of affairs. He was stumbling around in unfamiliar territory and didn't like it.

"Man, I think you're making too much of this," Aaron said, walking into the kitchen. "You want something to drink?"

"No, I'm good."

"Maybe you're just thinking the worst because she's been distant."

"Maybe. But my gut tells me that she slept with someone."

Aaron dropped back down in the oversized chair and popped open a soda. "What you need to do is talk to her. Because if you do, I'm sure you'll realize that this was all a big misunderstanding."

"We'll see. But as much as I hate to say it, I am not a man who can live without affection. I do love Charlotte, but I won't allow her to sleep around on me and get away with it. It's the one thing that will be the death of our marriage if she does it again."

"I'm sure everything will be fine before you know it."

"Oh, don't get me wrong, I am going to forgive her, but she's going to have to start being a much better wife than she has been. She's going to have to start spending a lot more time with me, and I'm talking intimately."

"Like I said, man, I'm sure everything will be fine."

"I hope you're right. For her sake and mine."

"Hello?" Charlotte said, answering the phone.

"Your preacher husband just left," Aaron said.

"And?"

"And I wanted to let you know."

"Why?"

"Because I thought you might like to strip naked and be ready for him when he gets home."

Charlotte didn't respond.

"Are you there?"

"Yeah, I'm here, but I'm not about to comment on your nonsense, Aaron."

"Okay, you're right. I'm sorry. As a matter of fact, I'm sorry for everything. For the way I spoke to you on Friday and for bringing Michelle around you today. But I told you before, you make me crazy. You make me do childish things that I'm not very proud of. And no other woman has ever had that much control over me. Probably because I've never loved a woman the way I love you."

"So, what did Curtis say that made you have this sudden change of heart?"

"That he only married you because you're Matthew's mother."

"Why are you lying, Aaron?"

"I'm not. And why would I lie about that anyway? Because you and I both know that Curtis probably wouldn't have ever called you again if he hadn't wanted to see his son. You've even said that yourself on more than one occasion."

"I still don't believe he told you that."

"Well, he did. He said it more than once."

"So what if he did?"

"And you still want to stay with him? Good it's you."

"Hey, Matthew is calling me. I have to go."

"Can I see you tomorrow?"

"I don't know."

"I'll make it worth your while."

"I have to go, Aaron."

"I'm not hanging up until you say yes."

"Look, I'll see you tomorrow evening. Now good-bye."

Charlotte hung up, traveling from room to room, erasing Aaron's number from the caller ID screen on every phone in the house.

Chapter 10

TODAY WOULD MARK THE FOURTH TIME IN TWO WEEKS THAT CURTIS had driven to the Chicago area. First, he, Charlotte, and Matthew had traveled there on Memorial Day to visit his in-laws; then he'd come back a few days later to preach at a Bible conference; then he'd picked up a guest minister from O'Hare; and now he was here again to pick up his daughter. It was the middle of June, school was finally out, and Alicia was coming to spend a week with him in Mitchell. Curtis had tried to convince her to stay for at least a month, but she was already registered for cheerleading camp and a few other summer activities. Only a couple of years ago, she'd wanted to spend all of her time with him, but now that she was sixteen, she had other interests and lots of friends to hang out with. She was growing up fast. Worse, she already had a driver's license and looked more like a twenty-year-old.

Curtis stepped out of his SUV and walked up to the front door. His ex-wife opened it and smiled.

"Hey, Curtis, how are you?" Tanya said.

"Can't complain."

"And how're Charlotte and Matthew?" she said, closing the door.

"They're fine. Matthew wanted to come with me, but he's already started summer day camp. He can't wait for his big sister to get there, though."

"I'm sure they'll have a great time. Alicia loves having a little brother."

"So how is James?" he asked.

"He's doing well. I took the afternoon off, but he's working."

"Well, isn't that special. You taking off an entire afternoon just to see me?"

"Right, Curtis," she said, laughing. "The truth is, I wanted to make sure Alicia packed everything she would need."

"If you say so," he teased.

"You haven't changed a bit."

After all these years, all the pain, all the arguing, all the terrible things he'd done to Tanya, there was still a certain chemistry between them. She was, without a doubt, his first love; he was hers, too, and nothing would ever change that. He was glad that they were now pleasantly cordial with each other and not the enemies they once were.

"Hi, Daddy," Alicia said, coming down the stairway with a garment and duffel bag.

"Hi, baby girl," he said, hugging her and kissing her on the cheek.

"Where's Matthew?" she asked.

"He's at day camp, but he'll be home by the time we get there."

"Oh yeah, he told me about that last week, when I spoke to him on the phone."

"So are you ready?"

"Yep. I just need to run into the family room to get my CD player. I think I need some new headphones for it."

"If you do, we can pick them up on the way."

Alicia left the room for a few seconds and then returned.

"Okay, Daddy, I'm ready."

"You be good," Tanya said, embracing her daughter.

"I will. And tell Dad James I'll see him when I get back."

Now, that was the one thing Curtis would never get used to, Alicia referring to another man as her father. Of course, James was only her stepfather, but the closeness he had with Alicia still bothered Curtis. It made him regret, that much more, the months and years he'd missed with his daughter.

"You take care, Tanya," Curtis said, hugging her.

"I will. And you take care of my baby."

"She's my baby, too, remember."

"I know."

Curtis placed Alicia's bags inside the SUV, they both got in, and Alicia waved at her mom one last time as they drove away. Curtis honked the horn.

"You still love Mom, don't you?" she asked.

"Why do you say that?"

"Because I can tell. She still loves you, too. I mean, she definitely loves Dad James, but she still cares about you a lot."

"But it's a different kind of love. No different than how I love Charlotte as my wife, and I love your mother as a close friend. I love her because we once shared a very special bond and because she is the mother of my first child."

"I'm just glad you guys can finally get along with each other. I hated it when you and Mom used to do all that arguing."

"And I apologize for that because we never should have done that around you. Not when we were married or after we got divorced. But the divorce thing was new and painful for both of us."

"I know."

"So, what do you want to do while you're visiting?"

"Matthew wants to go to Great America in Gurnee, and then there's some movie he wants me to take him to see."

"Figures. He's always got a list of things he wants to do. And he's been telling all of his little friends that his big sister is coming to stay with him for a week. It's almost as if Charlotte and I don't even exist."

Alicia smiled. "I love him, too. He's such a sweetie."

"The way you have accepted him makes me very happy."

"He's my brother, Daddy."

"I know, but I wasn't sure how you would feel about him at first."

"Why?"

"Because you were so used to being an only child."

"Actually, it did bother me for a while, but Matthew makes it very hard for anyone to dislike him."

"That he does."

"Charlotte said she's taking the day off on Thursday so we can go shopping."

"Yeah, that's what I hear. You like her a lot better than you did Mariah, don't you?"

"I guess. But it's probably because Charlotte is only nine years older than me. So, when I'm with her, it's almost like hanging out with my girlfriends."

"Does that make you feel uncomfortable? You know, having such a young stepmother."

"Not really. But it's not like I'm ever going to call her Mom or anything either."

Curtis laughed. "Point taken."

After stopping at an electronics store in Schaumburg to purchase a new set of headphones for Alicia, Curtis made it back to Mitchell in record time. The moment he pulled into the driveway, Matthew ran out of the house.

"Alicia!"

"Hey, Matthew," she said, holding her brother closely.

"Can we go to the movies tonight?"

"Not tonight, but what about tomorrow?"

"Matthew, why don't you let your sister get settled in first?" Curtis said.

"Okayyyy," he whined. "But can we order a pizza and rent a movie, then?"

"We'll see," Curtis responded.

"Hey, Alicia," Charlotte said as they walked inside.

"Hey, Charlotte."

"Your room is all ready. And there's a surprise in there for you, too."

"Really? Then I'm going up there right now. Come on, Matthew."

"I know what it is," he said.

"Matthew!" Charlotte warned him.

"I'm not going to tell her, Mom."

"Okay. Make sure you don't."

"Your son has such a big mouth when it comes to surprises," Charlotte told Curtis when the children left the room.

"Yeah, he does. And thanks for buying Alicia whatever it is you bought her."

"I bought her a pair of diamond earrings."

"Whoa. Then she ought to be screaming in just about—"

"Oh my God, Charlotte, thank you, thank you," Alicia said,

running back down the stairway and showing much love for her stepmother.

Nothing could've made Curtis more joyful than to see his wife and daughter so friendly with each other. Blended families were not always happy families, so this was a blessing.

Alicia and Matthew headed back upstairs so he could show his sister some of his new games and his new comforter set, featuring the Hulk.

"I know things have been awkward for us lately, but I do love you, Charlotte."

"I love you, too. But can I ask you something?"

"Go ahead."

"Is Matthew the only reason you married me?"

"Where is all this coming from?"

"Nowhere. But I need to know."

"In the beginning . . . that was the reason. But it was only because you made it clear that marrying you was the only way I could ever have a relationship with my son. But by the time we were married, I was definitely in love with you. And it was the first time I knew for sure that I could love a woman without being unfaithful to her."

"But if I hadn't given you that ultimatum, you would have been just as content not being married to me."

"That's not true, because I always wanted Matthew to grow up in a home with both his parents. I'd already messed things up for Alicia, and I didn't want to do the same with him. We may not have gotten together spontaneously, the way you wanted us to, but the love I have for you is very real. And you should know that by now."

"I just wish we could be as happy as we were when we first moved here. You had so many plans and so many dreams."

"And I still do. You may not believe that my column is good enough for syndication or that my book is going to be picked up, but I'm telling you, I have faith in what God has led me to do. Both opportunities are going to present themselves, and it's only a matter of time."

"You really think this is going to happen, don't you?"

"Yes. And you should, too. You should believe that God has great things in store for us. Everything is in divine order, and nothing can change that."

"I guess it's just hard for me, because very few people have a syndicated anything, let alone a newspaper column. And the odds are just as slim when it comes to having a book published."

"But not when God has His hand in it. You know my favorite motto is that 'we have little because we think little,' and I've made sure to never fall into that category. Not one day. I've thought big all my life, and I'm thinking the same thing about my writing."

"But if all this happens the way you say it's going to, how are you going to continue leading the church?"

"I don't know, but I'll figure out something. Even if it means having a couple of the associate ministers doing more sermons than they have been. Which they'll be fine with as long as they're compensated."

"I'm sorry."

Curtis wondered why she was teary-eyed. "For what?"

"For not supporting you and for not being the wife you want me to be."

"Every marriage has problems, but it's up to you and me to correct them."

"I know. But I just want you to know how sorry I am. For everything," she said, laying her head on his chest.

Curtis knew deep within his soul that what she was actually apologizing for was her infidelity. She would never admit it, and at this point, he didn't want her to. But maybe now she was ready to take her marital vows more seriously. Maybe now she finally realized that he was all she needed in a man, that she had no need for anyone else.

Maybe now they could get back to the happily ever after they were living a few months ago.

"Aaron. I just can't keep doing this."

"Well, that's not what you said at lunchtime today. And that's certainly not what you said two nights ago in the backseat of my Navigator."

"I know. But I can't keep living like this. I can't keep doing this to Curtis or to my son. And now with Alicia here this week, I feel even more guilty."

"Then, instead of screwing my brains out at that hotel today, why didn't you go with the good reverend to pick up your little stepdaughter?"

"Because you've got this crazy hold on me, Aaron."

"Charlotte, please. You sleep with me because you're not getting what you need at home. You like the excitement I create for you."

"But I'm in love with Curtis."

"No, you're not. You might care about him, but you don't love him."

"I do. I've been so confused about that, but after talking to him a couple of hours ago, I know that I love him and that I want to be faithful to him."

"Even though you know he only married you because of Matthew?"

"Maybe he did, but he explained all of that to me, and I know now that he does love me."

"Well, it's like I told you before, if I can't see you on a regular basis, then all this good lovin' I've been giving you will now become Michelle's."

Charlotte didn't know why the thought of Aaron being with another woman made her want him that much more. It was such an insane way of thinking, her obsessing over one man, knowing she was married to another.

"I don't want this anymore," Charlotte said.

"Is that right?" Aaron said, grabbing both of her arms. "Well, if that's true, then why in the hell are you standing here in my bedroom butt naked, when you're supposed to be picking up videos for your son and stepdaughter?"

Charlotte didn't even try to answer him. She couldn't.

She never even tried to resist him. She didn't want to.

She allowed him to love her the way he always did whenever she didn't have a whole lot of time.

When Aaron finished with her, she took a quick shower, left his condo, and drove away as if her life depended on it. When she pulled into the parking lot of the video store, she picked up her cell phone and dialed Curtis.

"Hey," he said.

"Sweetheart, I'm sorry it's taking so long, but the first store I went to didn't have the movies that Matthew and Alicia wanted, so I had to drive all the way on the other side of town to find them."

"No problem. The pizza isn't here yet, anyway. So just take your time."

"Do you need anything else?"

"Not that I can think of."

"Okay, well, I guess I'll be there in about twenty minutes or so."

"Love you."

"I love you, too."

Charlotte pressed the end button and wondered how many more lies she was going to have to tell.

She wondered when they were all going to catch up with her.

Chapter 11

CHARLOTTE, ALICIA, AND MATTHEW WALKED INTO WOODFIELD Mall. Charlotte had wanted to shop at Oakbrook but decided to come here instead, since the drive was much shorter. Last night, she and Curtis had argued once again about her not wanting to make love to him, and this morning, he'd barely spoken to her. He hadn't said anymore than he'd had to. She'd wanted to make love to him, but after dropping by Aaron's on her way to the video store, she just couldn't will herself to do it. She couldn't have sex with both of them on the same day, only hours apart, the way she had a few weeks ago. So Curtis had completely blown up and warned that she had better get her priorities in order or else. His tone and facial expression had spoken a thousand words, and Charlotte could tell he was serious. She knew it was just a matter of time before he found satisfaction in another woman's bedroom. He would do what he had to do the way he used to. But even knowing all of that, Charlotte couldn't stop thinking about Aaron. Either she couldn't or wouldn't, she didn't know which it was. But what she did know was that Aaron was her outlet, her exhilaration, her stimulation. He was the thrilling part of her life. But maybe if she could spend big money, the way she was planning to do today, that would be all the excitement she needed.

"So, Alicia," Charlotte said. "What do you want to look at first?"

"Sandals. I need at least a couple more pairs."

"Then let's go into Nordstrom. They had a pretty huge selection when I was here a few weeks ago."

"What about me, Mom?" Matthew said when they headed toward the department store. "Can I get a game for my Game Boy?"

"You really don't need any more of those, but maybe one and that's it."

A smile lit Matthew's face. There was nothing he loved more.

When they arrived in the shoe department, Alicia and Charlotte tried on one style after another.

"Charlotte, look at these." Alicia had on a red pair of Cole Haans.

"Those are too cute."

"Yeah, but they're eighty-nine dollars."

"And?"

"Mom would never buy me a pair of sandals that cost this much."

"Well, normally, I wouldn't spend that much either, but if you really want them, I don't mind paying for them."

"But you already got me the earrings."

"Yeah, but I'm telling you, you can have the shoes, too."

"Wow, Charlotte, thanks."

"No problem, sweetie. Plus, why shouldn't you get what you want, because I'm definitely getting these Donald Pliners and those Kenneth Coles," she said, pointing to the box sitting on the floor.

After Charlotte slipped back on the shoes she'd worn, she and the petite salesclerk walked over to the counter. When the clerk scanned the final bar code on the third box, she said, "Your total comes to three hundred twelve dollars and twelve cents. Would you like that on your Nordstrom account?"

"No, I think I'll use my Visa instead."

"Would you be interested in opening an account with us?"

"No, actually, I already have one."

The clerk printed the signature receipt. Charlotte signed on the bottom line and laid down the pen.

The clerk packed Charlotte's shoes in one shopping bag and Alicia's in another, and the three of them left the shoe area.

"So now what?" Charlotte asked.

"Can we go look at some shorts?" Alicia answered.

"Fine with me."

When they arrived in juniors, Alicia loaded her arms with five pairs of shorts, five shirts, one pair of jeans, and two T-shirts. Each piece was designed by J-Lo, Nautica, or Tommy Hilfiger.

Charlotte browsed through another rack and passed to Alicia a sleeveless jean dress to add to the pile. Then she gave her a pair of white capri pants she thought were pretty cute. Finally, Alicia went into the dressing room, and Matthew sat down in a chair nearby. Just as he did, Charlotte's phone rang.

"Hello?" she said, walking away from her son when she saw that it was Aaron.

"Why aren't you at work today?"

"I decided to take the kids shopping."

"Well, you could've told me, don't you think?"

"I didn't know for sure that we were going until this morning." Charlotte didn't like the way he was trying to keep tabs on her. He was acting as if she needed to report in to him.

"I guess I won't see you at all today, then, will I?" he asked.

"Probably not."

"And why is that?"

"Because we're in Schaumburg, and I don't know what time we'll be back."

"Come on now, Charlotte. It's not like you're going to be shopping late into the evening. Not when it's only eleven o'clock right now."

"But Matthew wants to see a movie, and then we have to get dinner," she said, looking around, making sure no one was listening.

"Let his sister or his father take him."

"What?"

"Let Alicia or Curtis take him."

"So what are you saying? That you want me to abandon my son so that I can come be with you?"

"No. But since you're with him now, I'm sure he won't mind being without his mother for a couple of hours. And to make sure he doesn't miss you, you and I can get together while they're at the theater."

"Absolutely not," Charlotte said. Betraying Curtis was one thing, but neglecting Matthew was another. She could certainly be categorized as a terrible wife, but a terrible mother she would never be. As a matter of fact, she would never again do what she did last night, stopping by Aaron's like some hooker when she was supposed to be picking up a video for her son. The scary part was that she'd never thought about her actions from this perspective until just now.

"Well, you do what you have to, and so will I," he assured her.

"You know, Aaron, I'm sick of you threatening me."

"Is that what you think? That I'm threatening you?" he said, cracking up laughing. "Girl, these aren't threats, these are promises I plan to keep. So, if you can't be here for me, then I'm calling Michelle."

"Good for you, Aaron. You be with whomever you want to."

"I will. Trust me, I will," he said and hung up.

Charlotte glanced over toward the dressing room and saw Alicia looking for her. She was wearing the dress Charlotte had given her to try on, and Charlotte knew Alicia wanted her opinion of it. So she hurried back in that direction.

"Let me see," she said when she arrived in front of her stepdaughter.

"What do you think?" Alicia twirled around.

"I like it," Matthew said, smiling. "It looks real good on you, Alicia."

"Matthew is right. It does. It really does become you."

"I like it, too," she said.

"What about the other things you tried on, did they fit?"

"Yes. I can pretty much fit anything if it's a size five."

"Okay, well, why don't you get dressed and we'll go pay for everything."

"All of it?" Alicia asked.

"Yes, if you want it."

"I do."

"Then there's nothing else to discuss."

Alicia smiled and walked away, and Charlotte could tell how happy she was. She could tell that Alicia wasn't used to being able to shop for so many items at one time. But before the day was over, Charlotte was planning to spend a whole lot more on all three of them. She loved having this kind of freedom. The kind that came from forging Curtis's name on a joint, preapproved Visa application. It had come in the mail just over a month ago, and she had quickly filled out the necessary information. Shortly after, she'd called the issuing bank to ask what credit limit they were authorizing and to ask when they would be sending the card. They'd given her an estimated time frame, and she'd stopped at home during her lunch break for four consecutive days until it had finally arrived last Thursday. She'd been worried to death that Curtis would end up getting the mail before she could, but it had all worked out in her favor. She'd been glad of the fact that they always received their mail around the same time every day, no later than twelve thirty.

But she had to admit, until two days ago when she'd purchased those earrings for Alicia, she'd been afraid to use the credit card because she didn't want Curtis yelling and screaming about it. He'd do so because of the way she'd maxed out two of his other major credit cards, the ones he'd added her name to right after they were married. Not long after, he'd closed both accounts and told her that her excessive spending had to stop. But what he didn't know was that she now had an account with every department store that would give her one. She also had her own Visa, MasterCard, and American Express cards, although each of those were nearing their limits, too, and the reason she was having her statements mailed to Anise's house. It was also the reason she never had the amount of cash Curtis thought she should have, since she was using a great deal of her earnings to pay the minimum payment requirements. She'd tried to live within her means, but it made her so unhappy. It made her do things she shouldn't have been doing. It made her sleep with Aaron.

But today she felt like a woman sitting in high places. Like she had control over her destiny and could buy anything she wanted. Right at this very moment, she didn't need Aaron in the least. Not when she was about to charge another seven hundred fifty dollars on Alicia. Not when the limit on this particular card was ten thousand dollars. But this was always her MO. If she spent a lot of money, she didn't need Aaron. If she slept with Aaron, she didn't need to spend a lot of money. She transferred one obsession for another when it was convenient. But this morning when she'd gotten up, she'd decided that spending money was a lot safer than having an affair. It was a lot easier to lie about money than it was about another man.

Charlotte paid for Alicia's new outfits and continued on her shopping spree for the next three hours. One hundred fifty on Game Boy cartridges. Three hundred on summer clothing for Matthew. One hundred thirty on two pairs of shoes for him. Five hundred on clothing for herself, and five hundred on two designer purses. One for her and one for Alicia. Then, just before leaving the mall, she'd purchased an eight hundred dollar suit for Curtis as a peace offering.

She couldn't wait for him to see it.

"Woman, have you lost your natural mind?" Curtis said.

"No, Curtis, I haven't. I wanted to take the kids shopping and that's what I did."

"Please. What you did was blow a lot of unnecessary money."

Charlotte couldn't understand why he was so upset. It wasn't like she'd spent any of his money. Not technically.

"I bought things that we needed and maybe a few things we wanted, but it's not like I killed anybody."

"You just don't get it, do you?"

"What?"

"That you can't go around spending money like some mad woman whenever you feel like it."

"But that's just it. I haven't spent any major money for months now, and I'm tired of living like we're in poverty."

"This is ridiculous," Curtis said, shaking his head at her. The man was fuming. But so was she.

"No, what's ridiculous is you thinking you don't have to do anything to better our living standard."

"How many times do we have to argue about this?"

"We'll be arguing about this until you figure out a way to make more money. The kind you used to make at your other churches."

"You've got issues, Charlotte. You know that? And I'm talkin' some real serious ones."

"Are you saying I'm crazy?"

"I don't know what to call it, but I do know that you've got some emotional problems. You're never satisfied with anything. And lately you haven't even been satisfied with me. I see this kind of behavior all the time when I counsel men in recovery. It doesn't matter what they're addicted to—drugs, alcohol, or whatever—they all have the same emotional behavior that you're exhibiting."

"Oh, so now you think you can talk to me like some mental patient?"

"Charlotte, don't exaggerate. Because it's not going to work. Whenever I call you on anything you're doing, you always try to turn it on me instead. No matter what you do, you never take responsibility for it. You always try to get away with everything."

"You're not my daddy, Curtis, you're my husband."

"And you think I don't know that?"

"Yes, because sometimes I think you forget. Maybe it's because you're fifteen years older than me. I don't know."

Curtis laughed right in her face, never taking his eyes off of her. She hated when he did this.

"I can't believe you're still trying to use psychology on me. Me, who has used every form of psychology and trick in the book when it comes to getting out of messes."

"Whatever, Curtis. I keep forgetting that you're the expert on everything."

"No, being an expert has nothing to do with it. This is about you being reckless."

"According to you, Curtis, everyone is. I mean, just thirty minutes ago, you wouldn't even let Alicia drive Matthew to the movies because you said sixteen-year-olds can be reckless when they first learn how to drive."

"I said it because it's true. You don't just go turning loose a brand-new car to a teenager when they haven't even been driving six months. Tanya was just telling me last week that Alicia still makes a lot of mistakes in traffic. She has her license, but she's definitely not ready to drive by herself."

"Well, my parents got me a car three days after I passed the test."

"And how many accidents did you have in the first year?"

"That's beside the point."

"No, tell me. How many?"

"It's not important."

"Yeah. I bet it's not."

"Why do we have to do this? I went shopping, and yes, maybe I spent more money than usual, but it's not worth arguing over."

"How did you pay for all of it?"

"My last couple of paychecks, and then I used my Nordstrom and Marshall Field's charge cards for the rest."

"Marshall Field's? I knew you had a card from Nordstrom, but when did you get one from Field's?"

She wanted to retract her statement, but it was too late.

"It just came the other day. I was in the store about a month ago, and they gave me fifteen percent off this suit I bought for opening up an account."

"What else haven't you told me?"

"Nothing."

"First, it was the thing on your leg and now this. And don't get me started on our sex life. It's practically nonexistent."

"I know, but that's all going to change. I know I've said it before, but I mean it this time. And that's part of the reason I bought you the suit. I wanted you to know how sorry I am."

Curtis sighed but didn't say anything.

"Let's not do this anymore, okay?" she said, wrapping her arms around his neck. "Let's just love each other the way we used to."

"You know we have to pick up Alicia and Matthew."

"Not for another two hours."

Charlotte kissed him, and although he resisted at first, he relinquished in a matter of seconds. They kissed with great intensity, and Charlotte wanted him inside her. She wanted him to take her without even removing their clothing. It would take too much time if they did. She wanted him to make love to her as roughly as possible. She needed him to excite her. She needed him to keep her mind completely occupied, so she wouldn't have to spend thousands of dollars just to be happy. She needed him to fill the void that she felt almost daily. If he could do that, and she prayed he could, they wouldn't have any more problems. Well, maybe some, the kind that all married couples experience, but they wouldn't have any major troubles. They could raise their son in the joyous way they'd planned and ultimately grow old together.

Charlotte wanted things to turn out perfectly. Or almost.

Chapter 14

CURTIS WALKED OUT TO HIS SECRETARY'S DESK, DISCUSSED A FEW items that he needed her to handle, and then walked back into his office and closed the door behind him. He'd been trying to concentrate on the writing of his column and the writing of his next sermon, but his mind kept wandering elsewhere. He'd been thinking about Charlotte and the problems they'd been having. When he wasn't thinking about that, he thought about the woman he'd seen during the church service. The one he was obviously attracted to and who couldn't seem to keep her eyes away from him either. He'd had to pray about the lustful thoughts he'd been having ever since that day. At one point, he'd even told himself that he had to have this woman and would. But he'd prayed about that, too, asking God to remove his sinful yearning. Sometimes, though, that yearning was strong and overbearing. It was almost uncontrollable. He knew Satan was on him like never before.

After relaxing and meditating for just over twenty minutes, Curtis picked up the phone and dialed Aaron's work number.

"Aaron Malone," he answered.

"Hey, man, how's it going?"

"I'm good, man, just trying to finish up this monthly report."

"I hear ya. I'm trying to get some work finished myself, so I can get out of here and go spend some time with Alicia."

"Now, how long did she say she was here for?"

"Just this week, and now it's already Wednesday and she'll be leaving on Sunday."

"Time flies."

"That it does. And hey, one of the reasons I'm calling is to see if you can teach Bible study for me tonight. This is my week to do it, but I'd really like to do something with Alicia and Matthew. Charlotte took them shopping yesterday, but I'd like to do something with them this evening. Maybe take them to that new arcade and then out for pizza. I tried calling each of the associate ministers, but all four of them have other commitments."

"No problem. I'll be glad to."

"I really appreciate it."

"So, how are things with you and Charlotte?"

"Better. Although we did have words last night because of all the money she spent shopping. But as they say, 'I'm not mad at her' because she definitely made up for it. She did some things to me that I won't even repeat to you," Curtis said, reminiscing.

"Really? Well, that's good to hear, man."

"Yeah, it is. Things aren't all the way back to normal but definitely better."

"I told you everything would work out."

"That you did. But these problems between Charlotte and me have really tested my faith."

"I can understand that."

"But the thing that has kept me in control is the fact that I love her. Regardless of what I say, what I think, or what I do, I really do love Charlotte and there's no way I can deny that."

"I hear you."

Curtis wondered why Aaron sounded sort of distant, but maybe he was concentrating on the report he said he was working on.

"Well, man, I guess I'd better let you go," Curtis said. "And thanks again for taking my spot at Bible study."

"Hey, that's what I'm here for. To support you in any way I can."

"You're a good friend, Aaron. You accepted me for who I was as soon as we moved here, and I have definitely come to depend on our friendship. It's not every day that a man can find a friend he can trust his life with."

"I feel the same way about you. You're a good man, Curtis, and a great pastor."

"Okay, now, I think we should end this before we both start crying like little babies," Curtis said, and they both laughed.

"I'll give you a ring tomorrow," Aaron said.

"Take care."

Curtis didn't have any other real friends he could think of. He'd bonded with a few ministers while in Chicago, but they were never the kind of friends he could trust the way he trusted Aaron. Once upon a time, he'd thought that Tyler, Cletus, and Malcolm were the closest friends he'd ever have, but now he looked at them a lot differently. Curtis had turned his life around, but the three of them were still running their massive churches in a corrupt way, and Curtis didn't have much to do with them. Occasionally, they spoke by phone, but for the most part, his connection with them was limited.

Then there was the estranged relationship he had with his family. He hadn't spoken to his mother or sister in over twenty-two years. He loved both of them, but the summer before he'd entered Morehouse, he'd stopped communicating with them completely. He'd explained to his mother that there were too many unpleasant memories regarding his childhood and that the only way he could be happy was to distance himself from anything or anyone who reminded him of it. His mother had begged and pleaded with him not to do it, but he'd purposely ignored her wishes. He'd even ignored the weekly letters she'd sent to him at school, by asking the postal service to return them. Then, during his sophomore year, his sister had called, saying that she wanted him to attend her high school graduation, but he'd told her in no uncertain terms that he couldn't make it. She'd promised him that she would never forgive him for as long as she lived.

Curtis wasn't proud of the way he'd turned his back on his family, but he hadn't seen any other way to block out his younger years. His father, his father's women, the way his father had mistreated Curtis, the way his father had allowed them to live—the way he had spent his money on his women. It had been a horrific time in Curtis's life, and he'd told himself that if he ever got a chance to leave home, he would never look back. He would pretend as though that period in his life never happened. He would work hard at building a life for himself, the kind every human being deserved.

But at least his mother had deposited every single check he'd mailed to her for Mother's Day for the last ten years. When he and Tanya had moved back to Chicago, Curtis had hired a private investigator to find out where she lived and had begun mailing her an annual check of a thousand dollars. He'd even had the PI locate his sister, who was married and had two beautiful children. But he still hadn't found the nerve to contact either of them. He thought about it from time to time but always settled on leaving well enough alone. Somehow, he truly believed it was better this way. And maybe his mother's feelings were mutual, because she'd never tried to contact him either, even though he always made sure to include his return address, just in case she wanted to.

Curtis finished the last paragraph of his column and leaned back in his chair. He sat there for a few minutes debating whether he should e-mail it to his editor now or read through it a couple of more times this evening. He glanced at his watch just as his phone rang.

"Pastor?" Lana said.

"Yes?"

"Your editor is on the line."

"Thanks. Put him through."

"Richard. How are you?"

"I'm wonderful, Curtis. And you'll feel even better than me once I tell you the news."

"Which is?"

"Your column is going into syndication. TBC News Service just made an offer for a frequency of three times per week."

"Richard, man, this is great news. When did you hear?"

"Just got off the phone with them about ten minutes ago. They wanted me to present the offer to you and then call them back with you on the line.

"Is it a good one?"

"A very good one."

"Which is?"

"They're starting you out in fifty cities and only with the top newspapers. They haven't discussed dollars and cents, but TBC is the best-known syndicate, so I'm sure the money will be what we want it to be."

"I've been waiting for this to happen, but now that it has, it seems unreal."

"Well, believe me when I say that this is only the beginning, because the subject of your book came up, too."

"Really?"

"Yes. I told TBC that you were finished with it and how once it's published, you'll be able to cross-promote. The book will turn readers on to the column, and the column will do the same for the book."

"And?"

"They agreed wholeheartedly, and Maxwell, the vice president, gave me the name of a top agent there in New York. He's going to call and make the introduction for you this afternoon and wants you to FedEx a copy of the manuscript to her for tomorrow morning's delivery. And Curtis, it sounds like this woman has connections with every major house there is. She used to run one of them herself before becoming an agent, so she definitely knows how to make things happen. As a matter of fact, Maxwell couldn't go on enough about how respected she is in the publishing community."

"I'm speechless."

"As you should be," Richard said, laughing.

"But I will say this, I'm not surprised. Because the one thing I know is that God is always true to His Word. Ask and ye shall receive. So my prayers have been answered."

"Congratulations, Curtis."

"Thanks. Thanks be to God."

"Hey, I need to get moving here, but if you can, I need you

to come down to my office so we can make a conference call to *your* new syndicate."

"I'll be there as soon as Lana prints out a copy of the manuscript. Shouldn't take me more than an hour or two," Curtis said.

"See you then."

"Oh, and Richard? What's the agent's name and address?"

"Geez. I guess I'm so excited, I can't even think straight."

Richard recited the information and Curtis jotted it down.

"I'll see you when I get there."

Curtis couldn't stop smiling if he wanted to. He couldn't stop praising God if someone asked him to. This was by far one of the happiest days of his life, and he couldn't wait to tell Charlotte. He couldn't wait to hear the happiness in her voice. Especially when she learned that his income would be increasing.

"Girl, can you believe Curtis's column is going to be syndicated?" Charlotte spoke excitedly to Anise. They were lounging at Anise's condo in the upstairs den.

"I know. It's a dream come true. I am so happy for you guys."

"I mean, it's only been a few hours since he told me, but it still doesn't seem real."

"I can only imagine, but you know Curtis believed in his column from day one and that just goes to show what can happen when you have faith. Mom says that all the time, and Curtis is living proof of it."

"And to think I doubted that any of this would happen. I feel so bad about not supporting him, but I just couldn't see any of this evolving. And now he might even be getting his book published."

"It's all such a huge blessing."

"I know. And I'm so thankful."

"And if I were you, I'd be out celebrating with my husband instead of sitting here pigging out on burritos."

"He asked me to come with them, but since he'd already planned to spend the night out with Alicia and Matthew, I told them to go ahead. He's been wanting to do something with just the three of them, and he definitely doesn't get very many opportunities. Plus, Alicia is leaving in a few days."

"That's true."

"Anyway, did I tell you that his cut will be almost a hundred thousand dollars per year?"

"Are you serious?"

"Yep. And he'll earn even more if the column is successful and more papers start buying it."

"That's a lot of money. Shoot. Maybe I need to come up with my own column idea," Anise said, and they both laughed.

"I know that's right. I wish I could come up with one, too."

"Before you know it, Curtis will be earning the same as Dave Barry, and I'm sure he's made hundreds of thousands of dollars and probably even millions from his column."

"Wouldn't that be a riot? And I would probably have a heart attack!"

"I'm sure you would, girl, as much as you love money."

"I admit it. I do. I don't know why, but I definitely love spending it, too. It makes life so much easier and so much more comfortable."

"But I keep telling you, it's not everything. We all like money to a certain extent and we all need a certain amount of it, but it is still the root of all evil. Especially if you become obsessed with it."

"Maybe. But I am who I am, and there's nothing I can do about it."

"You crack me up."

"I know. But you still love me, though," Charlotte said, leaning her head against Anise's shoulder.

"You're a trip. But yes, I do love you like a sister, and I would do anything for you. Including letting you use my address for all those credit card bills you get every month."

"Oops. Let's not even talk about that."

"Well, somebody needs to talk about it, because you've got a lot of 'em coming here. How much do you owe on all those, anyway?"

"I'm ashamed to even say. But with Curtis's new income, I'll be able to pay off everything in no time. And I'm going to close them out as soon as I do."

"I sure hope so, because if you keep this up, you're going to end up in bankruptcy."

"Not hardly. I owe more than I should, but it's nothing like that."

"If you say so."

"Really. I'm serious. It's not as bad as you think."

"Are you paying more than the minimum payments?"

"Anise, come on now. Of course I am," Charlotte lied.

"Good, because otherwise, you won't ever pay off any of those balances, and the interest will keep accruing for years to come."

"Okay, that's enough about money. Let's talk about you and your love life."

"That's easy enough. I don't have one."

"That's sad, girl."

"Although I did get a call from Frank two nights ago."

"And?"

"He called to see how I was doing, but that was about it."

"He didn't ask you out or anything?"

"He hinted around, but I'm not interested. I told you, he hurt me, and I won't ever allow him to do that again. I am not a believer in second chances once someone has violated me. When people show me their true colors, I pay attention."

"I guess. But people do change."

"Maybe. But like I said, I'm not interested. I'll be friends with Frank, but that's as far as I'm willing to go."

"Then we'll find you someone else."

"That would be nice, but it's not that easy. The pickings around here are very slim."

"There's someone for everybody."

"Supposedly, but we'll see."

Charlotte looked inside her purse when she heard her cell phone ringing. She tried to stay calm when she saw that it was Aaron.

"Hello," she said, decreasing the volume with her forefinger so Anise couldn't hear what he was saying.

"Where are you?"

"Oh, hi, William. I'm well. Is everything okay?"

"What are you talking about?"

"I think I left it somewhere near the right side of my desk."

"I know you're not with Curtis, because I called him as soon as I finished teaching Bible study."

"Did you find it?"

"Why are you playing these games with me, Charlotte?" he asked.

"I'm visiting with my cousin, but just call if you need to locate anything else. Otherwise I'll see you in the morning."

"No, I wanna hear from you tonight."

"Bye," Charlotte said, trying to keep her composure. "That

was one of the partners, looking for a document we've been working on," she told Anise.

"Oh. Work never ends, does it?"

"No. It never does."

Charlotte prayed that her heart rate would return to normal.

Chapter 13

CHARLOTTE DROVE OUT OF ANISE'S SUBDIVISION AND SIGHED. IT WAS now nine thirty and she was starting to feel exhausted. She'd worked ten hours today and couldn't wait to get home and climb into bed. Still, she was glad she'd had the opportunity to spend some girl time with her cousin. Being with a man was fine, and very needed, but spending time with another woman was special, especially when you could love and trust that particular woman and be yourself in the process. With Anise, Charlotte never had to watch what she said and never had to walk on eggshells when in her presence. Anise never judged her, and she never treated her any differently when they didn't agree on something.

Charlotte stopped at the red light and turned on the radio. She searched for AM 1370 and found it. *Live with Mary Ellen*, a syndicated talk show out of Detroit, was already in progress. The subject for this evening was "Is having an affair really worth the consequences?" Charlotte raised the volume. This was definitely a subject she could relate to, and she wanted to hear what advice Mary Ellen had for her callers.

"Next up, we have Lisa from Birmingham. Hi, Lisa," Mary Ellen said.

"Hi, Mary Ellen. It's so great to finally get through to you. I listen to your show every night and I just want to tell you how helpful you have been for me over the last year."

"I'm really glad to hear that and thanks for being such a dedicated listener."

"My question to you is, how do you end an affair with a man who gives you the best sex you've ever had in your life? I mean, how do you forget this man and simply go on like nothing ever happened? How do I start being faithful to my husband again?"

"Well, for starters, you need to understand why you decided to have the affair in the first place. Because there had to be some reason you made the decision to stray. Are you no longer in love with your husband? Does he no longer satisfy you sexually? Are you no longer attracted to him? Did you marry at a very young age?"

"I'm not sure if I'm still attracted to him or not, but yes, we did marry at an early age. We married during our third year in college, and I was a virgin when I met him. Of course, I ended up getting pregnant right away, so I never had the chance to finish school or start a career. I became a stay-at-home mom and eventually became pregnant with our second child when our first was only eighteen months. We've been married for ten years, but about a year ago I started paying attention to other men. My husband became this boring person who worked a lot of hours and traveled on business at least once every couple of weeks, and I needed some excitement in my life. I felt like I was going to go crazy if I didn't find it. So, the next thing I knew, I was flirting with one of my husband's coworkers, and he started pursuing me on a regular basis. He'd call me from

his office and sometimes my husband would come into his office while we were on the phone. And as terrible as this probably sounds, hearing my husband's voice in the background and
knowing that I was sneaking to talk to his friend started to turn
me on. Then, the next thing I knew, I was meeting him at mo-
tels, meeting him in parks late at night, and doing whatever I
had to do to have sex with him. And then, oh God," she said,
sniffling. "There were even a couple of times I left the house
to go meet him late at night when my husband was out of
town, and I left my children at home by themselves."

"You have got to seek professional help, Lisa. Sleeping
around on your husband is bad enough, but leaving your children all alone is totally unacceptable. Your affair with this man
is completely out of control and if you don't do something
about it, it will only get worse. Your situation is very common
though. I hear from many women who married their first loves
right out of high school or right out of college and ten years
down the road they start wondering how it would feel to be
with another man. They start to tell themselves that there must
be something better outside of their households. They don't
know anything other than the relationship they've had with
their husbands, so of course, the grass begins to look golf-
course green on the other side. It looks like the best thing in the
world, and it's so easy to get caught up in fantasy. You start believing that there is such a thing as a perfect marriage or the
perfect man, when in fact, marriage is what you make it. Some
women fail to realize that marriage requires a lot of give-and-
take, and it requires a ton of hard work. But you have to start
working on it from the very beginning. You can't take it for
granted, not for one day."

"I hear what you're saying, but how do I end this thing with him? How do I get him out of my system, because it's to the point now where I don't even want to have sex with my husband. It's to the point where I think about my lover every single day. I feel like I need to be with him in order to survive."

"Like I said, you must get help. I think you should see someone individually, but I would also suggest that you and your husband find a good marriage counselor. Because clearly, your marriage was in trouble long before you started having an affair."

"Are you saying I should tell my husband?"

"Coming clean would be ideal, but you have to decide. You know your husband better than anyone, and you'll have to determine if he'll be able to forgive you and move on. Some things are better left untold. It just depends on each individual. But before you do anything, I suggest you call up your lover and end things with him for good. You need to make it clear that your affair was a mistake and that you are going to make things work with your husband. And no matter what he says or how he tries to make you see otherwise, stick to your guns. You will need to say what you mean and mean what you say. Period."

"Thank you for speaking to me, Mary Ellen. I really appreciate it."

"All the best to you, Lisa."

Charlotte was in shock. This Lisa woman was in the same boat that she was in with Aaron. There were some differences, but the key similarity was the fact that she and Lisa both started having affairs because they needed more excitement in their lives. The other likeness they shared was the type of men they were sleeping with. Lisa's lover and Aaron both knew how to pleasure Lisa and Charlotte in a way their husbands couldn't. These men knew how to please them in ways that were unexplainable. And for Charlotte, it wasn't that she didn't enjoy making love with Curtis, because she did. But there was something just a bit more thrilling when it came to Aaron. She'd told herself that she was finished with Aaron, but ever since he'd called her cell phone one hour ago, she'd felt completely out of sorts. His voice alone had been enough to stir her. It was enough to make her go to him.

"Let's take one more caller, and then we'll go to a commercial break," Mary Ellen said. "Good evening, Melanie from Newark."

"Hi, Mary Ellen. How are you?"

"Wonderful. How about you?"

"I'm doing well. Actually, I'm doing a lot better for the first time in two years, and I wanted to share something that might help your last caller."

"Sure. Go ahead."

"I know exactly how she feels, because I've been there. I was only twenty-five when I married my husband, and all of a sudden when I turned forty, I wasn't attracted to him anymore. It was almost as if I wished I wasn't married to him. But after seeing the close relationship that my two boys have with their father, I decided to stay married and find love elsewhere. I decided it was time to get sex from someone who really knew how to give it to me. And I did for two whole years. But then one day, about six months ago, I met my lover at a forest preserve in broad daylight. He arrived before me; I parked next to him and then followed him on foot down a long hill and into a secluded, bushy area. We tore into each other like our lives depended on it, and before long we were completely naked, and my lover started pounding into me from behind like there was no tomorrow. I was down on my hands and knees begging him to do it harder, but when I looked up, I saw my eighteen-year-old son, staring at me. I saw tears flooding his face, and in seconds he ran away from us as fast as he could. I don't remember much else after that, because I fainted."

"Oh, Melanie," Mary Ellen said from the airways.

"Oh my God," Charlotte spoke out loud.

"But the real reason I'm calling is because Lisa needs to know how damaging an affair can be if a child finds out about it. Her children are still under the age of ten, but at eighteen, my son decided to do something about it. So I'm here to tell Lisa and any other woman who is sleeping around on her husband . . . my son committed suicide one week later, in that same forest preserve, in the same spot he caught another man with his mother. He even left a note that said, 'This is for you, Mom. What a nasty whore you turned out to be.' "

Charlotte waited for Mary Ellen to comment, but she didn't. Tears flowed from her own eyes, and she thought about Meredith Connolly Christiansen and how Meredith's daughter had ended her life, too, at such a young age. Charlotte thought about Matthew and what would happen if he ever discovered that she was sleeping around on his father.

"I am so sorry," Mary Ellen finally said.

"Not more than I am. Because not only did I lose my son, but my husband has moved out and filed for a divorce. And my other son has moved in with him."

"How devastating. I can't even imagine. But I do hope you're seeing someone professionally."

"I am, but I don't think I will ever be happy again. It's been six months, and I'm still as numb as the day it happened. Which is why I hope your listeners are really paying attention to what I'm saying and that they will stop the madness before it's too late."

"Thank you for sharing with us, Melanie, and please take care of yourself."

"You, too," she said and hung up.

"We'll be right back" was all Mary Ellen said.

Charlotte drove onto North State Street, wiping her face. She had to end this thing with Aaron for good. She could never allow what happened to Melanie and her son to happen to her and Matthew. She continued driving and heard her phone ringing. She was afraid to look at the caller ID screen.

"Hello?"

"When did you leave your cousin's?"

"Maybe ten minutes ago."

"Well, why didn't you call me?"

"Because there's nothing for us to talk about."

"You think you can just decide something like that without me having any say-so about it?"

"When you called me on the phone at the mall I made it very clear that you could be with Michelle or whomever you wanted to. And you said that's what you were going to do."

"But you know you don't want that. You know the thought of me being inside another woman makes you insane."

"Aaron. I don't know any other way to say this, but you and I are over. What we had was special, and I appreciate you being there for me these last few months, but I can't take the chance of Curtis finding out about us, and I won't allow Matthew to be hurt. We have to end this before something bad happens."

"You're serious, aren't you?" he said, sounding much more polite.

"I am. I know it's not what you want, but this is the way it has to be."

"But why?"

"I just told you. Curtis and Matthew."

"After all we've been to each other?"

"I'm sorry, Aaron. I really, really am."

"Baby, this hurts. I mean, this is truly going to tear me apart."

"Maybe for a while, but you'll find someone else. Or maybe you can spend more time with Michelle, because she really seems to like you."

"I'm not in love with Michelle. I'm in love with you."

"Like I said, I'm sorry for all of this. I'm sorry that we even started seeing each other, because it was never fair to you."

"You're damn right it was never fair to me, because you always had Curtis to run home to."

"I know, I know. And I hope that one day you can forgive me."

"Okay, look," he said, sounding calm again. "Your mind is obviously made up, so the least you could do is tell me all of this in person. You owe me at least that much."

"I don't think that's a good idea. I think we need to make this our last conversation. If we see each other face-to-face, it will only make things harder."

"I promise I won't try to change your mind, but please don't end this so coldly. Please let me see you one last time."

"I don't know."

"Please, baby, don't make me beg like this. It's so humiliating."

"Okay. Fine. But it can't be tomorrow, because we're taking the kids to Great America."

"Then what about Friday?"

"Where?"

"Wherever you want."

"What about your friend's house in the country?"

"Call me on Friday morning to let me know what time you want to meet."

"I will. And again, I'm sorry, Aaron. I can't say that enough."

"I'll see you on Friday, all right?"

"Take care."

Charlotte pressed the end button on her phone and dropped it onto the seat. As soon as she did, it rang again. She wondered what Aaron wanted now, until she saw her home phone number illuminated.

"Hey, baby," she said to Curtis.

"Where are you?"

"Only five minutes away. I just left Anise's."

"Did you guys have a good time?"

"We did."

"The kids and I had a great time, too. I'm missing Alicia already, and she hasn't even gone home yet."

"I know. She's going to have to start visiting us a lot more often."

"I agree."

"So are they ready for Great America?"

"Matthew definitely is. He hasn't talked about anything else since we got home. He keeps bragging to Alicia about all the huge roller coasters he's going to get on with her, but you and I both know it's all talk. Unless something has changed pretty drastically with him since last summer."

Charlotte laughed. "I really doubt that, because if I remember correctly, he was scared to death."

"He's funny. But hey, I'll see you when you get here."

"I love you, Curtis."

"Love you, too."

Chapter 14

THE TRIP TO THE AMUSEMENT PARK YESTERDAY HAD PROVEN TO BE A LOT of fun, and, to Curtis's surprise, Matthew had gotten on more roller coasters than he'd expected. Curtis was sure, though, it mostly had to do with Matthew's need to impress his big sister. It seemed as if he was willing to do whatever he had to in order to win her approval; however, what he didn't know was that Alicia loved him regardless. She never treated him like a half brother; she treated him no differently than if they shared the same father and mother and lived in the same house together, which, of course, made life a lot easier for Curtis.

As Curtis flipped through the first few pages of his manuscript, ironically enough, Joan Epstein, the agent his editor Richard had connected him with, called.

"This is Curtis," he said after Lana hung up.

"Curtis Black," Joan announced in a smiling voice.

"How are you?" he asked, admiring her attitude already.

"I'm batting a thousand after reading that book of yours. I tell you, I started it yesterday and finished it before going to bed last night. And I'm in total awe."

"Well, thank you."

"I truly believe you have a winner here, and I'd like to offer you representation."

"Excuse me for asking, but it's hard for me to believe that this could all be so simple."

"Well, normally it isn't, but you've got the makings of a best-seller, and there's no reason in the world why we should wait on this."

"This is amazing. But can I ask you a question?"

"Go ahead."

"What do you think of the book personally? I'm asking because I've heard that it's important for an agent to feel a certain passion for a book if the agent is going to be successful with getting a publishing house interested."

"This is true. So let me give you a general rundown of what I think about your work. To start, your voice is very bold, very powerful, and, most of all, very different from any other motivational and inspirational book I've seen from a Christian perspective. The fact that you have been connected with and spoken at so many megachurches throughout the country is reason enough to believe that you will sell thousands and thousands of copies. In addition to that, I believe your book has a mainstream vibe that will attract Christians and non-Christians alike. So the vibe you're projecting, your new syndicated column, and you agreeing to go out on speaking engagements is all I really need to convince any major house to pay you a pretty hefty advance and give your book what we call the big push."

"Meaning?"

"That you'll get all the marketing and publicity that this book deserves. The promotional budget will coincide with your advance."

"You mentioned speaking engagements?"

"Yes."

"How many of those do you think I'd be required to do?"

"As many as you can, but during the first year of release, it would be good if you could go out at least a few times per month. And this would be in addition to the national book tour the publisher would be sending you on right after publication."

Curtis understood why this would all be necessary, but he wasn't sure if it was the best thing for his marriage or the church. He'd figured he would have to travel, but not as much as Joan was explaining. But whenever large sums of money were involved, there was always some trade-off. It had always been that way for him.

"Sounds to me like writing the book is only half the battle," he said.

"Truthfully, it's probably only about twenty percent. Because right after an editor acquires your work, the editing process will begin. Then, copyediting, production, tour scheduling, and a lot more."

"So what do I need to do now?"

"If you give me your fax number, I'll fax you a copy of my agent-author contract. It's an agreement that protects both you and me should we ever part ways for any reason. It also outlines my commission."

"When do you need to have this back, because I'd like to have my attorney look it over before I sign it?"

"I encourage that. But if there is some way you could have him look at it this morning, that would really help. This way, I can get copies made and get them to the five editors I know will be interested. A couple of them only work part of the day on Friday, and I'd like to have them take the manuscript home to read over the weekend."

"I can call him now. Actually, my wife works for his firm, so if he's in, I'm sure he'll look it over as soon he gets it."

"Sounds good," Joan said, and they exchanged fax numbers. "Just call me when he gives you the go-ahead, so I can be looking for it. In the meantime, I'll have my assistant make copies. I'm sort of jumping the gun here, but I don't think you'll see any reason why you shouldn't sign the contract. It's pretty basic for the most part."

"If I may ask, what other clients do you represent?"

"Tara Lockhart—"

"The mystery writer?"

"That would be her. And I also represent Willie and Michael Tomlinson, the brothers who co-author *The Cubicle* sci-fi series."

"Enough said." Curtis was astounded and didn't need any more proof regarding Joan's legitimacy as an agent.

"I don't mind telling you anything you want to know, so all you have to do is ask."

"That's good to hear. I'm going to call my attorney right now, and as soon as you fax me the contract, I'll fax it over to him."

"I'm sending it now. Talk to you in a while."

"Thanks, Joan."

Everything was happening much faster than Curtis had anticipated, but he wasn't complaining. First the syndication offer and now this. And Joan was sounding as though her selling the book was a done deal.

Curtis phoned Charlotte to tell her the great news.

"Baby, this is wonderful."

"I told you this was going to happen."

"I know, and I was just telling Anise last night that I am so sorry for not supporting you the way I should have. I didn't believe in what you were doing, but I promise you, that will never happen again."

"I forgive you. And actually, I'm calling to see if William is in because I need him to review a contract that Joan wants me to sign."

"He is but only for the next half hour. So send me the contract and I'll have him look it over."

"I think Lana is sending it now."

"I'll have William call you in a few minutes."

"I'll be waiting."

"Oh my goodness, baby, I am so excited. Life is really about to change for us."

"Yeah, but in a very positive way. And maybe now you can stop complaining about the small amount of money I make," he teased.

"It's not that you make small money, it's just that I've always wanted so much more for us. Not just for Matthew and me, but for you, too."

"I guess."

"How much do you think a publisher will offer you?"

"I don't know. Joan sounded pretty hyped, though."

"Wow. Well, hey, I'll call you after you've had a chance to speak to William."

"Love you."

"I love you more."

Curtis smiled, pressed the flash button, and called Aaron. He couldn't wait to tell his best friend what was going on.

"Mom, you won't believe this," Charlotte said into the phone.

"What? You sound like you just won a million dollars."

"Maybe not a million, but things are definitely looking up

for us. Remember two days ago when I told you about Curtis's syndication deal?"

"Uh-huh."

"Well, they connected him with this big-time New York agent, and she called him this morning. And she just got his manuscript yesterday."

"Oh my. That's great news."

"And she's almost positive she can sell it to a publisher for good money."

"That's wonderful, sweetheart, and please tell Curtis I said congratulations."

"You should call him yourself, Mom."

"I will. Is he at the church?"

"Yes, he's waiting for one of the partners here to look over his agent contract."

"Who's that?" Charlotte heard her father ask.

"Your only child, and I'll let her tell you the news."

"What's going on, sugar?"

"Curtis found an agent and she's pretty sure she can sell his book to one of the publishing houses."

"Is that right? You know I never liked that Curtis after he got you pregnant, but I have a lot more respect for him now. He really has been a good husband to you and a good father to my grandson. Plus, I can tell he really does love you. I can see it in his eyes whenever you all come visit."

"I'm glad you feel that way, Daddy, because Curtis is a good man, and I love him, too."

"You tell that Curtis I said God bless him."

"Mom's going to call him, so maybe you could talk to him, too, when she does."

"I will. And how's my grandson?"

"He's fine. And actually, this week, he's in hog heaven because his sister is visiting. We took them to Great America yesterday, and they both had a blast."

"Well, you tell him his grandpa loves him and that I can't wait for him to get here on Sunday."

"He's already looking forward to it. We're going to bring him over right after we take Alicia home."

"I wish he was staying with us for more than nine days."

"He has a science camp that we signed him up for, but he'll be back to stay with you for three more weeks at the end of July."

"Your mother and I have got some big plans for him."

"I can only imagine how spoiled he'll be when he gets back here."

"Well, sugar, I need to get to a dentist appointment, so did you want to speak back to your mother?"

"No, I need to get back to work, but tell her I'll call her later."

"Okay, sugar, I love you, and kiss Matthew for us."

"I will, Daddy, and I love you, too."

Charlotte missed her parents a lot. She especially missed seeing them with Matthew. He gave them so much joy, and they did the same for him. Her father was a high school principal and spent most of his summer break out on the golf course, and her mother was a high school English teacher who tutored some of her students during the month of July. So both of them had plenty of free time to spend with Matthew once he arrived.

Charlotte heard her cell phone ringing and pulled it out of her handbag. She rolled her eyes toward the ceiling when she saw that it was Aaron. She'd told him they could meet one last time this afternoon, but now she'd decided against it, partly because she'd already apologized and explained her position to him on the phone and didn't know what else they had to talk about. It was better if they ceased communication so he could move on without her. He claimed he loved her, but she hoped his love was only an infatuation and something he would get over pretty quickly.

The phone rang one last time and shortly after, she heard the voice-mail signal. She would listen to his message at some point, but right now she had better things to do.

She ordered a dozen roses and a cluster of balloons and had them delivered to the church. She looked forward to the beautiful love she and Curtis would make when the day was over.

Chapter 15

ALL WAS QUIET AND WELL FOR THE REVEREND AND MRS. BLACK. Matthew was happily visiting with his grandparents, Alicia was back in Chicago, and life couldn't have been happier. They'd both taken the day off, something they hadn't done in months, just the two of them, and Curtis felt like they were on a second honeymoon. The utter chemistry and strong passion between them were refreshing. It reminded him of the way their relationship had once been, practically flawless. Charlotte even looked at him differently. He saw a gleam in her eyes that he hadn't seen for months. Even now, she was downstairs fixing him breakfast, preparing to serve him in bed, which was a privilege in itself because he couldn't remember the last time she'd done it. Then, there were the flowers and balloons she'd sent four days ago. So out of the ordinary for her, yet so special to him as a man. Special to him as her husband. Special, no matter how a person looked at it. Of course, her noticeable turnabout had a lot to do with his new syndicated column and possible book deal. It had a lot to do with money. Still, Curtis was just happy to have her acting the way a wife ought to. He was content just having a certain amount of peace and the feeling that there wasn't anything to worry about. It was good having her home when she was supposed to be and not working after office hours. It was good not having to wonder what was really going on after dark.

Curtis looked up when he saw his wife strolling into the bedroom, smiling.

"What do we have here?" he said when she placed the tray on his lap.

"Fresh strawberries, scrambled eggs, waffles, sausage links, and orange juice."

"Come here."

Charlotte sat next to him and he kissed her. "I love you so much, you know that?" he said.

"I do. And I love you. With everything that I have. And from this day forward, I'm going to be the wife that you want me to be. I realize now that I haven't been as of late, but that's over."

"We have such a great life together, and if we stay happy with each other, Matthew will continue being the happy child that he is. And that's extremely important to me. I pray for his happiness and his health every single day."

"I pray for the same thing. I've always prayed for that," she said, feeding Curtis a strawberry. He chewed slowly, enjoying it, and then lifted a forkful of eggs from his plate. Charlotte flipped on the television and turned it to *The View.* Barbara Walters, Star Jones, Meredith Vieira, Joy Behar, and the new host from *Survivor* were discussing current national news.

"Star has lost a lot of weight, hasn't she?" Curtis asked.

"Yep. She still isn't saying, but the rumor is that she had gastric bypass surgery."

"Well, whatever she's doing, she looks good."

"She really does."

They watched through the end of the segment, but right at the commercial break, the phone rang.

"Hello?" Charlotte answered. Curtis looked over at her. "Yes, he sure is, he's right here." She passed him the phone, seeming almost ecstatic.

"Hello?" he said.

"Curtis, this is Joan," his agent said. "How are you?"

"I'm good, and you?"

"Couldn't be better. And for your sake, I hope you're sitting down."

Curtis raised up, sitting at attention. "What's the word?"

"Remember yesterday when I told you there was so much interest that I was going to take your manuscript to auction?"

"Yeah."

"Well, I just got off the phone with Renee Kiley at Wexler-Adams, and she's made a preemptive offer."

"Which means?"

"She wants the book so badly, she doesn't want any other houses bidding on it."

Curtis wanted to speak, but since he didn't know what to say, he hoped Joan would continue. He felt a sudden wave move through his stomach. He hadn't been this nervous in years.

"Don't you want to know what the offer is?"

"Yeah, but I'm almost afraid to ask."

"Renee is offering you an advance in the amount of seven hundred fifty thousand dollars."

Curtis cracked up laughing.

"It's no joke. They're putting three-quarters of a million dollars on the table, and you have to decide today before the close of business."

"Decide?" Curtis said, moving his feet onto the floor, flabbergasted.

Now Joan was laughing. "They want world rights, but they've agreed to pay you two hundred on signing."

"Thousand?"

"Yes."

Curtis turned toward Charlotte. "They're offering me seven hundred fifty thousand dollars with two hundred of it on signing."

Charlotte covered the front of her face, shaking her head, obviously more stunned than he was.

"So, is the answer yes, because we can certainly take our chances and go ahead with the auction?"

"Do you think someone would be willing to pay more?"

"Possibly, but the thing is, WexlerAdams is one of the top houses, and Renee Kiley is probably one of the best editors you'll ever meet. She's really on top of her game, and I think you'll be happy working with her. She never acquires anything at this level unless she's going to take it under her wing completely. She will definitely do everything in her power to keep her bosses behind your book, and it will get all of the attention it deserves. I've dealt with her for years, and it's always been a memorable experience."

"Well, if you think we should take it, then let's go for it."

"I still need to finalize some minor details, things like what the other three payout amounts will be, delivery date, publishing date, and a couple of other items."

"Sounds good to me."

"This really is an exceptional offer, and I know you'll be pleased. So, congratulations, and I'll be in touch probably again this afternoon."

"Thanks, Joan. Thanks for everything. Especially for making this happen so quickly."

"These are the sort of deals that make me proud. Every now and then, I connect with authors who have great potential for overnight success, and I knew you were one of them the moment I started reading your work."

"I appreciate hearing that."

"Well, I'm going to let you go, but again, congrats, and please give your wife my best."

"I will."

Curtis hung up the phone and stared at Charlotte.

"Oh my God, baby," she said, hugging him and trying not to cry, but it was too late.

"God is so awesome."

"I can't believe they offered you so much money and this is only your first book. And it happened in less than a week."

"I know. It's strange, but when God is in control, nothing should surprise us. I mean, just as Joan had asked them, each of the editors she gave it to on Friday read it over the weekend and called her first thing yesterday morning."

"Maybe now we can start looking for our dream house."

"At some point, but not until the contract is signed and the check has cleared the bank."

"But you'll start getting paid from the syndicate very soon, too."

"Yeah. But getting six figures all at once has to be handled responsibly. We're going to have to meet with our accountant and investment firm to get things in order. I never cared that much about saving anything when I had those other two churches, but I learned my lesson. We will never be broke again if I can help it. And I will never blow money the way I used to."

"This is only the beginning. I can feel it. They'll be asking you to write another one before the year is over."

"I'm going to have to do a lot of traveling in the beginning."

"Maybe Matthew and I can go with you some of the time."

"Definitely."

"This feels like a dream. It's so unreal."

"I know. Who would have thought?"

"I can't wait to tell my parents. And Aunt Emma and Anise."

"I'm calling Aaron right now," Curtis said, already dialing the number.

Charlotte didn't want to, but Aaron had told her that if she didn't meet with him, she would be sorry. He'd left several messages on her cell phone, and as soon as Curtis had left for the hospital, Charlotte had gotten dressed. She and Curtis had planned on going out to dinner to celebrate the book deal, but Brother Hardaway, one of their members, had been given less than forty-eight hours to live. The family had wanted Curtis to come pray for him and the family.

She turned into the parking lot of the hotel and walked inside. Aaron had left the room number on her cell phone, so she walked through the lobby and into the elevator. When she stepped off of it, she walked down the hallway and stopped in front of the suite she'd been summoned to. She took a deep breath, dreading what was sure to be a confrontation, and knocked. Aaron opened the door immediately. He must have been standing there, waiting like a watchdog.

"Why did I have to threaten you? Why couldn't you just do what you said you were going to do last week?"

"I told you. There's nothing else to discuss. We can't ever see each other again. Maybe as friends, but not sexually."

"You're a true piece of work."

Charlotte stayed silent.

"You think you can waltz your ass in here, dump me like garbage, and then go back home to Curtis with no problems?"

"What are you talking about?"

"I'm telling you that I'm not having it. You knew what you were doing when you started seeing me, and you knew you were married."

"But it was a mistake. We were both wrong for betraying Curtis the way we did."

"No, there was no mistake. There was no mistake at all. We were meant to be together from the start. But somehow you've forgotten about that. I rocked your world the first time we were together, and from that day on, you were hooked. And then we fell in love with each other."

Charlotte didn't know why he was talking crazy. She'd never been in love with him and if she'd ever slipped and said she was, it would only have been in the heat of passion when he begged her to tell him. But she certainly didn't mean it. She loved what he did to her, the way he made her feel, but she never loved *him*.

"Why are you doing this, baby? Come on. Tell the truth. What's the real reason you're trying to drop me like this?"

"I keep telling you, it's because of Curtis and Matthew. I really want my marriage to work, and I don't want to hurt my son."

"Stop lying," he said, grabbing her shirt collar.

"Aaron, don't!" She was scared to death.

"You're trying to end this because of money, and I told you before how angry I get when I have to keep hearing about your preacher husband and all this money he can make. Oh yeah, baby, I know about everything. The syndication offer and the book deal. He told me everything, and that's why I told you to get your ass over here or else." He released her shirt and folded his arms. They were still standing near the door. Charlotte hoped she could break and run before he tried to hurt her.

"Aaron, please listen to me. We can't do this anymore. I know you don't see it now, but it's all for the best."

"Don't you dare say what's best for me," he said, standing toe-to-toe with her. "Don't you ever in your life say that to me again."

Charlotte swallowed hard, gazing toward the floor.

"You know, I should put a bullet in your head for playing games with me all these months. You strung me along all this time, and now you want to leave me? I mean, do you think I should let you get away with something like that?"

"I'm so sorry, Aaron. I'm really, really, sorry."

"Not as sorry as you're going to be."

Charlotte stepped back. "What do you mean?"

"Maybe I'll tell Curtis what his sweet little wife has been doing behind his back."

"Aaron, no," she pleaded.

"Maybe I'll tell him *everything*."

Charlotte's heart skipped a beat.

"Maybe I'll tell him every single thing I know about his innocent little Charlotte," he said, twirling a section of her hair with his finger. "Whaddaya think?"

"Why are you being so cruel?"

"Why are you trying to get rid of me?"

"I have to go," she said, reaching for the doorknob. But Aaron stepped in front of her, blocking her escape.

"You're not going anywhere until I tell you. You hear me? I'm running things now. I let you toy with me and lead me on for far too long, and now it's payback time. It's payback like you wouldn't believe."

"Aaron, what do you want me to do?"

"I want you to go home and ask Curtis for a divorce. And then I want you to file for a legal separation."

"What?"

"You heard me."

"But I won't do that."

"You will or I'm giving Curtis the four-one-one. When I finish unleashing all those skeletons you've got stacked on top of each other, Curtis won't give you the time of day. And he'll probably have grounds to take Matthew from you."

"I won't let you do that."

"You don't have a choice."

"Move out of my way, Aaron." She was still terrified but thought maybe a show of confidence might make a difference.

But Aaron laughed hysterically. And stopped abruptly.

"You'd better thank your God that we're here at this hotel. Otherwise, I would beat you down to the floor. I would make sure you left here on a stretcher or in a body bag."

"What's wrong with you, Aaron? Why are you acting like this?"

"Because I can. Because this is what you deserve."

"Please let me go. I'm begging you."

"Sure, baby. But I'm giving you two days to take care of your business. And if you haven't asked Curtis for a divorce by then, I'm singing like Luther. I won't leave out one detail. Okay?"

He stepped away from the door. "Now, go on. Run home to your preacher man."

Charlotte reached for the doorknob again, and this time she opened the door.

"Remember," he said. "Ticktock, ticktock. Better keep your eyes fixed on the clock."

Charlotte rushed out of the room and toward the stairway. She couldn't chance waiting for the elevator and went down five flights in record time. She was out of breath, but she wasn't about to stop until she was inside her car. Safe from that lunatic. What was she going to do if Aaron told Curtis any of what he knew? Any of what she'd confided to him so irresponsibly? What had she been thinking? Surely, her life would be over if Curtis ever found out that . . .

"Oh dear God, please. Please don't let this be happening. Don't let this be happening now."

"I am in so much trouble," Charlotte said as soon as Anise let her in.

"What's wrong?"

"It's bad. It's really, really bad." Charlotte was frantic and didn't know how she was going to tell Anise about her and Aaron. But she had to tell somebody before Aaron tried to ruin her.

"Girl, settle down. Come in here, and tell me what's going on."

Charlotte followed Anise into the kitchen, and they both sat at the table.

"I'm not even going to beat around the bush, because if I do, I'll never get it out. Aaron and I have been sleeping together for months now."

"Charlotte, no. Please tell me you're lying."

"I'm not, and now he's threatening to tell Curtis. He told me that if I don't ask Curtis for a divorce, he's telling him everything."

"This can't be true."

"Well, it is. I've been seeing Aaron several times a week, and last week I decided to break things off with him. Then, today, he left me a ton of voice messages saying that I'd better meet with him or I'd be sorry. He even grabbed my blouse and threatened to hurt me physically."

"But why? I mean, why were you messing around on Curtis in the first place?"

"Because I wasn't happy. I needed more than what he was giving me. But now I know it was all a mistake, and that's why I told Aaron it was over."

Anise shook her head in denial.

"What am I going to do?"

"I have no idea."

Charlotte wondered why Anise was sounding sort of short with her. It wasn't like this really had anything to do with her anyway, not to mention that Anise was supposed to support family first. She was *her* cousin, not Curtis's.

"I need you to help me, Anise."

"But how?"

"I need you to talk to Aaron. Maybe you can talk some sense into him."

"If he didn't listen to you, Charlotte, why would he listen to me?"

"Because he was angry with me. But maybe if you call him, it'll be different."

"I don't know. And if you want to know the truth, I really don't want to get involved with this. Because it's very hard for me to understand why you did this in the first place. Not when you have a husband who practically worships the ground you walk on."

"Anise, look. I didn't come here to be lectured. I came here because you're the only person I can trust enough to tell this to. You're the only person who can help me deal with this madness. And if you won't do it for me, then please do it for Matthew."

Anise stared at her disappointedly. "You're wrong, Charlotte. You're wrong for having that affair, and you're wrong for asking me to get in the middle of it."

"I'm begging you. And I promise you, I won't ever do anything like this again. I know I was wrong, and I'm sorry. But you have to call him for me. You have to make him see that telling Curtis is not going to be good for any of us. Especially not for Matthew."

Anise sighed heavily. "What's his number?"

Charlotte rattled it off, and Anise dialed Aaron at home.

"Hi, Aaron, it's Anise."

Charlotte wished she could hear what he was saying and wished she'd thought to pick up another extension before Anise had made the call.

"Aaron, I know this isn't my business, but Charlotte just told me what's going on."

Anise paused.

"Well, don't you think it would be best if you and Charlotte went your separate ways since she is a married woman? And if you tell Curtis anything, a lot of people are going to be hurt. Mainly their son. So I'm asking you for his well-being if for no one else's, please let this go. Let Charlotte go on with her life and you do the same with yours."

Anise paused again.

"I understand that, but no good can come of you doing—"

Anise paused midsentence.

"Aaron, I know you're upset and I sympathize with what

you're feeling. Believe me I do. But this isn't the way to handle your pain."

Anise paused and raised her eyebrows.

"But maybe if you really thought this through—"

Anise listened longer than usual and then hung up the phone.

"What did he say?" Charlotte asked.

"It really doesn't matter, but the bottom line is this: Aaron Malone is going to be a huge, huge problem. Mega."

A sharp aching whipped through Charlotte's chest.

Chapter 16

CHARLOTTE WAS THE LAST TO WALK IN, BUT AS SOON AS SHE DID, everyone greeted her, and then Sister Mason, chairwoman of the annual churchwide picnic committee, called the meeting to order. The very popular and well-attended event was less than one week away, and Sister Mason had called a final assembly. There would be a few other short discussions regarding last-minute details, but this would be the last meeting that all eight on the committee would come to.

"First off, I wanted to tell everyone that we now have more than enough volunteers," Sister Mason started. "We were lacking in the number of cooks we needed, but two of the members came forward just this week, offering their assistance."

"This is great," Charlotte said. "And we now have all the dessert we need, too. I was looking for at least three others, but my aunt has agreed to make two large pans of peach cobbler and one banana pudding."

"Well, bless her heart," Sister Mason said. "I've had Miss Emma's cobbler before and her banana pudding, and both are to die for."

"You can say that again," Aaron agreed, and Charlotte's heart raced. She'd purposely not looked in his direction since sitting down at the conference table. She couldn't wait to get out of there. She wanted to be as far away from him as possible and wished he would find another church to worship at.

Still, Charlotte ignored him and thankfully, he didn't say anything more.

"Sister Simmons, are we all set with the games and the people who are going to coordinate them?" Sister Mason asked.

"As a matter of fact, yes. I still need to purchase a few other prizes, but that's pretty much it."

"Remember to keep your receipts this time," Sister Mason joked.

"What do you mean by that?" Sister Simmons snapped.

"Don't get upset; I'm only teasing you because last year you asked to be reimbursed for more than the amount on those receipts you submitted."

"And like I told you *last* year, I misplaced them, but I still knew about every dollar I spent. I kept track of everything mentally, and I had no reason to lie about it."

"Which is why we went ahead and paid you what you asked for." Sister Mason was no longer smiling. There had been a lot of talk about Sister Simmons and the way she connived and schemed when it came to money. She was always involved with every event and program the church sponsored, but she never had all of the receipts to prove what expenses she'd incurred. Five or ten dollars was one thing, but fifty and seventy-five were another.

"Well, it sounded to me like you were trying to insinuate that I was lying."

"Well, I wasn't. But just so everyone here is on the same

page, any expenses over twenty dollars will not be paid without a valid receipt. Pastor Black wanted me to share that with all of you, so that there won't be any misunderstandings when the picnic is over."

"Hmmph," Sister Simmons grunted. "Whatever."

Charlotte always wondered how Sister Simmons could do so much passing out in the aisle every Sunday, claiming to be filled with the Holy Spirit and then be so rebellious on every other day of the week. Charlotte knew she wasn't perfect herself, but she never walked around acting holier than thou either.

Sister Mason turned her attention to Aaron. "So, Brother Malone, are we all set with the audio equipment?"

"We are. The guy we hired is planning to arrive hours ahead of time to get everything hooked up."

"Good, good. You know, I really want to thank all of you for being so cooperative and so diligent with your efforts. Chairing a committee of any kind can be trying but not when you have so many wonderful people helping. You made a commitment and you stuck by it. So God bless all of you."

"I think I speak for all of us, Sister Mason, when I say that you are quite welcome," Aaron said. "And I know for me, a commitment means exactly that. We should all do what we say we're going to do and it will eliminate so much confusion. In some cases, it will eliminate a lot of unnecessary trouble. Isn't that right, Sister Black?"

"Yes, it is," she answered reluctantly. Aaron was definitely going too far. He was actually sitting there, taunting her right in front of everyone. She could tell that some of the members were wondering why he'd geared his lesson on philosophy toward her. He'd tried to make it sound like general information, but that question he'd specifically asked her at the end was enough to make people talk. It was enough to start rumors floating throughout the congregation. Aaron knew exactly what he was doing, and Charlotte was starting to hate him.

They discussed a few more items over the next half hour and then adjourned the meeting. Most of them talked among themselves and were planning to stay for Bible study, but Charlotte excused herself immediately. She headed straight out the church and over to her car. Unfortunately, Aaron followed behind.

"Sister Black, hold up," he said when he saw Brother Sanders, another committee member, walking out to the parking lot. "I need to talk to you for a minute."

Charlotte wanted to get in her car and speed off, but she knew it wouldn't look right to Brother Sanders if she did. She was trapped and that was all there was to it.

They both waved at Brother Sanders when he drove by them.

"Baby, I need to see you," he said.

"Aaron, I won't do this. Not here, not anywhere. You and I are over. Do you hear me? We're over for good."

"I'm asking you nicely."

"Look, I have to go."

"You think I'm playing with you."

"I don't think anything. But unless you have something important to say, I'm leaving."

"Oh, so now you're trying to play the tough role, huh? Well, let me tell you something. You know that clock I warned you about yesterday? Well, it's still ticking. It's ticking louder and louder all the time, and if I were you, I'd pay attention to it."

Charlotte opened her car door.

"You and I weren't just lovers, baby, we were also close friends," he said. "So don't think for one minute that our affair is the only thing I'm going to tell Curtis about. I thought I'd made myself clear yesterday. I'm telling every single thing I know."

Charlotte got in her car and closed the door. Aaron stepped back and waved good-bye to her when she drove away. He smiled at her the way lovers smile at each other when things are great between them.

But Charlotte was a nervous wreck. She was mortified at the thought of Curtis finding out anything he didn't already know about her. She was sorry she'd ever trusted Aaron so willingly.

And what was she going to do if she was pregnant? For two weeks now, she'd tried to tell herself that this just wasn't possible. But as of today, her period still hadn't shown up. At work, she'd visited the restroom at least a dozen times, hoping for the smallest sign. But there hadn't been any. There hadn't been any sign of anything that would clear her conscience. She'd chosen to be in denial, but the reality of it all was now staring her straight in the face. It was time she owned up to what just might be. Time she realized that the walls were closing in on her very rapidly.

It was time she realized the worst of all nightmares.

That Aaron had never once used a condom when they were together.

After leaving the church, Charlotte drove about thirty miles to a small pharmacy in a rural area to purchase a pregnancy test. She didn't want to chance running into someone from the church. Once home, she removed the white tube from the package. At first, she debated whether she should wait until tomorrow, but with Curtis teaching Bible study tonight, she figured it was better to get this over with. It was better to find out what was what as soon as possible.

She pulled out the instructions, read them, and then saturated the feltlike tip with urine for five seconds. It would take only three minutes to see the result, but her stomach was already stirring. Her hands had been shaking during the whole process, and she'd almost dropped the tube in the toilet.

Charlotte leaned against the bathroom vanity with her eyes closed, praying that she wasn't pregnant. She hadn't seriously prayed about much of anything in a long while, but now she had no other alternative. It wasn't that she didn't believe in God, because she did. But she just didn't see a reason to pray all day every day the way a lot of people she knew did. The way her mother and Aunt Emma had done for years. When Charlotte was a child and was adamant about things she didn't feel were necessary, her grandmother would say, "Chile, just keep on livin'. If you do, you'll end up seein' and doin' a whole lot of things you never thought you would. I'll be gone on to glory, but one day you'll realize what I mean."

And how right her grandmother had been. Before marrying Curtis, she'd sworn she would never commit adultery. But she had. Before marrying Curtis, she'd sworn that she would never lie to the man she married. But she had.

Before today, she'd sworn that she would never have an abortion.

But now, she would go back on her word again. She would do so because the end of that test tube was as pink as pink could be. She was definitely pregnant, and there was no way she could have a baby. Not when she couldn't guarantee who the father was. Not when there had been many weeks when she'd had sex with Aaron more than with her own husband. And she could blame only herself, because the reason she hadn't wanted Aaron to use any protection was that she'd wanted to feel the real him inside her. She hadn't wanted anything getting in the way of that. She'd wanted to feel him skin to skin in the most natural way possible. Plus, she hadn't been worried because she'd been taking the pill ever since Matthew was born. Sometimes she missed one here and there, but she always made up for it the following day. Her mother had told her that being careless would eventually catch up with her, but Charlotte hadn't thought it was a big deal. She hadn't thought she would ever get pregnant again. How wrong she had been though, and now she was suffering the consequences.

Feeling sorry for herself, Charlotte threw on her gym clothes and stepped onto the treadmill. She was in the habit of working out at the health club at least three days per week, but sometimes she exercised at home, too. Walking always energized her, and it made her feel better when she was having personal difficulty, even more so when she felt on edge like she was now. About a year ago, she'd read an article about sadness and depression and had learned that working out could help alleviate those emotions. It enhanced the production and release of endorphins, an important stress hormone.

But after walking briskly for forty-five minutes, she wasn't feeling any happier, so she turned off the machine and walked through the house, trying to cool down. When she entered the kitchen, preparing to grab a bottle of water from the fridge, she heard the doorbell ringing.

She cringed when she saw that it was Aaron at the door. Her first thought was to walk away, ignoring him, but somehow she knew he would never leave if she did. So she opened it.

"Hi, baby," he said, forcibly brushing past her.

"Aaron, what are you doing here?"

"Because I want to be."

"Do you want Curtis to kill us both?"

"Please. I just left him at the church, and he's the one who told me to meet him here in an hour. But you know me," he said, grabbing her and pulling her close to him. "I decided to show up a little early."

"Stop it," she said, pushing against his chest.

But it did no good. Aaron slipped both his hands inside her athletic pants and underwear, caressing her butt and kissing her neck. She fought him as hard as she could, but she wasn't strong enough to escape him. She screamed when he moved his hand to her vaginal area and groped her roughly. But that only made him angrier. He slammed her onto the living room sofa and then pulled her down to the floor.

"Aaron, don't," she yelled.

"I told you I wanted you," he said, breathing heavily. "But you wouldn't listen. No, what you did was cut me off."

Charlotte continued fighting until she saw a light flash through the window.

"Oh God, it's Curtis."

Aaron looked up and saw the SUV waiting to enter the garage.

"Lucky for you, but this isn't the end of this," he said, standing up.

Charlotte got up and ran. She went upstairs and did everything she could to keep from crying. She had to or otherwise Curtis would know something was wrong. He'd start questioning her and doubting her again, and she couldn't have that. But maybe telling him the truth was the only way out of this. She would never tell him about the pregnancy, but maybe it was time she came clean the way that talk-show host had suggested to one of her callers. What she would do was take Curtis to dinner, so they could officially celebrate his new publishing deals. They would enjoy themselves and then she would tell him everything as soon as they were back at home. She would explain things to him and ask him to forgive her. She'd pray for his understanding and hope that his love for her would outweigh any possibility of divorce.

But regardless of what the outcome was going to be, she couldn't go on like this. She couldn't allow Aaron to keep blackmailing her and torturing her the way he was. Tonight, he'd almost succeeded at raping her.

She would never allow something like that to happen again. Not under any circumstances.

Chapter 17

GIRL, HE ACTUALLY TRIED TO RAPE ME IN MY OWN HOUSE."

"He what?" Anise said.

"Yes. He was supposed to meet Curtis after church, but before Curtis got there, he tried to rape me. And if Curtis hadn't come home when he did, I'm telling you, he would have hurt me. He would have done whatever he wanted to do."

"So what happened after Curtis came into the house?"

"He came upstairs to let me know he was home, and then he and Aaron sat around in the family room for another hour or so going over some new ideas for the church. And Aaron was laughing and talking like normal."

"He's insane, Charlotte, and if I were you, I'd tell Curtis everything. Because if you don't, things are only going to get worse."

"I am. Right after dinner. I'm taking him to Antonio's, and then I'm going to tell him the truth."

"You have to."

"I know, but it will be the hardest thing I've ever had to do. And I'm so afraid that he'll try to leave me. Especially since I was the one who told him I would never accept him messing around with other women. I made that very clear before we got married, and now I'm the one who ended up having the affair."

"It's unfortunate, but at this point, you have to take care of this no matter what Curtis decides to do."

Charlotte sighed. "I just can't believe I allowed this to happen."

"It was definitely a huge mistake, because like I told you the other night, you have a good man. A man who loves you dearly."

"I know. And even though I was angry at you for saying that, I know you were right."

"Well, the only thing you can do now is pray for the best."

"Actually, I've been doing that since Wednesday. And since Aaron didn't try to contact me yesterday and hasn't tried to call me here at work this morning, maybe my prayers have been answered. Maybe he's through with all of this for good."

"Anything is possible, but I wouldn't get too comfortable with that. Because the Aaron I heard on the phone that night sounded like a madman. He sounded like he was capable of doing anything to anybody."

Charlotte leaned back in her office chair and closed her eyes. She'd tried to think just the opposite of what Anise was saying, but in all honesty, she agreed with her completely. Over the last week, Charlotte had seen a side of Aaron that she hadn't even known existed, and she could tell he was someone to be afraid of. She was starting to realize that when she was alone, she needed to be more cautious. At the office, at home, and anywhere else she could think of.

"I hear what you're saying, and I'm definitely planning to be careful."

"That's good, because you never know what people like Aaron will do. You never know what to expect."

"This is true. And hey, thanks for listening to me and for not writing me off."

"You're my cousin, girl, and I love you. I don't agree with what you did, but that doesn't change our relationship. So know that I'm here for you if you need me."

"I love you, too. And Anise, please, please don't tell Aunt Emma. She would be so disappointed, and I would never be able to face her again if she found out about this."

"I understand, and I won't."

"I mean it, Anise. Because I know you and Aunt Emma share just about everything."

"But if you don't want me to tell her, then I won't. I promise. It wouldn't be good anyway because she'd be worrying herself to death about you."

"I know, and that's why I'm not going to tell my parents either. They would do the exact same thing. And you know Daddy would get in his car and drive over here."

"You know he would. And you couldn't blame him because this is serious. People get killed by lovers all the time."

"I know. Look at what that Adrienne chick did to Curtis, and then she killed herself."

"Exactly. So just hang in there, girl. But call me if you need me, no matter what time it is."

"I will. I love you, cousin."

"I love you, too."

Curtis slipped on the new Ralph Lauren polo undershirt and briefs that Charlotte had surprised him with. When he'd gotten home from the church, he'd found a huge box wrapped in beau-

tiful silver paper with a black satin bow. Inside was everything
he needed to go with his suit, the one she'd bought for him just
a week ago. Underwear, socks, a dress shirt, a tie, and platinum
cuff links. She'd gone on another one of her spending sprees,
but he just couldn't be upset with her tonight because they were
still so happy with each other and had been for days now. She'd
even made reservations for dinner at the best Italian restaurant
in the area so that they could celebrate his new career accom-
plishments. And he had to admit, it was nice being able to dress
in fine clothing. The suit alone brought back a lot of great
memories. He still wore expensive suits, but they were mostly
suits he'd owned for a few years. Which was more than accept-
able, though, because the suits he owned never went out of style,
not the ones that he'd paid at least a thousand dollars for.

He was pulling on his socks and then his dress shirt when
Charlotte walked out of the bathroom.

"Baby, can you button this for me?" she asked.

"You look beautiful."

"Thanks."

Curtis couldn't tell if Charlotte was wearing it or if it was
wearing her, but she had on the most beautiful black dress he'd
seen in a while. It was sleeveless, had a yoke that dropped toward her back, and the length stopped just above her knees. It
fit perfectly. She looked exceptionally elegant, the way he liked
her to. When they were first married, she'd dressed "okay," but
her taste had been no different than the average twenty-year-
old, which she couldn't help because she'd only been twenty-
three at the time. But now, two years later, she'd grown up in a
lot of ways, and Curtis was happy about that.

"You need to get your suit on so we can get out of here," she
said. "The reservation is for six thirty."

"I'll be ready before you know it."

Charlotte turned to go back into the bathroom and the phone rang. Curtis walked over and picked it up.

"Hello?"

"Hey, Dad."

"Hey, son. How are you?"

"I'm good. What about you and Mom?"

"We're fine. Just getting ready to go to dinner."

"Oh. Grandma and Grandpa and I had cheeseburgers and fries from that restaurant down the street."

"Really? And they liked that?"

"Yep. They like anything."

Curtis laughed because he knew that was the furthest thing from the truth. But he also knew his in-laws would do anything to make Matthew happy. They allowed him to run their entire household whenever he visited. Whatever he wanted to do they did with no questions asked.

"What did you do today?"

"We went to the movies and then to the arcade. And then they bought me a Game Boy Advance."

"Is that right?"

"Yep. And they said I could bring it home with me, too. It's so fun."

"Well, it sounds like you're having a good time."

"Yep. But I can't wait to come home because I miss Jonathan and Elijah."

"What about us? Your mom and me?"

"I miss both of you, too."

"And we miss you. A lot."

"I know."

Curtis couldn't help chuckling. Matthew had so much confidence in himself because Curtis had made sure of it. He'd made sure that Matthew knew he was loved by his parents and was worthy to be loved by anyone for that matter. A self-esteem issue he would never have if Curtis could help it. He would walk with his head held high at all times and know that he was just as good as the next person.

"Well, son, I need to finish getting dressed, so I'm going to let you speak to your mom."

"Okay. Bye, Dad. Love you."

"Love you, too."

Charlotte came back into the bedroom and Curtis passed her the phone. She talked to Matthew for maybe five minutes before hanging up.

"I miss him so much," she said, and Curtis could tell she wanted to cry.

"I know," he said, hugging her. "But he needs that time with your parents, and he'll be back on Tuesday. The days will pass by before you know it. Plus, we needed some time alone to ourselves."

"You're right. This has been one of the best weeks of my life."

Curtis had to agree. He'd learned that he would soon be able to give Charlotte some of the luxuries she wanted, and they were loving each other like wild animals. What more could a man ask for? Not a single thing. He was in excellent health, had a beautiful wife, a handsome son, a great church, and a comfortable income. There wasn't a thing he could truly complain about. Finally.

When they arrived at the restaurant, they were seated immediately. It was a bit crowded, which was the norm on a Friday evening, and Charlotte was glad she'd made reservations.

"So what are you having?" she said.

"Prime rib, I think."

"Then I'll probably have the same."

"Why don't we order a couple of appetizers?"

"Whatever you want. It's your night, remember?"

"Does that mean you're paying, too?"

"As a matter of fact, my published author, it does."

"You mean, *almost* published."

"You will be. And soon."

The tall and slim waitress walked over to the table.

"What can I start you with?"

"How about the stuffed mushrooms and bruschetta?" Curtis answered.

"Okay. And to drink?"

"I'll have cranberry juice mixed with 7UP or Sprite," Charlotte said.

"I'll have the same," Curtis told her.

"I'll be right back with your drinks, and then I'll take your dinner order."

"Thank you," Curtis said. "So. How was work today?" he asked.

"It was good. It's always good, but yesterday I made a major decision about my career."

"Meaning?"

"On Monday, I'm planning to give the firm a one-month notice of my resignation."

"Whoa. Now don't make me have a heart attack. Where is all this coming from?"

"It's true. I'm quitting."

"But why?"

"Because you've been asking me to and because I know now that you're really going to need me at the church full-time. Especially once you start traveling to more and more speaking engagements."

"True. But actually, that's what I was talking to Aaron about the other night when he came over. I told him that I'll need him to play a much larger role at the church than he has been. I wanted to discuss it with you first, but within the next few months, I'd really like to offer him a full-time position, so that he can leave his current job for good. He's not that happy with it anyway, and not only does Aaron care about the church, but he cares about you and me. And that's the type of person we need to run things."

Charlotte was stunned and felt somewhat disoriented. Curtis had always been such a great judge of character when it came to men, but he didn't have a clue about that maniac he called his best friend. He had no idea how much Aaron despised him and how he envied everything about Curtis. She knew she had to tell him the truth before the night was over.

"But Deliverance is our church, Curtis," she said. "And I don't think it's a good idea to give anyone other than you and me that kind of control. So, as much as I hate to disagree with you, I don't think hiring Aaron full-time is the right thing to do. And even though I know you trust him, you really can't trust anyone when it comes to money."

"I guess I don't know what to say. I mean, I hear you, but I was so sure you would be even more happy than me about this, especially since hiring Aaron would mean I could stop harassing you. It took me a while, but I finally realized that you deserve the opportunity to work wherever you want to."

"And I appreciate knowing that, but my mind is made up. I'm giving my notice and taking over whatever you want me to at the church."

"Wow. Well, if you're sure. Because you know I've wanted that all along, but you were so against it."

"I was just being rebellious is all. But those days are over."

The waitress set down their drinks and took their prime rib orders. Shortly after, she brought out their appetizers. They took turns, sampling each.

Curtis scanned the restaurant and then smiled at Charlotte.

"This was such a great idea," he said. "You know Antonio's is my favorite. No matter how many times I come in here, I'm still fascinated by the waterfall in the lobby and that marble flooring."

"I'm glad you're enjoying it. Because, baby, from now on, things are only going to get better. Life is much too short, and we need to start living it to the fullest."

"I agree."

"The thing is, I love you with everything in me," she said, holding his hand. "I haven't always been the best wife, but you've always treated me like a queen. And most women will never know how that feels. You made such major changes in your life, and I know they were all because of Matthew and me."

"But I'm glad I did. I'm glad that I finally learned how to love one woman and stay faithful to her. I was so terrible to Tanya and Mariah, and even now, I still regret it. They deserved so much better than that."

"But at least you learned from your mistakes. Some people never do."

"I even did wrong by you before we were married, and I'm just glad you forgave me."

"We all deserve to be forgiven," she said, hoping he felt the same way. "And you said yourself we all deserve a second chance when we mess up."

"Actually, I've been given a third, so I'm even more thankful than most people."

"I'm just glad we were able to reconnect after five whole years."

"I am, too. It was the best thing that could have happened, because you slowed me down, girl. Wayyyy down."

They both laughed.

"Yeah, you were pretty wild," she said.

"But everything happens for a reason, and our marriage is no different."

Charlotte squeezed his hand tightly. She knew she had a tough night ahead of her, but she felt confident that Curtis would be there for her in the end. He would be hurt at first and then angry, but everything would work itself out in no time. She had to believe exactly that because there wasn't any other way.

Chapter 18

CHARLOTTE SAT INSIDE THE SUV, AND THE VALET ATTENDANT CLOSED her door. Curtis tipped him five dollars and drove away from the restaurant. They would be home in a matter of minutes, twenty to be exact, and Charlotte was already trying to prepare her words. Nothing would soften what she had to say, but still, she wanted to say what she had to say in the best way possible.

"I'm full," Curtis said.

"Does that mean I won't be getting any loving tonight?"

"No, I'm not saying anything like that. Not at all."

"I didn't think so. And you won't regret it either."

"Don't make me fly through all these red lights out here."

They both laughed.

But in the midst of their humor Curtis's phone rang. Not his cell but the one inside the Escalade. Charlotte wondered who had passed away because the answering service only called this number in case of an emergency.

"Hello?" he said.

"Hey, man," Aaron said, his voice booming through the

speaker just above Curtis's head. "I just saw you guys leaving the restaurant and thought I would call to congratulate you again. Man, I'm truly proud of you."

"Thanks, man. You know how much I appreciate that, and it's good to know somebody has my back and is happy for me."

Charlotte wanted to jump out of the car while it was still moving. She knew Aaron was purposely calling Curtis's car phone and not his cell because he wanted her to hear his voice. He was doing that taunting thing again, and she wished she could strangle him. She wished he would have some fatal accident. If he did, it would make life a whole lot easier.

"True," Aaron commented. "But sometimes even people who have your back have to rain on your parade. They have to tell you things you need to know even if it hurts."

Charlotte's body trembled.

"Rain on my parade?" Curtis said. "Meaning what?"

"That I wonder when Charlotte is planning on telling you that Matthew might not be your son."

Charlotte slowly closed her eyes and felt tears running out of them.

Curtis was speechless.

"Did you hear me?" Aaron continued. "Because I know your wife hears me loud and clear."

Curtis pulled to the side of the road and turned on the interior light, but he still didn't respond.

"I know you can't believe what I'm telling you, but it's true. And just so you know, Charlotte, I already called Anise an hour ago and told her the whole story. And I have to say, she wasn't very happy when I told her how you'd slept with her husband in her own house in her own bed eight years ago. She wasn't happy about it at all."

"Aaron, are you crazy?" Curtis finally said. "Joking about my wife and son like this?"

Charlotte stared straight ahead. Her insides were burning up.

"Joking? Man, if you don't know anything, you should know I wouldn't joke about anything this serious. I'm telling you what *your* wife told me a few months ago. And I won't even go into how she slept with some guy she used to date the night before you married her. Or how she slept with one of her college professors just so she could get an A in his class. No, I won't go into any of that."

"Is all of this true, Charlotte?"

"Hell, yeah, it's true," Aaron said. "Tell him, Sister Black."

Charlotte looked at Curtis and wept silently. Veins were bulging at his temple, and she knew life as they'd known it was over. It would never be the same for as long as they lived.

"Anyway, good people," Aaron said. "I do hope you enjoy the rest of your evening. I know I've certainly enjoyed mine."

Charlotte felt as though she was having an out-of-body experience. She wanted to say something to Curtis, anything, but she didn't want to anger him any further. She didn't want him to beat her down the way he must have wanted to.

But to her surprise, he pulled back into traffic and drove home in silence. She'd tried to read his facial expression, but it told her nothing. Only a few minutes had passed, yet he was already acting as if nothing had happened. She knew his defense mechanism had kicked in because there was no way he or any man could remain this calm, not after hearing that his only son might be someone else's. Charlotte had known all the time that when Aaron had sworn he would tell everything, her fling with Anise's husband, David, and the fact that David might be Matthew's father would rise to the top of the list. But she'd told herself he would never do that. He would never try to hurt Matthew. He would never try to hurt any child he knew.

How wrong she'd been, though, because now Curtis knew everything. Everything except that she'd been sleeping with Aaron. It was so amazing how he'd conveniently kept quiet about that part of the equation. He'd said all that he could to damage her and said nothing to incriminate himself. But in all honesty, it was probably best he hadn't mentioned anything more. It would only have made bad matters worse.

Curtis drove into the driveway but didn't open the garage door.

"Get out," he demanded.

"But Curtis—"

"I *said* get the hell out!"

"Curtis, baby, I'm so sorry."

"Charlotte, I'm warning you. Open the door and get your ass out, before I do something crazy."

She did what he asked and as soon as she did, Curtis sped out of the driveway, screeching his tires and flying through the subdivision.

Charlotte stood there, wondering what he was going to do— to her, Aaron, or both of them.

Curtis was so furious, he burst into tears. He'd been driving around town for more than an hour, trying to piece things together, but he couldn't. He couldn't understand why Charlotte would lie to him about Matthew. Why she'd done any of what Aaron had told him. But more than that, he wondered why Aaron had felt the need to disclose what he knew in such a cold and sarcastic manner. Almost as if he was deliberately trying to hurt both Curtis and Charlotte for different reasons. Nothing was adding up, and Curtis was to the point now where he needed to talk to someone who could identify with what he was going through. He needed to speak to someone who had a level head, someone he admired and had a lot of respect for—someone who was much more respectable than Charlotte.

Curtis loosened his tie, drove another five miles or so, and pulled into Anise's driveway. He got out of his vehicle, took off his suit jacket, laid it across the driver's seat, and set the alarm system. As he walked up the sidewalk, leading to the condo, his cell phone rang. But when he saw that it was Charlotte, he turned it off and pressed the doorbell. He pressed it four times before Anise finally opened the door.

"Hey," he said.

"Hey," she responded.

"I'm sorry for showing up over here unannounced, but I need someone to talk to."

"Come in," she said.

They walked into the great room and sat down. Anise on the sofa and Curtis on the loveseat.

"So do you believe any of what Aaron is saying?" he said.

"At first I didn't, but he knew way too many details about the time Charlotte was visiting David and me. And there's no way he could have known any of it without Charlotte telling him. Plus, it's not like Charlotte is ringing my phone off the hook, trying to deny anything."

"All she said to me was that she was sorry. Can you believe that? Matthew might not be my son and all she has to say is that she's sorry?"

"Well, I'm telling you right now, Curtis. I'm through with her."

"I'm feeling the same way, because she knew from the very beginning how much I loved Matthew, and she took advantage of that. She wanted me to think he was my son so that I would marry her."

"Charlotte will do and say whatever she has to to get what she wants, and the more I think about her sleeping with David, the more I hate her. I hate everything about her and to think she slept with my husband in our own bed. I mean, nothing gets much lower than that. And on top of that, we're family."

Curtis could see the pain and rage in Anise's eyes. He'd never seen her like this before, but he totally understood what she was feeling. He understood because he was feeling the same or worse.

"You know, Aaron even told me that she slept with some guy the night before we got married and that she slept with some college professor," he said.

"I wouldn't be surprised. Not now."

"I really underestimated her. And I've been so committed to her. I haven't been with another woman since the day I was shot."

"Well, not every woman realizes what they have, and I just told Charlotte that the other day."

"Now I'm wondering what else I don't know."

"A lot."

"Really?"

"Yeah, like the fact that she's been using my address to hide bills from you. I always knew it was wrong of me to let her do it, but I loved Charlotte like my own sister. And sisters do things for each other."

"What kind of bills?"

"From credit card companies."

"Credit cards?"

"Yeah, she gets at least eight different statements every single month. From both major banks and department stores. And three of them have your name on them as a joint owner."

"What? How?"

"I'm assuming she's been signing your name on the applications and then changing your address to mine once the accounts have been opened. But who knows with Charlotte."

"She's unbelievable."

The saga was still continuing, and Curtis didn't know how much more news he could digest. He wondered who Charlotte was. Because from the sound of it, he was married to a stranger. He was married to a woman who told one lie after another whenever it was convenient. A woman who was no different from the way he used to be years before. From this day forward, Charlotte deserved whatever she got—from him and anyone else.

"What still bothers me is why Aaron called me on a car phone to tell me all of this crap and then basically just hung up. It doesn't make any sense, because even if he wanted to let me know what Charlotte was up to, I'd think he would have told me when she wasn't around."

Anise looked away from him with no comment.

"Do you know why?" he asked.

"What you need to do is talk to Charlotte."

"But if you know something, I really need you to tell me."

"Just talk to her. Ask her why Aaron did what he did."

Curtis didn't like what he was sensing because this was the first time since he'd arrived at Anise's that she wasn't giving him direct eye contact. She looked at him, but she kept looking away and then back at him, which definitely meant she knew something. She knew something he wasn't going to be happy about.

Anise stood up quickly and went into the kitchen. "Can I get you something?"

"Some juice if you have it."

Curtis watched her from the living room and saw her wiping her eyes. He could tell that she was crying, so he walked over to where she was and embraced her.

"Why did she do this to us?" Anise said, laying her head against Curtis's chest.

"I don't know why, but I do know how badly it hurts."

"My heart is so broken. Especially since I've gone out of my way to be there for Charlotte ever since you guys moved here."

"I know," Curtis said, stroking her hair. "You've been there for both of us, and I've always been thankful for that. You're a good woman, Anise, and a good friend. So don't feel bad about anything. This is all about Charlotte and the way she manipulates people. Nothing else."

"I'm sorry for breaking down like this," she said, trying to pull away from him.

But Curtis kept her close and kissed her. They kissed intensely, and their passion was strong. Their chemistry was undeniable, and Curtis didn't want to let her go. He needed someone to hold him until all the pain was gone. He needed someone to love him now when his life was falling apart.

"Oh God, Curtis, what are we doing?" she said.

"I don't know. But it's my fault and I apologize."

Anise backed away from him, but he could tell she didn't want to.

"We can't do this," she said. "We can't let this thing with Charlotte make us do something we're going to regret."

"You're right. I shouldn't have kissed you like that."

"We're both guilty."

"But I initiated it."

"But I didn't resist, and if you stay here any longer it's going to mean trouble. We're both too vulnerable right now, and we're not thinking clearly."

Curtis knew she was probably right, but he still wanted her. They were attracted to each other; it was now out in the open, and nothing was going to change that. And why should they care about betraying Charlotte anyway, because she certainly hadn't cared about betraying them? She hadn't even cared about the possibility of hurting her own son, the child she claimed she loved so much, and the thought of that enraged Curtis all over again.

"Hey," he said when they arrived at the entry. "You've got my cell number, so call me if you need me."

"I will. And you try to calm yourself down before you get home, okay? I know it's going to be hard, but at least try to keep in mind that Matthew might really be yours."

"I'll try," he said, kissing her on the forehead. "Take care."

He backed out to the street and saw Anise still standing in the doorway. As much as he loved Charlotte, he couldn't help wondering why he couldn't have married someone like Anise, someone who was mature, responsible, and compassionate. But the more he thought about it, the more he realized that Tanya had been all of the above. She had loved him and only him, and he'd lost her. He'd done a lot of dirt over the years to his wives and significant others, and maybe this situation with Charlotte was the ultimate payback. Still, he wondered why God would take his son when he'd been so faithful to Him and the ministry for more than two years. But for the first time in those two years, he wondered if being faithful to anything or anyone was really worth it.

He honestly didn't know.

Chapter 19

CURTIS WALKED INSIDE THE HOUSE AND UP TO THE BEDROOM AND started in on Charlotte immediately. He wanted answers and he wanted them now.

"Why did you lie to me like this?"

"Because I really believe Matthew is yours," she said. Her eyes were bloodshot, mascara was streaking her cheeks, and her hair was a mess. But Curtis didn't care.

"But you don't know for sure, so you lied. You lied to me and thought nothing of it."

"And I'm sorry. I should have told you, but I just couldn't."

"Why? Because David used to be married to your cousin and you knew you couldn't be with him? Is that why?"

"No, Curtis. I wanted to be with you because I love you. And it's not like I was with David all the time."

"Was it more than once?"

He could see her clamming up.

"Was it? Or were you screwing him every chance you got?"

"I slept with him maybe three times, but that was it."

"Uh-huh. And when was the first?"

"It . . . was at Anise's."

"When?"

"Where did you go when you dropped me off?" she asked.

"Don't even think about trying to change the subject, and don't you ever ask me again where I've been for as long as you live. Now, like I said, when were you with him?"

"We had a family reunion here one year and I stayed with them for a couple of days while it was going on. Anise went over to her mom's that Sunday morning, I think to say goodbye to some out-of-town relatives, and when she left, it happened."

"So you waited for your own cousin to leave, and then you slept with her husband like it was nothing."

"No, it wasn't like that. I mean, it happened, but I was young and dumb. And I would never have tried to hurt her. It was a stupid mistake, but David didn't mean anything to me."

"Then why were you with him two other times after that?"

"I don't know."

"Do you know anything?"

"Yes, but I don't know why I did what I did. The same as I don't know why I slept with you back then either. All I can say is that I didn't know any better. I was only seventeen, and you know that."

"You're right. I'll give you that, and I was definitely wrong for having sex with you, but that still doesn't change the fact that you don't know who Matthew's father is."

"I'm sorry. I know you don't want to hear that, but I am."

"When you slept with David those other two times, was that at their home, too?"

"No. David commuted to work from here to Chicago, and we met at a hotel near the company he works for."

"And what about you sleeping with some guy the night before we got married, because you certainly weren't seventeen then?"

"Aaron is lying about that. And he's also lying about me sleeping with one of my professors."

"But why would he lie, Charlotte? Or no, I have a better question. Why did he break this news to me the way he did? With you sitting right in the car?"

She was speechless again.

"Answer me," he yelled. "Why did he do it?"

"Because . . ."

"Because what?"

"Because I've been sleeping with him."

Curtis picked up a ceramic vase from the dresser and slammed it against the wall, only a foot from where Charlotte was standing.

She leaped out of the way, sobbing. "Curtis, please. I'm so sorry. You have to believe me."

"You make me sick. You know that. And now, I can't stand the sight of you."

"But we've both made mistakes."

"Don't even try it. Because regardless of what I did in the past, I've done right by you since we got married. And you know it, Charlotte. You knew how much I loved you and Matthew and you've got the nerve to be sleeping with a friend of mine? A man I called my best friend?"

"But I'm not sleeping with him anymore. I broke things off with him for good, and that's when he started threatening me. That's when he said he was going to tell you everything."

"Why?"

"Why what?"

"Why did you stop sleeping with him?"

"Because I didn't want to keep doing this to you, and I wanted us to get our marriage back on track."

"No, you stopped sleeping with him because you know that I'm about to earn a lot more money than I have been."

"That's not true."

"It is true. You've been all over me ever since you found out about my syndication offer. And ever since you heard about the book deal, you've been acting like you love my dirty underwear."

"I stopped seeing Aaron because I love you. And that's the only reason."

"Girl, you're going to make me hurt you if you keep lying to me like that," Curtis said, wrinkling his forehead. She was pissing him off more and more by the second.

"Well, what do you want me to say?"

"I don't want you to say anything else, but what I do want is for you to schedule a DNA test. And I want you to do it as soon as possible."

"Curtis, I know you're upset, but I really don't think a test is necessary. Especially since Matthew is the spitting image of you. Everybody always says that, even you."

"Look, either you schedule the test, or I'm calling your parents and telling them everything. Now, do you want that?"

"No, but what are we going to tell Matthew?"

"You're a good liar, so tell him whatever you want to."

"You don't mean that."

"I do. Tell him anything except that I might not be his father. It will kill him just as much as it's killing me, and he doesn't deserve that."

"I'm telling you, he's your son."

"I'm finished arguing with you about this. But all I know is that he had better be. You'd better pray like you've never prayed before that he is. Because with the way I'm feeling now, your life depends on it. You hear me?" Curtis said and left the bedroom.

He wanted to murder Aaron. Charlotte, too, for that matter.

Charlotte felt like she was in a time warp. It had been only two hours since Curtis had left the house again, but it seemed like a whole day had passed. She'd been jumping out of bed and dashing over to the window every time she heard a car go by, but he never showed. It was now one o'clock in the morning. She'd even tried to call him on his cell phone, but he wouldn't answer it. She'd left multiple messages, begging him to call her back, but it hadn't done any good. She'd tried not to think the worst, but she knew her husband. She knew what he was capable of when it came to women. Her affair with Aaron was all the ammunition he needed to do whatever he wanted. For the first time ever, Charlotte wished she'd never messed around with another woman's husband. But most of all, she wished she hadn't slept with David. She would give anything to take it all back and do the right thing, but it wasn't possible.

She'd never seen Curtis as violently upset as he was tonight, and it was that very reason that she'd lied to him about David and the number of times she'd been with him, which was easily ten to twelve times. There were even days when she'd been with David in the afternoon and Curtis that same evening. But she would die before ever admitting any of that to Curtis or Anise. She would never admit that she'd slept with one of her college professors the way Aaron had said or the guy she'd been with the night before marrying Curtis. She would never admit a whole list of sins she'd committed because it wasn't going to help her. It would never change the predicament she was in currently.

She debated whether she should call Anise and finally decided to go for it. But Anise wouldn't answer. Charlotte knew she was home and just didn't want to be bothered. Maybe she would try Anise again tomorrow. But she couldn't help wondering if Anise would ever speak to her again. She wondered how much of the story Anise had told her mother. Chances were, she'd spilled everything. She probably hadn't left out one sentence. Charlotte didn't know how she would ever make this up to either of them.

But she wished everyone would consider the fact that these were grown men having sex with a minor, because that's exactly what David and Curtis had done. She'd brought that particular truth to Curtis's attention many times before, but it didn't seem to matter to him. All he cared about was what she'd done and what she'd better correct. And how was she going to tell her son that he needed to have blood drawn? What reason would she give him? She was shocked that Curtis would actually put Matthew through all this, especially when she was sure that Curtis was his father. She couldn't prove it, but deep down she knew that he was.

Charlotte tossed and turned until two o'clock and dialed her husband again. Still he didn't answer. She did the same at three, four, and five and decided to give up. But then the phone rang. She grabbed it without checking the caller ID screen.

"Curtis?"

"No, baby, this isn't, Curtis," Aaron said.

"Why are you calling here?"

"Because I know you're alone. I saw the preacher man leave hours ago. He must *really* be pissed off at you, huh?"

"Why did you do it, Aaron?"

"Because I told you to ask Curtis for a divorce. But instead of listening, you tried to play me for a knucklehead. And this is what it got you."

"I'm hanging up, and if you ever dial this number again, I'm calling the police."

"Talk to you tomorrow. I love you, Charlotte."

What a sicko. The man desperately needed help, and she was starting to wonder if he would ever leave her alone. She'd been so sure that she'd never hear from him, now that he'd ruined her life with Curtis. But here he was still calling and tormenting her. And watching the house, checking to see when Curtis was coming and going. There was no telling what he was planning to do next.

She glanced over at the security system keypad to make sure it was on. She was sometimes lax when it came to setting it, but she would never be again. She couldn't afford to, not with the likes of Aaron on the loose. She had to start being a lot more aware of her surroundings than she had been.

What an outrageous life she was living.

Chapter 20

CURTIS WALKED INTO THE BEDROOM, REMOVED HIS CLOTHING, AND headed straight for the shower. Charlotte was lying in bed, staring at him, but he'd purposely ignored her. As far as he was concerned, she didn't even exist. Not until that DNA test was administered and the results were in. He knew she'd been agonizing over where he'd been all night, and it served her right. Actually, the whole reason he'd stayed out was just so he could mess with her. He'd wanted her to wake up every hour on the hour, looking for him—even better, he hoped she hadn't slept at all. He wanted her to feel the pain he was feeling and then some. Before it was over, she would wish she had never met him. She would never sleep around like a whore, not again. Not on him or any other man. When he was finished treating her the way he planned on treating her, she would be the perfect wife to her next husband. She would think twice before betraying any one person she knew.

When he finished drying his body, he went into his closet and removed a cotton pullover and a pair of khaki shorts.

After slipping them on, he searched for his sandals and walked toward the bed where Charlotte was still watching him.

"Where were you?"

"Out."

"Out where?"

"Didn't I tell you last night not to ever ask me that again?"

"But it's eight o'clock in the morning, Curtis."

He smoothed his hair down in the mirror, pretending not to hear her.

"And you know the church picnic is today," she said.

"Yep. And that's where I'm on my way to."

"So what am I supposed to do, drive separately?"

"Exactly. Or do whatever you want for that matter, because I really don't care."

"We need to talk, Curtis. We have to work this out."

"No, the only thing *we* have to do is find out whether I have a son or not. But other than that, I don't want anything to do with you."

"So, are you saying that this is it for us? Our marriage is over just like that?"

"Don't talk to me anymore, okay? Because I'm really not in the mood," he said and walked out of the room.

Then he went downstairs, got in his car, and left. He headed toward the park where they were holding the picnic and called Matthew while he was in transit.

"Hello?" Charlotte's mother said.

"Hey, how are you?" he asked.

"I'm fine, Curtis. Did you and my baby have a good time last night?"

"The restaurant was as elegant as always, and the food was the best I've had in a long time."

"Well, I'm glad."

"I'm on my way to the church picnic to help with the meat and figured I'd holler at Matthew for a few minutes."

"Okay, hold on a second. Matthew," she called.

"Hello?" he said.

"Good morning, son."

"Hi, Dad. What are you doing?"

"On my way to the church picnic."

"Aw man, I forgot about that."

"Remember, we told you that you were going to miss the picnic if you went to Chicago this week."

"I know. Maybe you could come get me and bring me back when it's over."

Curtis laughed. "Do you realize how far away you are? It would take three hours round-trip. You know?"

"Okay," he said, sounding disappointed. "Where's Mom?"

"She's at home."

"Is she going to the picnic?"

"Yeah, she'll be there in a little while."

"Oh."

"Have you been watching TV this morning?"

"Yep. I'm watching it now."

"Figures," Curtis said, laughing. "Well, I'd better let you go, but I just wanted to check in with you."

"Okay, Dad, but call me when you leave the park, okay?"

"I will."

"Love you, Dad."

"Love you, too, Matthew."

Curtis was so tired of shedding tears over his son that he didn't know what to do. He couldn't remember ever feeling so sad, so hurt, and so angry all at once. There were so many emotions boiling inside him, and he was terrified that the DNA test would prove what he didn't want to hear. He wanted to know the truth, but then again, he didn't want to. He dreaded thinking about the possible outcome.

He pulled into a gas station, placed his gear in park, and dialed Alicia's line but didn't get an answer. Then he tried Tanya and James's number, since Tanya was the person he really wanted to speak to.

"Hello?" she said.

"How are you?"

"I'm fine, Curtis. How are you?"

"Can you talk?"

"Sure. What about?"

"What I mean is, is James there?"

"No, he's out golfing, and Alicia is at a carwash fund-raiser for cheerleading."

"Oh."

"So what's up?"

"No, the question is, what isn't?"

"Is this something I need to sit down for?"

"Maybe."

"You're not sick, are you?"

"Hmmph. No, nothing like that."

"Okay, now what's going on?"

"You know my friend Aaron?"

"Yes. Your best friend."

"Well, Charlotte has been sleeping with him."

"No way."

"She has. And worse than that, she doesn't know for sure if Matthew is my son, because she was sleeping with her cousin's husband during the same time she was with me."

"What?"

"It's true. And it's taking everything in me not to kick her out."

"I know you're hurt and you have a right to be, but Charlotte is still Matthew's mother."

"And if it wasn't for him, I'd be filing for a divorce on Monday. And if I could take Matthew away from her, I would."

"Have you spoken with her?"

"Last night, but then I left and got a hotel room. And this morning when I came back, I didn't say any more to her than I had to, because I don't see where there's anything to talk about."

"What about Aaron? Have you spoken to him?"

"Not since he called to tell me about Matthew."

"I'm confused."

Curtis explained the whole scenario to Tanya, and of course, she was stunned.

"I can't believe this," she said.

"Well, believe it, because it's all true. And I'm telling you, Tanya, the more I sit here thinking about Aaron and the way he smiled in my face, the more I know I can't let him get away with it."

"Look, I know you're upset, but you can't start thinking like that. Going to jail just isn't worth it. And if you don't consider anything else, you need to remember Alicia and Matthew. They need their father, and there won't be a thing you can do for them behind bars."

"But if Matthew isn't my son, then what?"

"Then you're going to have to accept it and figure out how to deal with it. Because regardless of whether he is or not, you still need to be there for him. He's only a child, and none of this is his fault."

"But it won't be that easy. I know you don't understand, but finding out that Matthew belongs to someone else will be no different than cutting off my right arm. It will be the worst thing that has ever happened to me."

"You said the same thing when you had to leave our church and when we got divorced, but eventually you were able to move on."

"This is different. This is about my being completely dedicated to a woman and having her betray me in the worst way. Not only did she sleep with my best friend, but she led me on about Matthew. She used and manipulated me to get what she wanted."

Tanya didn't comment.

And Curtis knew why.

"As much as I hate to say this, you did the same thing to me," she finally said. "You did the same thing to Mariah, and you and I both know you hurt a lot of other people along the way."

"And I'll be sorry for that for the rest of my life. There's not a day that goes by that I don't regret what I did to you and Alicia. What I destroyed."

"It took me a long time to get past the pain, but I did. And so will you."

"No, that's where you're wrong. I won't ever get over this. I won't ever trust another man or woman."

"But what if Matthew is your son? Because there is a good chance he is."

"I don't know. Because I just don't know if I could stay married to Charlotte. I resent her too much, and I'm not sure I could even stomach her on a daily basis."

"But she's your wife, Curtis."

"And?"

"You need to try to work things out with her."

"Please. She should just be happy she still has a house to sleep in or that I haven't slit her throat."

"Okay, look. You're taking this too far. I know Charlotte was wrong, but Curtis, you've done just as much or worse than she has. I'm not saying that that justifies her actions, because it doesn't, but you slept around on me for years, and I forgave you. It took me a while, but still, I forgave you. But most of all, you asked God to forgive you for everything. And Curtis, you and I both know, you did a lot of terrible things. Some things are too terrible to ever bring up again."

He knew she was telling the truth, but he didn't want to hear it. Not when this truth about him wasn't eliminating his pain. Not when nothing he'd ever done could compare to the sins Charlotte had committed. Not when Aaron was probably sitting around right now laughing at the way he'd deceived Curtis. It was all enough to make Curtis ill. He wanted revenge more than ever.

"I hear what you're saying, but it's not helping me," he said.

"Then what you need to do is pray. You're a minister, Curtis. A pastor of a church."

"But I'm also human just like everyone else."

"I realize that, but you're supposed to react a lot differently to adversity than the average person. I'm not saying you can help the way you feel, but as a minister, you should be asking God to help you. You should do exactly what you tell your members to do when they find themselves in unbearable situations. You need to listen to your own advice."

"That's easier said than done."

"But it's possible."

"I don't know whether it is or not, because at the moment,

I'm not sure of anything. I don't even know if returning to the pulpit again was the right thing to do."

"Why? Because you're having a few problems in your life?"

"No, because I don't see what good the pulpit is doing for me. I don't see how being a minister and preaching the Word is helping anyone, because it certainly isn't helping me."

"What you need to do is find a quiet place to meditate. And you need to do it immediately."

"Maybe."

"Promise me that you will."

"I'll try."

"Trying isn't good enough."

"Well, that's the best I can do."

"You know that's not true. And if you won't do it for yourself, then do it for your children. You need to be there for them, and you can't be there when you're feeling like this."

"Hey, Tanya, thanks for listening, okay. I really appreciate it."

"So what does that mean? You don't want to hear any more of what I'm saying?"

"No, it's nothing like that. But I really need to get to the park. Our church picnic is today."

"Whatever you say, Curtis. I just hope you don't do anything you'll have to pay for later."

"I won't."

"I'm serious."

"So am I."

"Then I'll let you go."

"Take care, and tell Alicia I'll speak to her later."

"I will."

Curtis sat quietly, yet furiously, trying to figure out which direction he should drive in. To the picnic, back home, or over to

Aaron's. If he went back home, he couldn't be responsible for what might happen to Charlotte. If he ended up over at Aaron's, he couldn't guarantee much different for him. If he went to the picnic the way he'd planned, he wouldn't have to hurt anybody. He wouldn't have to do something drastic. At least not today, anyway. But the two of them would get what they had coming to them. There just wasn't any way around it.

After praying for just over an hour, Charlotte picked up the phone and dialed Anise's number. It rang a number of times, until the voice system answered. Charlotte wanted to leave a message but couldn't. She wanted to apologize profusely and explain her side of the story, but she simply didn't have the strength to. So she called Curtis instead.

"What?" he answered.

"Curtis, please don't hang up. Please come back and talk to me."

"No."

"I'm so sorry. I'm so, so sorry."

"Charlotte, how many times are you planning to say that?"

"As many times as I have to."

"Well, I wish you would stop it, because it's not helping you, and it doesn't change the way I feel."

"But I love you, Curtis. I've always loved you no matter what."

"And? What do you want me to do, give you some prize for it?"

"No. I'm just trying to make you see that this was all a mistake."

"Call it whatever you want, but you and Aaron knew exactly what you were doing."

"Curtis, you and I have been through so much together, so please don't throw our marriage away like this."

"You're the one who threw it away when you lied to me about Matthew and when you decided to sleep with another man. Now, unless you have something important to say, let's end this pointless conversation."

"What about tonight at home, can we talk then?"

"I won't be there."

"Curtis, please. I'm begging you."

"And you're wasting your time, too."

"But what about Matthew? What is he going to think if he comes home and realizes that things aren't the same between us?"

"That's your problem. You caused all of this, so you figure it out."

"Fine, Curtis."

"And when you see me at the picnic, don't come over to me acting like we're so in love with each other, because if you do, you'll get your feelings hurt. Right in front of everybody. Now, good-bye."

Charlotte hung up and tried to pretend that none of this was real. It was the only way she could keep her sanity.

Chapter 21

AN ENTIRE WEEK HAD PASSED; IT WAS NOW SATURDAY AGAIN, YET CURTIS still hadn't said more than two words to Charlotte—that is, outside of answering her questions. He'd even kept his promise about the church picnic and hadn't acknowledged her one time. He hadn't even cared that some of the members had noticed it. Then on Tuesday, he'd driven over to Chicago to pick up Matthew, but he'd made it very clear that he didn't want her riding with him. She'd asked him why he was being so cruel, but he'd given her a very strong look of hatred. He'd told her in no uncertain terms that he didn't care how badly she wanted to see Matthew, she wasn't going. He hadn't even flinched when he'd seen her doubled over in tears. He'd grabbed his keys, walked out of the house, and started on his way without her. She hadn't even had the strength or the will to try and reason with him. She knew it wouldn't have made any difference if she had.

But now, she was headed over to her aunt Emma's, preparing to apologize for all the confusion she'd caused with Anise. Charlotte had phoned her aunt first thing that morning to see if it would be okay for her to drop by, and her aunt had told her to come any time after two. Currently, it was only minutes before three o'clock. She'd planned on getting out of the house somewhat earlier, but she'd been trying to spend as much time with Matthew as Curtis allowed. Ever since Matthew had returned home, Curtis had been spending every single evening with him, right up until bedtime, not leaving any quality time for her. But it was almost as if Curtis dared her to say anything about it. And she didn't. He'd become even colder when he'd learned yesterday that the DNA test was scheduled for the day after tomorrow.

Charlotte drove in front of her aunt's home and regretted choosing today as the day she would visit. Anise's SUV was parked in the driveway. Charlotte turned off the ignition and sat in her vehicle for a few minutes, praying that Anise wouldn't go off on her. She hoped that Anise would listen to what she had to say and then find it in her heart to forgive her.

She stepped out of the car, set her security system, and waved at the woman who lived next door. She was an elderly woman who no one ever seemed to visit, not even her three grown children, so Aunt Emma always went over to check on her or take her food when she cooked. But that was just like Aunt Emma to do for others who couldn't necessarily help themselves.

Charlotte walked up the three steps, rang the doorbell, and waited. Her heart rate picked up speed slowly but surely, and Charlotte hoped with everything in her that her aunt would be the one to open the front door. She simply didn't know how she would ever be able to face Anise without talking to her by phone first. She wanted to and, of course, had tried to call her many times since that wretched incident with Aaron, but Anise

had refused to answer the phone. Charlotte had even tried calling her at work, but each time Anise's assistant had told Charlotte that Anise wasn't available. Charlotte could tell the
assistant was lying and hadn't felt comfortable doing so.

When Charlotte heard the door being unlocked, she looked
up, saw her aunt Emma, and felt somewhat at ease. She walked
in and hugged her immediately. She held onto her longer than
usual and didn't want to let go.

"Charlotte, please," Anise said. "You can stop the drama any
time now."

"Anise!" Aunt Emma scolded. "Don't."

Charlotte walked into the house and looked at Anise, who
was standing in the dining room.

"All of a sudden, you're so pitifully innocent," Anise continued. "Well, sweetheart, you might have Mom fooled, but I
know exactly who you are. A lying, manipulating adulteress
who will sleep with anything that walks. In a word, you're a
straight-up whore." Anise turned to Emma. "And Mom, I'm
sorry for speaking this way in front of you, but I'm not about to
let Miss Thing waltz in here, acting like she's the victim. I can't
believe you had the nerve to drive your butt over here in the
first place. Why don't you go visit your own mother? Because
we all know that she would clearly understand what it's like to
sleep with someone else's husband. Hell, she slept with her own
sister's fiancé herself. But as they say, the apple *never* falls too
far from the tree, and you're proof of it."

"Anise, look," Emma said. "I know you're upset, but try to
calm yourself down. Charlotte, you come in and have a seat."

"Hmmph," Anise grunted, rolling her eyes at Charlotte and
leaving the dining room.

"Aunt Emma, I am so sorry. I'm so sorry I don't know what

to do. But I can't change what happened. I wish I could, but I can't."

"I know, baby, but you have to understand how Anise feels, too. She's loved and trusted you like a sister for years and even more so since you and Curtis moved here. And I have to tell you, Anise is the type of person who will be there for you for all eternity until you cross her. She is not good with forgiving people who betray her. It's the one thing I've always had to talk to her about."

"But I was so young back then. I mean, I know I was wrong for what I did with David, but he was the adult."

"What did you say?" Anise roared, walking back into the dining room.

Charlotte was afraid to blink, let alone answer any questions.

"Did you say, you were young and David was the adult? Because if that's the case, then why have you been sleeping around with Aaron, knowing that you're married to Curtis? And what about some man you supposedly slept with the night before your wedding? And don't get me started on some professor Aaron said you were sleeping with when you were in school."

Charlotte wanted to turn around and rush out the door. She'd known that Aaron had probably told Anise everything the same as he'd told Curtis, but she didn't want her aunt hearing about any of it. She didn't want her aunt thinking badly of her from now on. She wished Anise would stop this rampage she was on.

"And what about all those credit card applications you forged your husband's name on? I mean, I had to be out of my mind to let you use my address. I was just as wrong as you were, and I regret letting you use me to go behind Curtis's back."

Charlotte was speechless, yet still in tears.

"You might as well stop all that crying, because the bottom line is that you slept with my husband, and you did it in my bed. I mean, what were you thinking?"

"Anise, I know how you feel," Emma said. "Lord knows I do, but you and Charlotte are blood cousins, and blood relatives should try to get along with each other. Everyone makes mistakes, but we all have to get past them."

"Maybe. But not in this case. And for the record, I'm through with Charlotte for good because I don't want anything to do with a person who lies and cheats just to get what they want from people. Charlotte cares about Charlotte and nobody else."

Anise was discussing Charlotte as if she wasn't even sitting there. Charlotte wanted to explain herself, but she knew there was little if anything she could say that would make Anise listen to her. Anise was fuming, and Charlotte realized it was probably better to just keep quiet. Anise looked as though she was ready to fist-fight.

"Mom, I'm really sorry for disrespecting you and your house," Anise continued. "You know I've never done that before, but this whole thing is far too much for me. And that's why it's probably best that I go," she said, lifting her handbag from the chair she was standing in front of.

"Lord, Lord, Lord," Emma said. "Lord knows I hate seeing you and Charlotte into it like this."

"Well, Mom, Charlotte should have thought about that before she slept with David. But like with everything else she's done, she thought she was slick enough to get away with it. She thought she could do whatever she wanted with no regard for anyone else. But now she's the one who is going to be left out in the cold."

"Anise, why won't you just talk to me directly?" Charlotte asked softly.

"Girl, you've got a lot of nerve, saying anything to me. And if I were you, I wouldn't say anything else. And if I were Curtis, I'd pack up Matthew, leave Mitchell, and make sure you never see him again. Because as far as I'm concerned, Matthew deserves a much better mother than you. He deserves to have a mother who is decent and one who cares about more than just herself."

"I love Matthew more than my own life, Anise, and you know that."

"Whatever, Charlotte. Whatever you say. But let me make myself clear once and for all. Don't you *ever* dial my phone number again, and don't you ever step foot near my home. If you do, I'll be filing a harassment complaint with the police."

Emma shook her head in disappointment.

"I'm sorry, Mom. I know you hate seeing this, but this is what happens when people become consumed with themselves and start thinking they're on top of the world. They start thinking they can treat people any way they want to. But I'll call you later," Anise said and left.

"How am I ever going to get past this?" Charlotte said, clasping her hands together beneath her chin.

"You're going to have to pray your way out of it. Because if I know my daughter, prayer is the only chance you have with her."

"I just don't know what I'm going to do if I end up losing Curtis and my friendship with Anise all at the same time."

"Well, as much as I hate saying this, baby, you were wrong. I love you with all my heart, but you were wrong for sleeping with your cousin's husband and wrong for lying to Curtis about Matthew."

"But I just know that Matthew is Curtis's son. I'm all but sure of it."

"I know you want it to be, but the truth is, David could actually be Matthew's father. And just so you know, Anise called David, and he told her that you came into their bedroom and got in bed with him as soon as she left that day. Said you were always trying to flirt with him behind her back even before then."

Charlotte couldn't believe David had fixed his lips to say such awful things about her, especially since he'd slept around on Anise with other women, too, and basically treated Anise like nothing when they were married. What he'd said about Charlotte was actually true, but Charlotte didn't see a reason for him to talk about it. By doing so, he'd only made bad matters worse between her and Anise, and no matter what anyone said, she still blamed David since he, like Curtis, had been the adult when she was with him. Nonetheless, she could barely look her aunt in her face.

"I know I was wrong, but I can't change what I did."

"That's true, but it's up to you to try to fix these problems with Anise and Curtis."

"But how? Anise doesn't want me calling or coming near her anymore, and Curtis pretty much walks around the house ignoring me. As a matter of fact, he won't talk to me at all unless I ask him a question, and even then, he replies with short answers. He looks at me like he wants to kill me."

"Curtis loves Matthew, and I'm sure the thought of Matthew not being his son is destroying him emotionally."

"But what about me? I was only seventeen when I got pregnant."

"I hear what you're saying, but now you're twenty-five, and

you have to take responsibility for your actions. We all have to take responsibility for what we do whether we want to or not."

Charlotte thought about Matthew and how hurt he was going to be if, by some slim chance, Curtis wasn't his father. She broke down all over again just thinking about it.

"Baby, come on." Emma reached out to her. "Come on, and let's go into the den."

They sat on the sofa, and Charlotte laid her head in her aunt's lap, weeping like a child. She cried until there were no more tears, and her aunt kept trying to counsel her. She tried to make Charlotte see that this, too, would pass eventually. She told her that for every wrong there were consequences and the reason we all have to try to do the right thing. Charlotte heard what she was saying and agreed with her, but it still didn't help the way she was feeling. She was thankful that her aunt was trying to console her, but what she really needed was for Curtis to forgive her and at least stop despising her the way he did. She needed him to treat her like his wife and like the mother of his son—a son that just had to be his.

She wanted that so desperately, and if everything worked out in that respect, she could finally focus on the child she was carrying and the date she was having an abortion. She tried hard not to think about it, but she knew it was time she scheduled the appointment. It was time she ended this pregnancy before there was more confusion to contend with. They just didn't need that in their lives right now.

Curtis heard Charlotte come into the house and into the family room, but he never even looked up. He and Matthew were playing one of Matthew's video games and were deep in competition.

"Hi, sweetheart," she said.

"Hi, Mom. I can't talk right now, because Dad is right on my tail."

Curtis could tell she was expecting him to say something, anything, but he didn't.

"Curtis, have you guys had dinner?"

"It's after seven, so I hope so." He still didn't turn to look at her.

"Sorry," she said and then walked upstairs.

Soon after, Matthew won the game, dropped his controller, and said, "Dad, what's wrong with you and Mom?"

"Nothing."

"Well, how come you don't hardly talk to her anymore?"

"We've had some disagreements, but everything is fine. Adults do that sometimes."

"Well, I don't like it because Mom looks real sad. And she didn't look sad before I went to stay with Grandma and Grandpa."

"Some things are hard to understand, but there's nothing for you to worry about, okay?" Curtis tried convincing him that nothing was going on, but he could tell that Matthew was still uneasy. The child loved both of his parents, and nothing bothered him more than when they seemed upset with each other. The thought of Charlotte and her skeletons made Curtis want to do unspeakable things to her—none of which would be expected from a pastor.

Curtis and Matthew started a new game, but the phone rang. Curtis hoped it wasn't an emergency situation with one of the church members. Not that he didn't want to help them, but he was enjoying his time with Matthew and didn't want to leave him.

"Curtis," Charlotte said, walking down the stairway. Curtis didn't like the look on her face.

"Who is it?"

Charlotte passed him the phone but didn't respond.

"Hello?"

"Curtis, this is Trina."

Curtis could already feel the nervousness in his stomach. He couldn't believe it, but his sister was actually calling him. He didn't know whether to smile, jump for joy, or what.

"How are you? It's so good to hear your voice."

"The only reason I'm calling you is to let you know that my mother passed away this afternoon."

Curtis dropped down onto the chair. His muscles tightened one after another, and he felt paralyzed. He needed to wake up from what had to be some nightmare he was having.

"Are you there?" she asked.

"Yes."

"I'll be making the arrangements tomorrow and will have someone call you with the details."

"Was she sick?" he asked.

"She had terminal cancer."

"For how long?"

"Almost a year."

"And no one——"

"And no," she interrupted. "No one took the time to call you, because there was no reason to. You're the one who dropped out of our lives and disowned us, remember? And the only reason I'm calling you now is because my mother made me promise to."

Why did she keep saying *her* mother? She was speaking as if *her* mother wasn't also his. But what could he say? He had disowned both of them for years and treated them as strangers, just the way his sister had stated.

"Like I said," she continued. "I'll have someone call you with the details."

"Trina, I'm really sorry. I know my apology won't fix anything, but I am sorry."

"I'm sorry, too, Curtis. I'm sorry that you and I have the same blood running through our veins and that my mother asked me to call you."

"Is there anything that you need?"

"Nothing."

"Anything at all, Trina. Even if you want me to come over there tomorrow to help with the arrangements."

"I don't. And in all honesty, I need to end this conversation, so that I can notify some of the people who actually cared about my mother."

"I cared about her, too, Trina."

"No, you didn't. All you cared about was yourself."

Curtis was speechless. Unfortunately, any argument he had wasn't going to matter. Trina hated him with a passion, and he couldn't blame her.

"I have to go," she said and hung up.

Curtis pressed the button on the phone, set it down on the table, and didn't move.

"Sweetheart, I'm so sorry," Charlotte said.

Curtis broke down, and Matthew went over to hug him. Curtis held his son closely and cried like a newborn. He cried harder than he ever had in his life. Even more so than when he was a small boy and there hadn't been any food to eat. His mother's death was taking a major toll on him, and the guilt he felt was killing him. Why hadn't he called her or gone to see her when he'd had the chance? He'd wanted to and, then again, he hadn't wanted to, and now it was too late. It was too late to

see her alive, and he would never live down the way he'd neg-
lected her. He'd never live down the way he'd separated himself
from his mother and sister and pretended to the world that they
didn't exist. He'd done a terrible injustice and now he was paying for it.

His heart ached, and he wished he had someone to share his
pain with. He wished that anyone other than Charlotte was
standing in the room with him. He wanted to go over to Anise's
for comfort but decided it was best to stay there with Matthew.
Matthew had never met his paternal grandmother and didn't
know very much about her. It was time Curtis told him as much
as he could. It was time he told him how wonderful his grandmother was and how she would have loved having him for a
grandson.

It was time Curtis tried to accept that he'd lost his mother for
good and that he might also be losing his son in the same
month. What a tragedy his life had become.

Chapter 22

CURTIS HAD SPENT MOST OF THE NIGHT MOURNING THE LOSS OF HIS mother, and now he was heading toward the church. He'd told Matthew that he had some church business to attend to before the start of service and that Matthew should ride with his mother. Matthew hadn't been happy about not being able to go with him, and more than anything, he wanted to know why Curtis and Charlotte had to ride in separate cars. Curtis hadn't been able to offer him a straight answer, but he could tell that Matthew's questions were becoming more specific. He wanted to know what was going on with his parents, and it was clearly starting to worry the boy.

But Curtis had needed some time alone. He was trying to deal with his mother's passing as best as he could, but all he could picture were scenes from his childhood. Mostly, he thought about the bad times because there weren't very many happy ones. He thought about the way his father mistreated Curtis's mother and how he never tried to help out financially. He'd never thought twice as to whether they had clothing on their backs or if the rent was paid up. His facial expression had never even changed that day he'd walked into their apartment and realized that the electricity had been turned off. He'd simply looked around, shaken his head, and walked right back out. Curtis's mother had begged him to help her with the bill, but his response was "Bitch, it's *your* responsibility to get the lights turned back on, not mine."

Curtis could still remember the sad look on his mother's face, but what Curtis never understood was why she would never leave him. Why she never took him and his sister out of such a horrible situation. Right or wrong, he'd blamed his mother just as much as he'd blamed his father, because only months after Curtis had turned thirteen, his father had started beating him for no apparent reason. He would beat Curtis when he was as drunk as could be and would even laugh about it. Interestingly enough, though, he never laid a hand on Trina or even their mother. Of course, he spoke to his wife any way he wanted to, called her names, ones that Curtis didn't want to think about, and practically treated her like a slave. But he never touched her. Maybe it was because his wife knew what and what not to say, what and what not to do. Maybe it was because taking his frustrations out on Curtis was more than enough for him. Maybe it was all his father needed in order to feel like a man.

It was also the reason Curtis had waited for him to arrive home late one evening, the night Curtis hit him across the head with a baseball bat. He'd struck him multiple times until blood had streamed down both sides of his face, and Curtis's mother had pulled Curtis away. Curtis had hoped and thought for sure that his father was dead, but he wasn't. The ambulance had come and taken him away, and after resting comfortably in the hospital for seven whole days, the hospital had sent him home. Curtis had still hated him, but from then on his father walked around his son with caution, and he never raised another hand to him. In the end, his father had remained a drunk until the day alcoholism had claimed the last of his pathetic little life. Curtis had been seventeen when his father had died, but he still hadn't been able to forgive his mother. He'd tried to, but he'd blamed her for all that he'd gone through as a child. He blamed her because it was a mother's responsibility to protect her child at all costs. It was her responsibility to place her children before any man, even if that man was their father.

Curtis had tried understanding her position and how she was probably afraid to leave him, but it just wasn't enough of an excuse. It was the reason he had ended his relationship with her and his sister as soon as he had the chance. His sister hadn't done anything wrong, but there was no way he could truly put his past behind him unless he stopped communicating with both of them. Now, though, if he could turn back time, he would do things a lot differently. He would apologize to his mother and sister and spend as much time with them as possible. He would be the perfect son by any means necessary. He would have been there for her until she'd taken her last breath. But as he'd realized yesterday and then again this morning, it was much too late for that.

When Curtis arrived in the church parking lot, he drove into his reserved space and left his vehicle. Sunday school wouldn't be starting for another hour, so no one was on the premises. Curtis was glad because this way he could pray in peace. He could spend some time alone, speaking to God without any distractions. He didn't have the sanctuary to himself very often, and now that he did, he was happy about it. After dropping off his Bible and briefcase in his study, he came back downstairs and knelt directly in front of the altar.

"Father in heaven, I stretch my hand to Thee. I come before You with a humble heart and call on You in the name of Jesus. I ask You to forgive me for all my sins and that You would guide me during these very trying times I am experiencing. I know I haven't always been the best that I can be and that I still have a long way to go, but I really am a changed man. Which is why today, Father, with all the faith and belief in You that I have, I find myself confused and disappointed. I find myself wondering why my life is steadily falling apart, even though I keep trying to do what You would have me to do. I have been faithful to my wife, yet she's been sleeping with my best friend. I became a full-time father to my son, yet there is a chance that we're not even related. I've committed myself to the church, yet my mother is gone, and I never even had a chance to say good-bye to her. So, Lord, I ask You to give me understanding and meaning for all of this. You said that You would never place any more on me than I can bear, but right now, Father, it is surely starting to feel like it. Lord, I ask You to remove the lustful temptation which is building deep inside me. I ask You to remove the violent temptation I have toward hurting my wife and Aaron. Father, I ask You right now to give me the strength I need to overcome these trials. I ask that You please allow Matthew to be my son and not someone else's. Father, please hear my prayer. In the name of Jesus. Amen."

Curtis stood up and sat down in the right front pew. He sighed when he realized just how heavy his heart still was. He missed his mother and he wasn't sure how he would ever get past what he'd done to her. His entire body ached, and what he wanted most was to go back home and into his bedroom, shutting off the rest of the world. He certainly didn't feel like delivering a sermon to his congregation this morning.

Another half hour passed before the Sunday school atten-
dees entered the church for their weekly lessons. An hour after
that, general service began. Before the benediction, Curtis stood
at the podium to address his members.

"Some of you may have already heard, but today is a very
sad day for me. My mother passed on yesterday, and while I'm
ashamed to say it, I hadn't spoken to her in over twenty years.
My childhood was not what it should have been, but regardless,
my mother was still my mother, and I should have respected
that. The Bible says, 'honor thy father and thy mother: that thy
days may be long upon the land which the Lord thy God giveth
thee,' and I completely disobeyed that scripture. I've read the
book of Exodus many times, but for whatever reason, I made
the decision to ignore chapter twenty, verse twelve as if it were
never even written. It reminds me of my hypocritical days back
in Chicago and how I would fix and quote scriptures the way I
wanted to hear them. I would rarely quote any scripture verba-
tim from the Bible. I always added in or left out appropriate
words—words that allowed me to commit many, many sins
without feeling bad about it."

"Speak today," a woman said.

"That's all right, son. We've all made mistakes," Brother
Dixon stated.

"But I stand before you with much humility and shame,"
Curtis continued. "I stand here feeling more pain than I have
in years, and I ask that you would all please pray for me. I went
into deep prayer this morning, but I know now that I need all
of your prayers if I am to successfully deal with what I am
going through. I won't go into details, but I will say that my
mother's passing is not the only problem I'm dealing with and
that my plate is very full. It seems as though Satan is on a seri-

ous mission to destroy me. It has happened to me before, but right now, at this very moment, I feel weak. I feel as though all my faith and work in the ministry is in vain."

There were sounds of love and sympathy throughout the congregation and some of the female worshippers were in tears. The members of Deliverance loved their pastor, and it was obvious that they were prepared to stand by him. Curtis tried not to become emotional, but he couldn't help it. He stood for a few minutes longer in silence and then took a seat in the pulpit. One of the associate ministers reached for the mic and assured Curtis that they were all there for him. He told Curtis to feel free to take as much time off as he needed, because they sincerely understood. Thankfully, everyone else agreed with him.

Curtis wiped his eyes with a white handkerchief, stood up, and prepared to walk out of the sanctuary. He stopped when he saw Aaron strutting down the center aisle. Curtis's mind quickly flashed back to Adrienne and the Sunday she'd showed up at his other church.

"Well, well, well," Aaron said, smiling. "Doesn't everyone look so nice this morning."

Curtis couldn't believe this was happening all over again. He didn't know what Aaron was up to, but he knew it wasn't good.

"I apologize for interrupting the service, but I just didn't know when I would ever find the perfect time to get all of you together. I wasn't at the picnic last Saturday or here at church on Sunday, but it's only because I'm feeling a lot of pain. Isn't that right, Miss First Lady," he said, patting Charlotte on top of her head. Curtis felt those violent tendencies again. At the same time, he was worried that Aaron was feeling the same way.

"How are you, Pastor? I'm sorry to hear about your mother, and I wish you'd called me last night to let me know."

Curtis glanced at some of the church members and noticed the shock on their faces. Charlotte looked as white as a ghost. He was glad that Matthew was attending the children's service over in the educational center. The church held a separate service for the children, twice per month, and this was one of the Sundays.

"Don't worry," Aaron said to Curtis. "I know you're upset with me for obvious reasons, but I'm only here to let this great congregation in on a secret. Actually, it's one of the best-kept secrets in this city. You see, Miss Charlotte and I have become special friends. Actually, we became close friends a good while ago. However, now we're in love with each other, but unfortunately, she's confused about everything. We'd been spending a lot of time together, but all of a sudden, after I confessed some information to Pastor Black, she sort of tried to cut me off. And I have to say that while I will accept living without her if that's what she wants, I still thought I'd better let you, the tithing and offering contributors of this church, know who your first lady really is. So, Charlotte, baby, I ask you, once and for all, are you going to come with me or stay with Pastor?"

"Looorrrd have mercy," one woman said.

"Mmm, mmm, mmm," another added.

"Aaron, you need help," Charlotte said. "There's something wrong with you, and Curtis and I are more than willing to find some help for you if you want us to."

Aaron laughed loudly. "Help? The only person who is going to need any help is you," he said, turning and walking back down the aisle. "Again, everyone, I apologize for the interruption. I didn't mean any disrespect to any of you."

That Negro was completely insane. Curtis had seen Aaron stroll into the church, he'd heard every word that Aaron had said, and still, he was astounded. There was whispering throughout the entire building and most eyes were fixed on Charlotte. Curtis wasn't happy with what Charlotte and Aaron had done, but he hadn't wanted any of their personal business disclosed to the congregation. He hadn't wanted one soul to learn that Charlotte and Aaron had been sleeping together or that Matthew might not be his son. At least Aaron hadn't gone as far as exposing any particulars on that subject.

"Church, I'm sorry for what just happened," Curtis said. "I don't know what has gotten into Brother Malone, but we will make sure that nothing like this happens again. And while it's unfortunate that all of this has occurred, I think it would be best if I gave the benediction so that all of you can go home."

Curtis finished the last sanction of service and watched as each member left the church. Some of them came up and expressed their sympathy regarding his mother and their concern for whatever Aaron had been talking about. One woman told Curtis that he should call the police if there were future incidents. Charlotte stood speaking to two of her female acquaintances in private, but Curtis was sure that both women were only trying to find out what they could from her. Their concern had nothing to do with compassion and everything to do with nosiness. What they wanted was a hot topic to gossip about.

"Pastor, Pastor," one of the male members yelled, rushing toward him.

"What is it?"

"These flyers were stuck on the windshield of every car in the parking lot."

Curtis grabbed the fluorescent pink sheet of paper and read it.

SUNDAY MORNING NEWSFLASH:

Pastor Marries Ex-Mistress

Pastor Moves To Mitchell

Pastor Starts Deliverance Outreach

Pastor's Wife Sleeps With Pastor's Best Friend

Pastor's Wife Sleeps With Pastor's Best Friend A Lot!

Pastor's Wife Falls In Love With Pastor's Best Friend

Pastor May Only Have One Child—Not Two

Poor, Poor Pastor

Pastor And First Lady Divorce.

First Lady Marries Pastor's Best Friend

They Live Happily, Happily Ever After

Curtis was numb. He couldn't feel a thing if he wanted to. Charlotte looked over at him as did the remaining members. Everyone else had rushed outside to see what all the excitement was about. Matthew walked into the sanctuary and over to his father. Curtis's worst nightmare was happening.

"Dad," Matthew said, batting away tears. "Who's not your child? Me or Alicia?"

Curtis wondered why he'd ever been born. Not Matthew, but himself.

Chapter 23

THE ATMOSPHERE IN THE BLACK HOUSEHOLD WAS AS COLD AND awkward as a hundred-year-old mausoleum. The ride home from church, Curtis in his car and Matthew and Charlotte in hers, had seemed much quicker than normal. It was probably because Curtis dreaded facing Matthew and needed more time to figure out what he was going to say to him. He didn't want to lie to him, but how could he tell him the truth? How could he tell an innocent little seven-year-old that his mother wasn't sure who his father was? How could he tell his son that he could no longer live in the same house with him? Because Curtis just didn't see how he could stay with Charlotte after all of this. Not with all the lies and deceit and the fact that everyone at Deliverance knew the complete lowdown regarding them.

Curtis went straight up to the master bedroom and removed his clothing. He slipped on a T-shirt and a pair of shorts. It was the first of July and the temperature had to be almost ninety. The central air was running full force, but Curtis still wanted to dress in cool clothing. Charlotte changed out of her dress and high heels and into a shorts set but didn't say anything. Still, he saw her staring at him on and off through the dresser mirror. Curtis was on an emotional roller coaster. He could barely stand the sight of her, but he didn't want to hurt Matthew. Not to mention the pain he was still feeling about his mother or the rage he was feeling toward Aaron. It was one thing for him to sneak around with Charlotte, but humiliating Curtis during his own church service was another. It was enough to make Curtis consider something drastic. He wanted Aaron out of the way once and for all. Curtis had asked God to remove these unholy thoughts, but for some reason, these thoughts and desires were growing stronger. They were beginning to consume his mind in a scary sort of way.

"We have to sit Matthew down and talk to him right now," Curtis said.

"I know. But what will we tell him?" she asked.

"I'm not telling him anything, but you're going to tell him that his uncle Aaron is very sick and that he needs medical treatment. Then I want you to tell him that those statements in those flyers are not true and that you don't know why Aaron did what he did."

"I've never lied to Matthew since the day he was born," Charlotte said.

"Well, as of this moment, you're going to start, because I won't stand to see him hurt. It's bad enough that we may have to break the news about him not being my son, but I keep praying that things turn out fine with that. Still, there is no guarantee, and, Charlotte, as much as I love Matthew, I don't think I can stay married to you."

"I'm telling you, he is your son."

"Time will tell soon enough."

"I still hate putting Matthew through all of that."

"Well, Charlotte, you should have thought about that before you spread your legs open to all those men."

"Curtis, we were both sleeping around back then."

"You're right, but the difference between you and me is that I didn't lie about the father of my child, I didn't sleep with my cousin's husband, I never slept with anyone else the night before our wedding, and I certainly haven't been sleeping with your best friend."

Clearly, Charlotte knew she'd lost the argument, and Curtis was glad because he didn't want to talk about it anymore.

"Let's go," he said, heading toward Matthew's bedroom.

"Son, are you okay?" Curtis said, when they walked in. They both sat down on either side of him.

"Not really," he answered.

"I know today was sort of confusing, but your mom wants to explain it to you."

"Matthew, sweetie, your uncle Aaron is very ill. He has a mental condition and that's why he did that crazy thing at church today. He didn't mean to do it, but he couldn't help it. He needs to be hospitalized."

"But, Mom, he didn't look real sick to me."

"I know. When people have a mental illness, you can't always see how sick they are."

"But why did he say that Dad only had one child?"

"Well, actually, sweetie, he didn't say that. He typed up some crazy note on those flyers and stuck them on everyone's car. And even though you were over at the children's service, he walked into where we were, said some strange stuff, and then walked right back out. No one understood what he was doing or why."

Curtis had to give it to her, she was good. And oh so convincing. She was good at telling lies, almost as good as he'd been back in the day, and it was the reason she'd been able to betray him so easily. He'd believed every excuse she'd told him, including her claims of having to work all those overtime hours and her many stories explaining why she couldn't make love to him. It was all so ironic.

"I wish he would go back to being the uncle Aaron who used to come over to play my games with me."

"I know you do," she said. "And maybe he will when he gets better."

"I hope so, because I miss him."

Curtis breathed deeply and realized just how devious Aaron was and how he'd quietly gained both trust and admiration from everyone in their household. Curtis's fury rose to a whole new level.

Curtis hugged his son, and both Curtis and Charlotte left the room in opposite directions. Curtis went downstairs to the family room, and Charlotte headed to the kitchen to warm up leftovers. Now Curtis was dialing Alicia to tell her that her grandmother had passed away. With everything that had been going on, he'd totally forgotten to call her this morning. He hoped she wouldn't be upset about him not contacting her immediately, but she would probably be fine since she didn't even know her.

"Hey, Daddy," she answered.

"Hi, baby girl. How are you?"

"I'm good. We just got home from church though, so I'm starving. Can I call you back in a little while?"

"Sure. But I did want to let you know that your grandmother passed away. You know, the one you never met."

Alicia didn't respond, but he could tell she was still there.

"Are you okay?" he asked.

"I'm fine. But there's something I have to tell you."

"Which is?"

"I met Granny Pauline a long time ago."

"What? When?"

"Mom thought I should meet her, so when I was fourteen, she looked up the phone number one day and called her."

"Well, it certainly would have been nice if someone had told me."

"We thought you would be mad, because you never called Granny Pauline or went to visit her even when you lived here in Chicago. And, Daddy, please don't be angry, because I'm really glad I got to know my other grandmother. She was so nice to me, and now she's gone already."

"Did you know that she had passed?"

"Yes, Aunt Trina called us last night."

"Really? Well, even though I'm hurt, I'm not upset with you or your mom. I was the one who was wrong, because I never should have kept you away from your own family in the first place. I never should have treated them the way I did, and now I'm going to have to live with that mistake until the day I die."

"I'm sorry, Daddy. I'm really sorry that you didn't get to see her."

"It's all my fault, so don't feel bad. Trina said she was making the arrangements today, so if you want, I can pick you up on the day of the funeral."

"Okay. I think Mom is going, too. But I'll still ride with you guys."

"Is your mom there?"

"Yep. You want to speak to her?"

"If she's not too busy."

"Okay, hold on. Mommmm," she called out. "Bye, Daddy."

"I'll talk to you soon."

"Hello?" Tanya said.

"How are you?

"I'm fine. How are you?"

"Not well. You already know about everything else that I'm dealing with and now my mother has passed away. Alicia told me that she's been visiting with her for the last couple of years."

"She has. I wasn't sure if you would be okay with it, so I decided it was best if we didn't tell you. I'm sorry for going behind your back, but I have to tell you, Curtis, with Pauline dying at sixty, I'm glad I tried to find her. Otherwise, Alicia never would have gotten a chance to know her."

"I'm glad you found her, too. I just wish Matthew could have had the same experience."

Neither of them spoke for a few seconds.

"Well, I know you just got home from church, but I'll let you know when the funeral is unless you end up hearing first," Curtis said. "I don't have to tell you how cold and short Trina was with me, so I'll be surprised if she even calls me back."

"It's a tough situation, but try and be patient with her. She was very close to your mother and so were her two children. So she's really hurting over this."

"I know. And, Tanya, thanks for connecting my mother and Alicia. I probably would have been upset if you'd told me about it two years ago, but that's because I'm sometimes too stubborn for my own good."

"Don't I know it."

"But hey, I want you to know that you're still the best in my book. You always will be."

"Thanks. And keep your head up, okay. Stay prayerful."

"I will."

"Take care."

"You, too."

Curtis sat the phone on its base and looked over at Charlotte. She'd come into the room and had been listening to his every word and didn't look too happy about the conversation he'd just had with his ex-wife. But it wasn't like Curtis cared one way or the other. It wasn't like her opinion or feelings mattered to him in the least little bit. She had to know that and if she didn't, she might as well get used to it. She might as well get used to a lot of changes because life as she'd once known it was over. It would never be the same again for her or them as a couple.

Chapter 24

THE DAY HAD FINALLY ARRIVED. CHARLOTTE WAS A BUNDLE OF NERVES and couldn't wait for this whole DNA business to be over with. She couldn't wait to hear the good news, maybe a week from now, that Curtis was in fact Matthew's biological father. It would definitely make a whole world of difference. Curtis still wasn't speaking to her unless he had to, but she was sure his attitude would drastically improve once those test results were in.

Charlotte heard the doorbell ringing and walked toward the front door. When she opened it, a young female postal carrier asked her to sign for a box she was holding. Charlotte wrote her signature, brought the package inside, and immediately saw that it was from Anise. At first, she debated opening it, but since Curtis had gone to the church for a couple of hours and Matthew was upstairs watching cartoons, she took the box into the kitchen, pulled out a knife, and cut it open. Enclosed were a ton of credit card statements and the white gold and diamond heart she'd given Anise for her last birthday. Underneath, there was a note inside an envelope. Charlotte pulled it out and read it.

Charlotte: As of today, I still have not spoken to or seen you since I learned about you sleeping around with my ex-husband, and in all honesty, I don't plan to. It is my hope that you and I never have to cross paths again and that you will stay as far away from me as possible. To say that you hurt me terribly would be an understatement, but I think it is only fair that you know something about me. When I am finished with someone, I am finished with them for good. I do not believe in second chances because the first chance should never be violated in the first place—at least not at this magnitude. We all make mistakes, but this mistake of yours was a bit too much for me, and it is the reason we can no longer continue our friendship. We will always be cousins, but this is only because I do not have the power to change that. So, my only request from you is that you please stop trying to contact me by phone and through my mother. My suggestion is that we leave well enough alone and move on with our lives. It really is the best thing for both of us.

There wasn't much Charlotte could say, but it was obvious that Anise had mailed the package on or before Saturday when Charlotte had seen her at her mother's. The mere thought that they would never be close again bothered Charlotte, but she knew that there was nothing she could do about it. Anise had been hurt by David, Frank, and even some woman she worked with named Lorna. So of course this thing with Charlotte was the final blow so to speak. She wished that Anise would reconsider what she was doing, but Charlotte doubted it would ever happen. She knew that Anise was serious about every word she'd written.

Charlotte folded the note and dropped it inside the box. She carried the box up to her closet and placed it under some clothing she was planning to give away to the church for women who were in need. She couldn't take the chance of Curtis seeing all of the charges. All it would do was cause another commotion. It would give him another reason to leave her.

A couple of hours passed before Curtis returned from the church. Shortly after, the three of them headed for the testing center.

"So did you finish up everything you needed to take care of?" she asked.

"Pretty much."

"Is Lana still taking vacation next week?"

"As far as I know."

Charlotte was trying her best to lighten the atmosphere, but her best wasn't good enough.

"Mom, where did you say we were going again?" Matthew said from the backseat.

Charlotte looked over at Curtis, Curtis looked over at her, and then he switched his gaze back to the road. He didn't say a word, and Charlotte knew what he wanted her to do. He wanted her to lie to Matthew the same as she had yesterday, and she hated it. Still, she didn't have any choice. The look on Curtis's face confirmed it.

"Sweetie, we're going to a clinic so we can have some blood work done."

"You mean with a needle?" His face filled with terror.

"Yes, but it won't really hurt."

"Uh-huh. It always hurts. That's why I'm afraid of needles. I don't want them to take any of *my* blood."

"I'm sorry, honey, but we have to."

"Why, Mom?"

"Because we need to make sure that all of us are healthy. It's just like when I take you to the doctor and they give you an examination."

"But I already had that before school started last year."

"I know, but we have to do it again."

"Dad, do we have toooo?"

"Unfortunately, son, we do. I know you don't like needles and neither do I for that matter, but we have to have this done. It won't be as bad as you think, though."

Charlotte could tell that Matthew didn't believe a word of what she or his father was saying. He was completely afraid and Charlotte blamed herself. If only she hadn't slept with David. If only she'd told Curtis about it from the very beginning. But she hadn't planned on Curtis or anyone else ever finding out. For the life of her, she still couldn't understand why she'd confided so much information to Aaron. She'd asked herself that question over and over and still she didn't have an answer.

Curtis drove through a four-way-stop intersection and turned into the parking lot of the building that they were going to. Charlotte swallowed hard and silently prayed for all to go well. She prayed that Matthew wouldn't throw a fit once inside, since he truly was afraid of needles. She wished Curtis would take that into consideration and forget about doing any of this. But she knew that would never happen.

"Hi," Charlotte said when they walked up to the reception desk. "We have an appointment at three and the name is Charlotte Black."

The receptionist scanned her computer screen. "I have a few forms that I'll need you and the father to fill out."

"This is my husband," Charlotte said.

The woman looked at her strangely. Charlotte knew their situation wasn't normal. It wasn't every day that a husband and wife walked into a DNA clinic, trying to verify who their son's father was. She was so embarrassed.

"How are you, honey?" the woman asked Matthew.

"I'm afraid of needles."

"Really? Well, you won't have to worry about anything like that here. The test we'll be performing won't hurt at all. We won't need to use even one needle.

Matthew's face brightened. Charlotte was relieved.

Curtis seemed happier, too.

Each of them took a seat, and Charlotte filled out most of the documents. Curtis signed those that required his signature. When they approached the desk again, the receptionist asked them for photo IDs and then made copies.

"Okay, I think that's everything. We'll be calling you very shortly."

Charlotte flipped through a women's magazine, and Matthew tried to work a puzzle over in the children's corner. There was another little boy sitting at the table, and Matthew exchanged a few words with him. But it wasn't long before the boy's mother's name was called and they both left the room.

Charlotte continued flipping through her magazine and read an article on how to add more spice to a marriage. She looked over at Curtis, hoping that he was at least glancing at the page, but he was sitting next to her with his eyes closed. Lately, he did just about anything so he wouldn't have to pay her any attention. In the past, he would have chatted with her nonstop. It was amazing how radically everything had changed.

They waited another twenty minutes, and Charlotte realized that she hadn't called in to her office. She'd taken the day off, but she'd told her bosses that she would check in, making sure they didn't need anything. But then, they would never hesitate calling her if something came up. Still, she hadn't been herself of late, so she was worried that she might have made a few mistakes on some of the legal documents or filed something in the wrong place. Her home life was affecting her work life, and she was sort of glad she'd decided to quit the firm.

"Charlotte and Curtis Black," the very tall and beautiful nurse announced. Her haircut was very becoming, and it made Charlotte want to whack her own hair down about two inches.

They followed her down a carpeted corridor and into an average-size room.

"How is everyone? And please have a seat."

"We're fine," Charlotte said.

"Can't complain," Curtis said.

"What about you, Matthew?" the nurse asked.

"I'm good. The lady outside said I didn't have to get poked with any needles."

"And she was right. We do something here called a buccal swab procedure. Have you ever seen a Q-tip?"

"My mom uses them when she cleans out my ears."

"Oh, that's not good, Mom," the nurse said.

"Why is that?" Charlotte asked.

"You should never use Q-tips to clean out anyone's ears, not even your own. There are so many dangers involved, like causing infection, pushing earwax even farther into the ear canal, and damaging the skin inside. There have been many cases where permanent damage has been done, including hearing loss."

"I had no idea. My mom used them on me, and so do a ton of other people I know."

"I'm not surprised, but believe me when I say that it's very unsafe."

Charlotte felt like an unfit mother, and Curtis stared at her like she was.

"Okay, now, back to the buccal swab. The two benefits of this particular test are that it is quick and painless. All we have to do is rub it around the cheek area inside the mouth."

"Is the swab method just as accurate as taking blood?" Curtis asked, folding his arms.

"As a matter of fact, it is. All sample types give the same results."

"When will we have the results?" he said.

"The usual turnaround is five to seven days, but for an additional fee, we can probably have them in three. We have actual lab capabilities right here and won't need to send them outside."

"Whatever the charge is, I'll pay it."

"Not a problem. But with Thursday being a holiday, you still won't have it until Friday."

"That'll be fine."

Charlotte hadn't even thought much about the Fourth of July. Probably because she knew they weren't doing anything special. Her mother-in-law's funeral was arranged for Wednesday, so she knew Curtis wouldn't be in the mood for celebrating.

"Okay, then, unless you have any further questions, we can get started," the nurse said.

Then she asked one of her coworkers to come in and assist her. They took samples from Charlotte, Curtis, and Matthew, and the procedure was over in no time. Before leaving, Charlotte stayed back and asked the nurse why they needed her DNA, since this was strictly a question of paternity and not whether she was the mother. The nurse explained that although her DNA wasn't actually required, without it the samples would involve much more analysis and would take a few days longer to complete.

When Charlotte went outside and got in the car, Curtis drove onto the street and said, "Matthew and I are going out for pizza. We would invite you, but we haven't had a boys' night out in a long time. Have we, Matthew?"

"Nope. Sorry, Mom."

"That's okay, sweetie. You go with your dad and have a good time. It's good when you guys spend quality time together."

Charlotte saw Curtis roll his eyes toward the ceiling of the car, but she pretended not to notice him.

When they arrived in front of the house, she stepped out of the car and Curtis pulled away from the curb. She went inside the house and considered calling her parents. She'd called them from work last Thursday and then again on Saturday morning so that Matthew could speak to them, but she'd made sure to keep their conversation short. She hadn't wanted them noticing anything different. She'd tried to be as upbeat as possible, but she'd been worried about overdoing it, especially when speaking to her mother, a woman who could detect trouble a thousand miles away. Actually, Charlotte wished she could confide everything to her, but she knew if she did, her father might find out and would probably threaten David with statutory rape charges the same as he had with Curtis. It just wasn't worth causing so much trouble. It wasn't worth getting her parents upset over something they couldn't do anything about.

Charlotte turned on the television and searched for something interesting. But no matter how many channels she flipped through, she felt awfully uncomfortable. And she knew why. She was already dreading the outcome of those test results. Until now, she'd been sure that there was nothing to worry about, but for some reason she felt edgy. She felt like there really was something to be concerned about, but maybe she was getting herself all worked up for nothing. What she needed to do was make that appointment with an abortion clinic. She'd found a place in Wisconsin, but by now they were probably closed for the evening. She'd make sure to call first thing in the morning from her office at work.

She rested her head against the back of the sofa, trying to relax her nerves. Just as she closed her eyes, her cell phone rang and she reached inside her bag and pulled it out. When she saw that it was Aaron, she set it on the table. Why wouldn't he leave her alone? And if he was calling her now, he had to have been watching when Curtis and Matthew left. She was shocked that he wasn't calling their home number.

Before long, her phone rang again. She debated whether she should answer it, and while she knew she shouldn't have, she did.

"Aaron, so help me God, if you don't leave us alone, I'm filing charges against you."

"What? Is that supposed to scare me?"

"I don't care what it does to you, but if you keep calling here, you're going to be arrested."

"And if you do, your life will be over as soon as I'm out of jail. You won't live more than a few hours afterward."

"What we had is over, and I told you that I was sorry. Why won't you just move on with your life?"

"Because my life is with you."

"Look, I'm not staying on here, Aaron. I'm hanging up, but if you call me again or come near my family, you'll be sorry. That stunt you pulled at church yesterday wasn't very smart because now the entire congregation thinks you're crazy."

"Is that right? Well, the congregation is mistaken. I'm a lot more than just crazy, and they don't have a clue as to what I'm capable of. And neither do you for that matter."

Charlotte didn't know why she was wasting her time on the phone with him. But in all honesty, she'd been afraid not to pick up the phone. She'd been afraid he might try to break in on her if she ignored him, especially since Curtis wasn't there with her.

"Aaron, please don't call here again. I'm begging you not to. At least think about Matthew and his well-being if nothing else. You know Matthew always looked up to you."

"You know what? You'd better stop trying to play all these head games with me, because it's starting to piss me off. Unlike you and your paternity charade, I would *never* do anything to hurt Matthew. I would never harm him in any way. And you've got a very sick mind if you ever thought I would."

"I'm sorry."

"You damned well should be, and don't you ever let me hear you make reference to Matthew around me again. He's an innocent child who can't even fend for himself. He never asked to come here, and neither did I. But my mother brought me into this world anyway and then gave me up to some child welfare agency. You didn't know that, did you? I was tossed around from one foster home to another, and every time I started to love my foster mothers, they always got rid of me. They always pretended like they really cared, but then they'd change their minds at the last minute. They lied to me the same way you did."

"I'm so sorry, Aaron." She tried to pacify him and show some concern. If she did, maybe he would have mercy on her. Maybe he'd leave her alone for good.

"I don't like that word *sorry* either. If people did what they were supposed to do, they would never have to apologize."

His philosophy was so similar to Anise's, and, strangely enough, he was making sense. But he was still insane. He was still someone to be frightened of.

"I'm finished talking to you for now, but I'll be calling you again very soon. And next time, make sure you sound a lot happier to hear from me. Love you."

Charlotte dropped her phone on the sofa and wondered what was next. Whatever it was, she knew it wouldn't be good. She knew something bad would have to happen before this was over.

Chapter 25

WHAT A SAD TIME THIS WAS FOR CURTIS. HE'D TRIED TO KEEP HIS mind fairly occupied over the last four days, but the day had finally arrived for him to see his mother. As a minister, he'd preached at a great number of funerals, too many to count, but this would be the most different and most painful that he'd attended. It would be the funeral he'd never forget for as long as he lived. Not to mention how heartlessly his sister was still treating him. She'd ended up calling him late Sunday night, telling him that the funeral would be on Wednesday, but when he'd tried to ask additional questions, she'd told him that she didn't have time for it. She told him that he didn't even have to come to her house if he didn't want to. It was her opinion that it would be better if he drove straight to the church and simply walked in with them once they got there. Curtis had been speechless and near tears right after she'd said it. But it was obvious that she meant every word.

He tried respecting the way she felt and knew she had every right to be upset with him, but he'd been hoping that she'd at least try to stay civil. He had hoped that she would let bygones be bygones for the sake of the family, because even he had decided to do the same in regard to Charlotte. He hadn't wanted Charlotte riding over to Chicago with him and Matthew, but he knew Matthew would never understand their leaving her. She'd been waiting on pins and needles, wondering whether she'd be able to go, and finally Curtis had agreed. He decided that he might actually need her support when all was said and done.

Now, though, they'd picked up Alicia and were just pulling up in front of Trina's massive brick home, located in the south suburbs. Thankfully, the church was just a few miles away.

Curtis turned off the ignition, and they all got out of the car. Matthew held his sister's hand, and Charlotte and Curtis walked behind them. Curtis noticed his mother's brother immediately.

"Curtis, is that you?" the man said, smiling yet tearful.

"Uncle Bradley? It's so good to see you," he said, embracing him.

"Boy, it sure is good to see you, too. It's been a long, long time. And who is this handsome little fellow right here?"

"This is my son, Matthew, and my daughter, Alicia."

"I already know Miss Alicia. I met her a couple of years ago. But it's nice to meet you, Matthew."

"It's nice to meet you, too, Mr. Bradley."

"That's Uncle Bradley to you."

Matthew smiled and looked at his father.

"And what about this beautiful young lady standing next to you?" Uncle Bradley asked.

"This is my wife, Charlotte."

"It's nice to meet you, Uncle Bradley," she said.

"Likewise. I'm sorry it had to happen under these circumstances, but it's still nice to know you."

"So who all is in the house?" Curtis asked.

"My wife, Samantha, and a few of our cousins. And, of course, Trina and her family. Go on in. I was just standing out here getting some fresh air and thinking about my baby sister."

"I understand," Curtis said.

Alicia opened the door, and they all walked in one by one.

"How's everybody doing?" Curtis said shamefully. He felt so out of place, and it was his own fault.

"Fine," most of his relatives responded, but it was obvious that they weren't too sure who he was.

"I'm Curtis, Pauline's oldest child."

"Oh, okay," one of the women said. "Pauline used to talk about you from time to time. I'm her first cousin, Etta Mae, and this is my sister, Rayzene. We live in Cincinnati, but you probably don't remember us. Your mother brought you and Trina over to see us a couple of times, but both of you were barely toddlers. Then, by the time we saw Pauline again, you had gone off to college."

"Well, it's nice to see you again," Curtis said.

"Boy, where you been?" Rayzene said nastily.

"It's a long story."

"What kinda story you talkin' about? Because all I know is that you worried your mother half to death. And that's probably the reason that cancer came back and got her."

"Rayzene!" Etta Mae shouted. "Leave that child alone. You always sticking your nose where it don't belong. And anyway, we didn't drive all the way here just so you could start up some mess."

"Hmmph. Well, quiet as kept, I think it's a shame when children disown they own mother."

Curtis felt as small as a church mouse. He wanted to shrivel up and die. Right then and right there. He didn't have the courage to look at Charlotte or his children. As strong as he was, he didn't even have the courage to defend himself. Rayzene was a monster.

"Now, who's this gorgeous little thing right here, Curtis?" Etta Mae tried to smooth things over.

"This is Charlotte, my wife. And this is my daughter, Alicia, and my son, Matthew."

"Pauline talked about Miss Alicia all the time. She was so proud of you, baby."

Curtis could see Alicia's eyes filling up, and Charlotte placed her arm around her.

"And Matthew, you're just about the cutest little boy I've seen in years."

"Thank you," he said, blushing.

"And I'm your aunt Samantha," the other woman offered. "I'm your uncle Bradley's wife."

"It's good to meet you," Curtis said.

Rayzene stared at Curtis but didn't say anything. She definitely didn't like him.

Now Curtis wondered if it would have been better for him not to come here. Maybe he should have taken Trina's advice about going directly to the church.

Charlotte took a seat on the plush, tan sofa, and Alicia and Matthew sat down next to her. A muscular-looking man walked out into the living room.

"You must be Curtis," he said.

"I am."

"I'm Jason. Trina's husband."

They shook hands, and Curtis said, "It's nice to finally meet you."

"It's good to meet you, also."

"How is my sister? Is she hanging in there?"

"It's hard on her, but she's trying. You can go in and talk to her if you want."

"Man, I don't know if that would be good."

"Go ahead. Our bedroom is at the end of the hall and to the right."

"Baby, go on," Charlotte said.

Curtis didn't respond to either of them, but he slowly walked toward the corridor. He braced himself for whatever Trina's reaction would be.

When he arrived at the door, which was half open, he knocked.

"Come in," she said.

"Hey. Jason told me I should come see you."

She turned her back to him and finished brushing her hair. It was still long—thick, wavy, and beautiful—just the way he remembered it. She was thirty-eight, but she didn't look a day over thirty. Interestingly enough, most people never guessed that he was already forty.

"Trina, please let me talk to you."

"About what, Curtis? The way you abandoned Mom and me? The way you left Chicago and deleted us from your life like we were nonentities?"

"Yes. That's exactly what I want to talk to you about. I was wrong. Dead wrong. But after what I went through as a child, I just didn't know how to deal with my pain. All I knew was that I couldn't wait to leave and that it was best that I never look back. At least that's what I was thinking at the time. I just didn't see how else I was going to heal if I didn't."

"I had scars, too, Curtis. But I never would have left you or Mom."

"I know. And like I said, I know that I was wrong."

"Well, I just hope you're happy. I hope you got whatever you were searching for and that you've enjoyed being without us."

"I'm not happy. As a matter of fact, my life started falling apart weeks before you called me on Saturday."

"Well, that's not my problem. And after I lay my mother to rest today, the only family that I'll be concerned about are my husband and children. And, of course, Alicia."

Curtis leaned his head back against the wall and silently prayed for God to help him with his sister. He opened his eyes and smiled when he noticed how elegant her master bedroom was. She was definitely a class act. He could tell from her diction and the way she carried herself and now from her excellent taste. She looked and acted the part of a woman who had everything together. He was very proud of her.

"If you'll excuse me, I need to finish getting ready before the limo arrives," she said.

"That's fine, Trina, but I'm not giving up on you. Mom is gone and regardless of what I did, I know she would want you and me to be here for each other."

"You're probably right, but it's still not going to happen. You and I have lived very separate lives since we became adults, and I'd really like to keep it that way. There's no reason to change what the reality is. It's true that you are my brother, but it's only in the biological sense. Emotionally, you don't mean a thing to me."

Curtis watched her turn her back to him again, and this time he started to walk out of the room. Before he did, he glanced over at her.

"No matter what you think of me, Trina, I do love you. You're my baby sister and nothing will ever change that. And although you don't believe it, I loved Mom, too. It's the reason I started sending her a little something every Mother's Day."

"Oh, you mean those thousand-dollar checks?"

"Yes."

"Well, just so you know, she did cash them, but she never spent one dime of it on herself. She saved all of it and then when she met Alicia and found out that you also had a son, she started two trust fund accounts for them. She split the total ten thousand between the two of them. And before she became ill, she purchased a second life insurance policy for one hundred thousand dollars and split it equally among Alicia, Matthew, and my two children. So don't think you were doing anything special for her, because you weren't. Your money didn't matter to her in the least."

Curtis was crushed. All along, he'd been hoping that his mother was using the money for something she really wanted. He hadn't cared what it might be, but he'd always hoped that maybe she would use the money to purchase something personal—items that would remind her of him whenever she used them. But it hadn't happened, and now he felt guiltier than ever before. His mother had died and he hadn't given her anything. He hadn't made any positive impact on her life in any way. Again, he wondered what he was doing there. He'd wanted to pay his last respects, but now he knew he didn't have the right to. He was no different than a stranger on the street. His feelings, his opinion, his pain, didn't mean anything. Not to Trina, certainly not to Rayzene, and probably not even to his mother.

He walked out of the room and back toward the front of the house. There were at least twenty new people standing in the living room. Everyone was dressed in black, and they were con-

versing in small groups. Some were even laughing, but unfortunately, Curtis didn't know most of them.

Charlotte stood and strolled over to where he was standing.

"Are you okay?"

"Not really."

"Do you want to go outside and talk?"

"No. Let's just stay in here until the funeral director gets
here."

Curtis saw Matthew playing what must have been his little
cousin's handheld video game, because they were both sitting
on the couch raving over it. Alicia was sitting next to another
teenage girl who looked to be her age. Curtis knew immediately
that these children were Trina's. The niece and nephew he had
never met, his own flesh and blood. Ironically, her children and
his children were very close in age. He and Trina had a lot in
common. They shared similar personalities, and they both
liked the finer things in life, even though he had toned his particular tastes down a few notches, right after moving to
Mitchell. He didn't want to admit it, but she treated him exactly the way he would have treated her, if she had been the
one who had walked out on him. He would probably never forgive a sister who walked out on their mother. It was no different from the way he was having a hard time forgiving
Charlotte for her actions. Curtis deserved every ounce of cru-
elty that Trina was offering him, and he didn't blame her for it.

The funeral procession moved slowly down the road with a
black Cadillac leading the way. Two black limos and a number
of other vehicles followed behind it. More than anything, Curtis had wanted to ride in the first limo with his sister and her
family. Not for any prestige, but he truly wanted to be in Trina's

presence. She didn't want him to, but still, Curtis wanted to be there for his sister if she needed him. She was trying to stay strong for everyone else, but he wasn't sure how she was going to take seeing their mother lying in a casket. She'd probably viewed the body at the funeral home sometime yesterday, but this wouldn't be the same. This would be the very last time she'd be able to see their mother physically. The mother she obviously loved and adored so much.

Alicia and Matthew exchanged a few words, but overall, they remained quiet. Charlotte didn't have much to say either, but he supposed it was because he still wasn't being very receptive. He'd been cordial, but his conversation wasn't anything to brag about. He just couldn't forget about the DNA test and how they wouldn't have the results until the day after tomorrow.

When they pulled into the church parking lot, each driver lined up his vehicle, one after another, forming a single-file line. By doing so, their departure would run a lot smoother.

Everyone exited their cars and followed the direction of the funeral representative.

"Could I please have everyone lined up in twos with the children in front, then brothers and sisters, and then grand-children," he said.

There were at least six other people standing in front of him and Charlotte, but he wasn't going to push the issue. Trina would never want him sitting in the front row with her, so he was going to stay put. But she surprised him.

"Curtis," Trina called back to him. "They want you up here."

"Will you and the children be okay?" he asked Charlotte.

"We'll be fine."

"I'll see you in there," he said to Matthew and Alicia.

He made his way past Etta Mae and Rayzene and a few other relatives and stood directly behind Trina and Jason. He ended up partnering with his uncle Bradley, who was already wiping a river of tears. His face was completely wet. Curtis tried consoling him, but it wasn't helping.

When everyone was ready, they proceeded up the stairs, into the church, and down the center aisle of the sanctuary. The entire left side was full, and Curtis could tell that his mother was cherished by many—had to be, since most of them had probably taken time off of their jobs just to be there.

The closer they moved to the casket, the more emotional and audible Trina became. She shook her head in disagreement with her mother's death. The volume of her cry grew louder, and Jason held onto her when she stepped closer to the casket. She wept uncontrollably, and it was this very thing that Curtis had been afraid of.

"Mommy, why?" she spoke mildly. "How can I possibly go on without you? Who am I going to talk to? Who am I supposed to turn to when things go wrong? Oh God, please don't let this be."

Jason tried pulling her away, but Trina rested her hand on her mother's face and just stood there. "I love you, Mommy. I love you from the bottom of my soul, and I miss you already."

When she and Jason moved along, Curtis and his uncle moved forward. Curtis sighed deeply. His emotions were running rampant, and while he was sorry that his mother had passed, he was happy that she looked so beautiful. Her skin was flawless, and she even had a semismile on her face. It was the kind of smile that said, "I'm finally home with the Lord, and what a marvelous day it is." Curtis was in awe of his mother and was completely in his own zone until his uncle bellowed out.

"Pauline, Pauline! Oh my baby sister. Lord have mercy."

Curtis grabbed his uncle's arm, trying to help steady him. Uncle Bradley wiped his face with a handkerchief but couldn't seem to settle himself.

One of the funeral reps led him to his seat.

Curtis took one last look at his mother.

"I'm sorry, Mom. I'm sorry for everything, and I hope you can forgive me. I'll love you always," he said, leaning over to kiss her cheek. Then he walked away.

As soon as he took his seat, Rayzene lost it.

"Oh, Pauline!" she screamed. "I cain't make it without you. Oh Lawd, why'd you take my cousin? Oh Lawd, what we gone to do? Oh Pauline, take me with you. Let me just climb in there and go with you," she yelled.

Curtis couldn't remember ever being more embarrassed. He hated when anyone clowned at funerals the way Rayzene was doing right now. It was so country, so uncalled for, and so disruptive for everyone else in attendance. The way she was carrying on was simply ridiculous.

"Oh, Pauline, chile, I wanna go with you," she said.

Well, Rayzene, why don't you do just that—crawl inside and let them bury you with Mom? At least that's what Curtis wanted to tell her. He wondered what she'd have to say to that. It was all a put-on, and Curtis had learned a long time ago that the loudest family members were the guilty ones or merely those who wanted to be seen. They'd either treated the deceased terribly or hadn't come to see about them when they should have. Curtis was guilty of all of the above, but even he wasn't standing in the middle of a church acting a natural fool, yelling at the top of his lungs. Rayzene needed to sit her obnoxious butt down, and if he was her, he would fix that crooked wig sitting on top of her head.

Etta Mae shed a few silent tears and forcibly escorted Rayzene to her seat. She tried to do it in a subtle fashion. Etta Mae definitely had a lot more sense than her sister.

Curtis looked on as Alicia and Matthew stood before their grandmother. Alicia was pretty upset and so was Matthew, but Matthew was probably crying because Alicia was. Charlotte didn't show any particular emotion, but it wasn't like she'd been close to her mother-in-law. She'd never even seen her until today.

The service was divine. The soloist sang beautifully, and, thankfully, Trina hadn't allowed every Tom, Dick, and minister to get up and say "a few words." Curtis had stopped families from allowing such nonsense whenever funerals were held at his church. He remembered the time one family had asked ten ministers to say a few words, and they'd each spoken for a minimum of five minutes. Most of them hadn't even known the deceased, so Curtis hadn't understood why they were up there. Some even used their "few words" as an opportunity to show that they could preach. They showed everyone what they could do, trying, he guessed, to recruit new members to their own churches.

Trina read a tribute to their mother, as did Alicia. Curtis was very proud of his daughter for doing so, but at one point, he'd wished that he'd had the opportunity to say something to his mother, too. He'd wanted to play at least a small part in her going-away celebration. But he never made it known.

When the eulogy was complete, the pastor turned the service back over to the funeral director. It was time to head out to the cemetery.

But how wrong Curtis was. The director and one of his assistants moved the blanket of roses on top of the casket down toward the end and raised the lid up. They were doing that big-city ritual again. Curtis called it big-city because it never happened in Mitchell or some of the other smaller cities he'd gone to. They were allowing the family a second viewing. Curtis was starting to get angry, because this was another one of those Chicago methods he didn't approve of. He just didn't see what the purpose of this drama was because all it did was upset everyone all over again. It rekindled lots of screaming and wailing with even those who hadn't screamed and wailed the first time around. Most people were pretty calm and relaxed after hearing the eulogies, so what was the point? Curtis stayed in his seat and waited for the commotion to end. He waited for Rayzene and a few others to stop their performances. He sat there wondering how his mother would have felt about any of this. He knew she would have been humiliated, the same as he was.

Chapter 26

CURTIS GLANCED AT HIS MOTHER'S OBITUARY, WHICH WAS SITTING ON his desk. Trina had given him five extra copies, and he'd found a frame for this one just before heading to work. He really did miss his mother, and he was saddened by the way some of his relatives had acted. It was the reason he hadn't bothered returning to the church for the repast. There was nothing he could do about missing his mother though, so he knew he had to get over it. Instead, he tried focusing on how beautiful and peaceful his mother had looked. She certainly hadn't looked like a woman who'd suffered with cancer. She looked as though she were asleep and hadn't been sick a day in her life. Curtis was glad he would be able to remember her that way.

He wrote the last paragraph of his weekly column and leaned back in his chair. The topic was death and how to deal with it. He'd made sure to cover how important it was to have strong faith and how even when the body was gone the soul would still remain alive and well—that is, if a person had lived his or her life right. He talked about people being there for their loved ones when they became ill so that there wouldn't be any guilt to contend with. He talked about how every human being needed to try and prepare themselves for the loss of someone they loved. It was important because it always made things easier when it finally happened. Some deaths were instant and caught people by surprise, but others allowed you weeks, months, and even years to get ready. He talked about how some people wanted to go to heaven but never wanted to die. He talked about how one had to be absent from the body to be present with the Lord. Curtis ended the column with a small tribute to his mother.

He reread the column one last time and moved it to the side of his desk. With everything that had gone on all week—his mother's death, the DNA testing, and the funeral—he hadn't prepared his sermon for Sunday. In all honesty, he still didn't want to. He just didn't feel like working today, and he knew it had a lot to do with the anxiety he was feeling. The testing center had advised that they'd be calling with the results by afternoon. This morning, Curtis had hugged Matthew so tightly that Matthew had asked if everything was okay with him. Curtis, of course, had told him that he was fine. He could tell that Matthew thought he was feeling sad because of the funeral and Curtis hadn't tried to tell him any differently.

As Curtis pulled out his notebook the phone rang. It was his assistant calling him.

"Hi, Lana."

"Hi, Pastor. I have your agent on the line for you."

"Thanks, Lana. Please put her through."

"How are you?" Joan said.

"As well as can be expected, I guess."

"I just wanted to express my condolences to you again and to make sure you received the flowers."

"We did and thank you for sending them. It's nice to know that someone was thinking of me."

"No problem. I was glad to do it."

"So is everything going well on the publishing end of the country?"

"As a matter of fact, it is."

"Anything new from WexlerAdams?"

"Well, actually there is, but we can talk about it next week. I don't want you jumping right back into business so soon after your mother's passing."

"I'm fine. Really. What's up?"

"Well, after Renee spoke with you a couple of weeks ago, she asked me if you might be interested in reading the script for the audio version of your book."

"Is that a good thing?"

"It's a lot of hard work, and it'll mean going into the studio with a producer for a lot of hours. But the one thing I can say is that no one can read your work the way you can. Only the author knows exactly the way he or she meant for a phrase or sentence to be heard, and readers respect that. Every now and then when we're dealing with novels, actors can sometimes do a great job, but with nonfiction, it's good to go with the author. That is, if they have a great voice and don't mind doing it."

"Sounds fine to me."

"Good. Well, again, I just wanted to let you know that I was thinking about you and if you need anything, even just to talk, please call me."

"I will, and you have a peaceful weekend."

"I'll try. You take care."

Curtis hung up the phone and wondered just how calm his

weekend really would be. It simply depended on what he found out in regard to that paternity test. He wouldn't love Matthew any less, but life for all of them would be different. He had wanted to know the truth, but as the hours and minutes continued, he wished Aaron had kept his mouth shut. If he had, Curtis wouldn't be in this stressful predicament. He wouldn't be trying to figure out what was what. He wouldn't be dealing with gossipmongers at his church—members who thrived on trouble in someone else's household.

Curtis spent the next two hours working on his sermon, but his mind kept drifting away from his subject matter. There was no way he'd be able to accomplish anything until the news was finally delivered. So he saved the document and signed off of his computer. He gathered together a few written notes, his Bible, and a couple of other companion texts and slid them inside his briefcase. Then he went over to the coatrack and lifted his blazer. But when he did, his cell phone rang. Curtis felt his heart beating a mile a minute, wondering if this was it. He'd asked the facility to call him directly, because he knew he couldn't trust Charlotte. She would never tell him the truth if that truth wasn't what he wanted to hear.

"Hello."

"Curtis, this is Aaron."

"And?"

"I think it's time we talk man-to-man about this Charlotte situation."

"Negro, you really don't know me very well, do you?"

"Actually, I know you exceptionally well, but you and I both know that Charlotte belongs with me. I realize you're upset, but I can't help how she feels. I can't help the way the two of us feel about each other."

"You're sick. And if you keep crossing me . . . well, just consider yourself warned."

"You're only saying all of this because you're hurt. And I understand. I really do."

"No, you don't understand anything. You slept with my wife and now you've tried to affect my relationship with my son, and somebody has to pay for it."

"Oh come on, Curtis. Be a good sport. Let her go. You fought a good fight, I give you that. But let her go."

Curtis slammed his cell phone shut and made a decision. Aaron Malone was going to be taken care of once and for all. Maybe not today or even this week, but it was inevitable.

It was another hour before Curtis actually left his office. He'd received a call from one of his members who was having problems with her husband, and he'd had no choice but to speak to her. She'd been having difficulties with this man from day one because of his obsessive drug use, and from the way she sounded, life for her was only getting worse.

Curtis sat inside his SUV and just as he wondered why someone from the DNA facility hadn't called him yet, his phone rang. The call showed up as private, and Curtis knew this was it. He allowed it to ring two more times before he took a deep breath and picked it up.

"Hello."

"Curtis Black?" the woman said.

"Yes. Speaking."

"This is Sherri calling with the results from your paternity test."

"Uh-huh."

"I regret that Matthew Black is not your son."

Curtis tried pretending that he hadn't heard her. But he knew he had. She'd spoken plainly and clearly, and he'd heard every single word of her sentence. Still he couldn't move or say anything. He couldn't respond without falling to pieces, and he didn't want to do that. He didn't want to weep dramatically like Uncle Bradley had done yesterday.

"Mr. Black, are you there?"

"Yes. Thank you for calling."

"You're quite welcome, and all the best to you."

He put the phone down without even closing it and stared across the parking lot.

"Oh God, no," he prayed. "Not my son. I know I've done a lot of wrong over the years, but please don't take my son from me. Lord, I'm begging you."

Curtis held the front of his face with both hands and cried silently. His cries came from deep within, and they were the same as he'd felt on Saturday when Trina had called to tell him about his mother. This just couldn't be happening, losing his mother and son all in one week. He'd asked God daily to grant him this one request, so he couldn't understand why God hadn't heard him. He knew that for whatever reason his desire must not have been God's will, but he didn't know how he would go on without Matthew. He didn't know how he would ever accept the fact that he no longer had a son. He loved his daughter, but his bond with Matthew had changed his life completely. That child had become his reason for being.

Curtis wiped his eyes, saw that it was shortly after five, and started the engine. He drove away from the church and kept driving for miles and miles. He drove around the city for over an hour, trying to alleviate his pain, but he never succeeded. If anything, he felt more vengeful and indignant than before.

He dialed Charlotte's cell number before he knew it.

She burst into tears as soon as she answered.

"I just called to tell you that I'm filing for a divorce as soon as possible," he said.

"But Curtis—"

"Just save it, Charlotte."

"But—"

"But nothing. There's not a thing you can say to me about anything. You lied, and now all of us are going to suffer the consequence. But I'm telling you right now, don't even think about telling Matthew, your parents, or anyone else. I'll decide when and how everyone should be told. And from this point on, I'll decide what you should and shouldn't do. You started all of this, but I'm going to have the last say."

"Curtis, please just meet me at home. I already asked Aunt Emma to pick up Matthew from camp."

"No. Don't you get it? Our marriage is over."

"You're not thinking straight right now, but if you just give me a chance, I'll make things right. You're the only father Matthew has ever known, and it will kill him if you leave us. I just know it."

The thought of what she was saying made Curtis loathe her even more. He wanted to call her every obscenity in the book. In truth, he wished he could create a few new obscenities because none of the words he could think of actually fit. The hatred and disgust he felt for her were unexplainable. Now, he knew exactly how Adrienne must have felt when she'd made the decision to shoot him. Her pain must have been far too much to bear. For the first time, he understood why she'd needed to get even with him. It had been the only way.

"I'm hanging up now," he said . . . and did.

He waited for the red light to change and pressed on the accelerator. He dialed Anise at the same time.

"Hello?"

"I know you won't think it's a good idea, but I really need to talk to someone."

"You sound strange. Are you okay?"

"No. And that's why I really have to see you. If I don't, Anise, I'll probably end up in jail."

"Oh no. It's not what I think, is it?"

"I'll see you when I get there, okay?"

"All right."

Curtis played a slew of mental tapes as he continued down the road. He pictured Charlotte and Aaron having sex until they were totally exhausted. He imagined how hard they must have laughed at him each time they'd gotten away with it. But nothing compared with the picture he was playing now—Matthew's face right after he'd been told that Curtis wasn't his father. It just wasn't fair, and it was at times like these that Curtis still didn't quite understand some of God's reasoning. He didn't understand why Matthew had to pay the price for his and Charlotte's sins when Matthew hadn't done anything. It was at times like these that Curtis felt his faith weakening and he no longer wanted a place in the ministry. He wished he'd stayed out of it when he'd had the chance. He would be much better off if he had.

Curtis pulled into Anise's driveway and sat for a few minutes. He wanted to go inside, and then again he didn't. If he did, he knew what would ensue. He knew that once he stepped across her front threshold, he would not be turning back. He had a feeling that Anise wouldn't want him to. Their attraction for each other was a given, and Curtis wanted her. He needed someone to make him feel like a man again.

He left the car and strode up the walkway. He rang the bell three times before Anise opened the door. She looked curious, and he could tell she didn't trust herself around him. She could barely look him straight in his eyes without glancing away.

"So what happened?" she said, leading the way into the family room. Curtis sat down next to her in the center of the sofa, barely leaving any space between them. Anise moved closer to the end.

"Matthew is definitely not my son."

"I'm so sorry, Curtis. I can't even imagine how you must be feeling. This is terrible."

"Yeah. It is, and right now I don't know what I'm going to do about it. I don't know how I can let Charlotte and Aaron get away with this."

"Poor little Matthew. Does he know?"

"Not yet. Your mom was picking him up today, and I told Charlotte not to tell anyone."

"This is unbelievable. It's a nightmare."

"Well, I really needed to see you because if I didn't, I probably would have ended up looking for Aaron."

"Well, if that's the case, I'm glad you came here instead. You certainly don't need to go after that fool. I heard about the way he showed up at church Sunday."

"That Negro is crazy."

"Have you heard from him?"

"He called me earlier, telling me to let Charlotte go because they were in love with each other."

"Really? He's acting like you and he were never even friends."

"I told you, he's crazy. The man needs to be in a nuthouse. Or six feet under."

Anise didn't respond, and Curtis knew she didn't approve of what he'd just said.

"Thanks again for letting me come by."

"Can I get you anything?"

"No. I'm too drained to eat or drink. All I want to do is be here with you."

Curtis slid closer to her.

"We can't do this," she said.

"Why? I told you before, Charlotte doesn't care about you or me."

"Still."

"Still what?"

"It's not right and you know it."

He stroked the back of her head. "I need you, Anise.

"Curtis, don't."

"I can't help myself. I've wanted you ever since that night I stopped by here."

"But you're married and regardless of what Charlotte has done, she's still my cousin."

He ignored her logic and kissed her roughly. He could tell she liked it. She was no longer trying to pull away from him. He pulled her body until she was flat on her back and he lay on top of her. He kissed her neck and slid his hand under her shirt. She moaned and begged him to stop what he was doing. He ignored her again.

He unzipped her pants and heard the doorbell ringing.

They both jumped up, straightening their clothing, and Anise tried to fix her hair.

"Were you expecting someone?" he asked.

"No," she said, walking through the house and to the front door.

His chest elevated rapidly, and he took deep breaths, trying to calm down. He couldn't believe someone had interrupted them.

He heard a voice that he didn't recognize.

"Curtis, you've met Monica before," Anise said, referring to her best friend.

"I have, but it's been a while. How are you?"

"I'm good. How are you?" she said. Curtis could tell she was suspicious. She seemed uncomfortable.

"I'm fine."

"Anise, I didn't realize you had company. I can come back if you want."

"No, not at all," Curtis said. "Actually, I've taken up too much of Anise's time anyway, so don't mind me at all. It was good seeing you again, though."

"Same here."

Anise walked him outside.

"Are you going to be okay?" she asked.

"I doubt it. Not after your friend just wandered in here and ruined everything," he said, smiling.

Anise smiled with him. "Some things just aren't meant to be."

"Maybe. But that still doesn't change the way we feel about each other."

She backed away from the car. "Good-bye, Curtis."

"Good-bye." He sat in his vehicle and backed out of the driveway, watching her the entire time.

Now what?

Chapter 27

CHARLOTTE TURNED THE TELEVISION TO SHOWTIME AND DROPPED the channel selector onto the bed. A rerun of *Soul Food* was in progress. She watched bits and pieces of it, but she had a hard time concentrating on the story line because her mind kept focusing on Curtis and Matthew. She'd lost her closest friend and cousin, and now Curtis insisted that their marriage was over. She had no idea how she would explain any of this to her son. He would never survive without Curtis, and her parents would jump through the roof once they learned what was going on. They would blame her for everything and rightfully so.

She'd spent the last two hours trying to figure out what she could do to save her family, but she hadn't come up with anything Curtis would go for. She'd even thought about swallowing a handful of Tylenol, anything to get his attention. She'd even considered packing up Matthew and taking him as far away as she could so that Curtis would see how much he missed him. But she wasn't sure whether that would actually work or not, since Curtis seemed dead set on divorcing her, anyway.

More than anything, she wished she could confide in another woman. She hadn't even told her aunt when she'd dropped off a set of clean clothing for Matthew. He was spending the night with her aunt for obvious reasons, but Charlotte had left her under the impression that she and Curtis simply needed some time alone together.

She turned down the volume of the TV, slid across the bed, and looked out the bedroom window. She thought she'd heard a noise of some kind, but she didn't see anything. She looked outside for more than a minute and then got back in bed. She glanced at the security keypad on the wall to make sure it was still on. She was glad they had access to it in two separate locations.

She tried getting back into *Soul Food,* but after a few minutes the phone rang. She grabbed it quickly, without checking the caller ID screen, hoping it was Curtis.

"I'm giving you one more chance to leave him," Aaron said.

This was it. Charlotte was going to put a stop to this once and for all. She would call the police as soon as she hung up on this maniac.

"Aaron, this is the last phone conversation that you and I will ever have. I don't want you, I don't love you, and I never did. So will you please stop calling here?"

"You don't mean that."

"Trust me. I meant every single word."

"Don't do this, Charlotte. I'm warning you."

"I'm calling the police, Aaron."

"If I were you, I wouldn't do that."

"Well, I am."

"Fine. Have it your way," he said and hung up.

Charlotte dialed the police immediately.

*   *   *

Curtis parked in front of the convenience store and walked inside. He went down the last aisle, pulled open one of the refrigerator doors, and pulled out a twenty-ounce bottle of Sprite.

"That's all?" he heard a woman say. "A bottle of soda?"

Curtis turned to look at her and couldn't help smiling. It was the woman he had been exchanging seductive stares with during service a few weeks ago.

"So how are you?" he asked.

"I'm fine. Shocked to see you, though."

"I guess we both are."

"Do you always hang out in stores like this?"

"No. Not especially, but since I was thirsty, I stopped at the first place I saw."

"Oh," she said. "Well, it's good seeing you."

She looked at him as though she wanted to have sex with him right where they were standing. Her big brown eyes and perfect body were driving him crazy. He was having those ungodly thoughts again. But what did he care?

Curtis followed her up to the cashier, where two teenagers stood in front of them. When it was her turn, the woman placed two bottles of water and a bag of cashews on the counter and paid for them. Right after, Curtis did the same and noticed that she was waiting at the door. When he started toward her, she walked outside.

As luck would have it, they were parked right next to each other.

Curtis leaned against his Escalade. "So what's your name?"

"Does it matter?"

"Well, yeah. I think it does. It's not like I make a habit of standing in store parking lots on Friday nights talking to strange women."

"But you've seen me at your church a couple of times, so technically, I'm not a stranger."

Curtis would never admit it, but he sort of liked the idea of *not* knowing who she was. Mystery was sometimes a good thing—kept life a lot more interesting.

"Are you married?"

She showed him a bare ring finger.

Curtis laughed. "Is that supposed to mean something? For all I know, you could have left it at home or dropped it inside your purse."

"What if I am?" she said.

"Then I guess you just are."

"But I do know that you're married, right?"

"Yeah. But I'm not denying it either."

"So are you headed home to your wife right now?"

"That depends."

"On?"

"You and whether you have something more exciting for me to do."

"Well, that was pretty straightforward."

"I meant for it to be. I've had a very long and frustrating day, so why talk in circles?"

"I hear you."

"So do you wanna go somewhere?"

"Where'd you have in mind?"

"If you're game, then just follow me."

"Whatever you say," she said and hopped in her Mercedes 500. There was definitely some major money involved here. She looked good in her Versace jeans and white T-shirt, but he could tell she wasn't the corporate type. If he'd been a betting man, he'd bet his money on her having a wealthy husband. But it wasn't his place to worry about it.

Curtis pulled onto the street and heard his car phone ringing.

"Hello?"

"Didn't I tell you and Charlotte what was going to happen if you didn't listen to me?" Aaron said. "Didn't I?"

"Your ass is mine, Aaron, the next time I see you."

"Really? Well, if I were you, I'd come see me right now, standing in front of your house. As a matter of fact, I would get here as fast as I could."

"Negro, what have you done?"

"I'm telling you," he sang. "You'd better come see about the little wifey."

Curtis hit the off button and pulled to the side of the road. He ran back to the Mercedes 500 and told the woman he had an emergency. He never even waited for her response. He jumped back into his SUV and drove well over the speed limit. He didn't feel good about that call from Aaron. He hung corners like a professional race car driver. When he pulled in front of his house, he was glad he had. His home was in flames.

He jumped out, leaving the door open, and ran toward the house. Neighbors had already formed a crowd, and sirens were screaming in the not too far distance. Curtis forced his way through the crowd and up to the front door. He was sure that Charlotte and Matthew were still in there.

"Hey, Curtis, man," Aaron said. "Did I do good or did I do good?"

Curtis punched Aaron with his right fist and shoved him to the ground. Then he slid his key inside the lock.

"Oh my God, I don't think you should go in there," he heard someone say.

"That poor woman and child," spoke another.

Curtis forced the door open and braced himself when the smoke hit him in his face. He held one of his hands across his nose and mouth and ran upstairs. He didn't see Matthew, but Charlotte was lying just outside of their bedroom. He picked her up and struggled back downstairs, coughing and choking. A fireman met him and helped carry her out.

"I don't know where my son is," Curtis said, preparing to go back in.

"Sir, please. Let us handle this. We've got other men in there right now, and if your son is in there, they'll find him."

Curtis prayed that Matthew wasn't in the house. He tried paying attention to Charlotte and to what the paramedics were doing, but he couldn't stop looking toward the doorway of the house. When he saw one of the firemen come back out and shake his head, he pulled out his cell phone and called Charlotte's aunt.

"Aunt Emma, this is Curtis. Is Matthew with you?"

"Yes. He's been here all evening. Why? Where is Charlotte?"

"Our house is on fire, and we're heading over to the hospital. I'll call you from the ambulance to let you know which one."

"Oh dear God," she said. "I'll get Matthew ready right now. And you make sure you call me."

"I will."

Curtis silently thanked God. Matthew was safe and in good care. Curtis watched the medics start an IV on Charlotte, and they'd started oxygen before that.

"Will my wife be okay?"

"She's unconscious, and we really need to get her to the hospital."

Curtis followed the stretcher toward the ambulance and then saw Aaron lurking in the crowd. He wanted to kill him with his bare hands. The satisfaction he would gain would be worth serving a life sentence. Aaron had officially ruined his life in every respect. But Curtis had a son, daughter, and wife who needed him, so it was better to let the police handle Aaron.

"Officers," Curtis said. "That's the man who set our home on fire." Four police officers rushed toward Aaron and forced him to the ground. They handcuffed him and then pulled him back to his feet. Without hesitation, they dragged him to one of the squad cars while reading him his rights.

"Officers," Aaron said. "You're arresting the wrong man. You want that guy over there." He nodded his head toward Curtis. "He's the one who slept with my wife and tried to take my son, Matthew, from me. And wait a minute, where are they taking Charlotte? Where are they taking my wife?"

The medical personnel lifted Charlotte into the ambulance, and Curtis hopped inside with her. As they drove away, he watched the firefighters working. Hopefully, the fire wouldn't destroy the entire residence, but he could already tell that the smoke damage was going to be horrendous. The entire house was filled with thick black clouds. But that was the least of his worries now. He'd been angry and hurt and wanted to leave Charlotte, but at this very moment, he couldn't deny that he still loved her. Maybe not in the way he once had, but he did care about her. He couldn't deny that even she deserved to be forgiven the same as Tanya had told him. Regardless of what that DNA test had determined, she was the mother of his son, and it was time he started acting like it. He was sorry for the episode with Anise and sorry for what he had been planning to do with that woman in the 500. He was ashamed to think what he would have done with her if Aaron hadn't called him.

Curtis watched his wife all the way to the hospital and prayed that she would be fine.

Chapter 28

AS SOON AS THE PARAMEDICS HAD ANNOUNCED WHICH HOSPITAL THAT they were headed to, Curtis had called Aunt Emma again. Now, they were rushing Charlotte through the emergency entrance, and Curtis followed alongside her. He followed until one of the staff members politely stopped him and told him that he would have to wait outside. He wasn't too happy about it, but he understood. He paced the hallway for maybe ten minutes until one of the registration clerks asked him to sign a few documents. They asked him general questions about insurance and Charlotte's medical history and then made a copy of his insurance card. He was glad they'd purchased a health-care policy that covered hospital stays in their entirety because at times like these it was worth it.

When he finished, he took a seat in the waiting room and scanned the area. For a Friday evening, the emergency department wasn't all that full, and Curtis was relieved. He wasn't really in the mood for a group of strangers. He was worried to death about Charlotte, he was still thinking about Matthew, and he needed some quiet time for meditation. He prayed silently for a few minutes and then realized he hadn't called Charlotte's parents. He dialed the number and waited.

"Hello?" his mother-in-law answered.

"Hey, Noreen, it's Curtis."

"Hi, Curtis. How are you?"

"Not good. We just brought Charlotte into the emergency room."

"For what? Is she okay?"

"We don't know yet. She was still unconscious when we got here, but they're in there working on her now."

"Oh my God. What happened?"

"Somebody set our house on fire, and she was there when it happened."

"What? And where's Matthew?"

"He was at your sister's house."

"Joe and I are on our way."

"We're at Mitchell Memorial."

"We'll call for the directions to the hospital when we get there."

"Sounds good."

"You call me on my cell phone if she gets worse."

"I will."

"We'll see you in a couple of hours."

Curtis leaned his head back and breathed deeply. He glanced at the doorway and then closed his eyes. He knew they'd just gotten started with Charlotte, but to him, minutes were starting to feel like hours. What if something happened to her? How would he explain any of it to Matthew? But Curtis knew this wasn't the way for him to be thinking. It was better for him to execute his faith and hope for the best.

He walked over to the doorway, the one that they'd wheeled

Charlotte through, but he couldn't see anything. He was so anxious to know what was going on and his nerves were getting the best of him. Guilt was eating at him even more so. He couldn't help wondering if his latest actions were the reason God had allowed another tragedy to evolve. Maybe if he'd willfully forgiven Charlotte, this wouldn't be happening. Maybe if he hadn't tried to get with Anise or the woman he'd connected with a few hours ago, Charlotte would be home safe and sound. But he knew there were no answers to his questions or theories.

"Dad," Matthew said, running toward him. "Where's Mom? I wanna see Mom."

"She's in there with the doctors, son, and they haven't come out yet."

"What's wrong with her?"

"Our house caught on fire and she got hurt."

"I want to see her." Tears rolled down Matthew's face.

"I know, son. I want to see her, too, but we have to wait."

"No word yet?" Aunt Emma asked, rubbing Curtis's back.

"No. Nothing."

"Well, we'll hear something soon. And don't you worry, God is running this."

Curtis smiled and hoped she was right. He knew that God was in control, but the human side of him wasn't too sure how this would work out. He needed one of those doctors to explain Charlotte's condition.

Shortly after, Anise and Monica arrived.

"Curtis, I am so sorry," Anise said, hugging him.

"Thanks."

"I'm sorry, too," Monica added.

"Thanks for coming," Curtis said.

"Why don't we all go sit down?" Aunt Emma suggested.

They each found a seat.

"What do you think started the fire?" Anise asked.

"We don't know yet," he lied. He would certainly tell them, but he didn't want to discuss anything in front of Matthew.

"Is our house burned down to the ground, Dad?"

"I don't think so. But I'm not sure, because I rushed over here with your mom."

"Where will we live if it did?"

"I don't know. But we're going to be okay. I promise you."

"But what about Mom?" he asked, sobbing again.

Curtis wanted to cry with him, but he didn't.

"Your mom is going to be just fine."

Matthew leaned his head against his father's shoulder, and Curtis placed his arm around him. He held him and knew that he could never leave Matthew the way he'd contemplated. During the ride over in the ambulance, he'd decided that he wouldn't leave him or Charlotte, but watching and holding his son confirmed his decision. He could never live without Matthew under any circumstances.

The waiting game continued for another half hour, and then finally someone came out to speak to them.

"Mr. Black?" said a late fortysomething man.

"Yes?" Curtis said, standing and shaking his hand.

"I'm Dr. Rivers."

"How's my wife?"

"Well, she's a tough young lady, and it's a good thing she got here when she did. There were no burns, but she did have smoke inhalation. It was very minor, but it still knocked the wind out of her."

"Is she going to be okay?"

"It will take a few days for her to gain her strength, but she should be fine after that."

"Thank you, Lord," Aunt Emma commented.

"Can I go see her?" Matthew asked.

"Not for a while," Dr. Rivers said, smiling. "But I'll make sure to tell her about the young man who's dying to see her."

"She's my mom, and my name is Matthew."

"Well, Matthew, I know she can't wait to see you, too."

"How long will it be?" Curtis asked.

"We want to do a few more tests, monitor her vitals, and then get her admitted to a room. After that, you should be able to look in on her for a few minutes."

"How long do you think she'll be here?"

"Depending on how she does tomorrow, we should be able to release her the day after. But I definitely want to follow up with your family physician tonight, so hopefully he's on call."

"Is she awake?"

"As a matter of fact, she came to a short while ago, but now she's out again. The medicine we're giving her will keep her slightly sedated for the rest of the evening. But this is a good thing because it will allow her to get the rest that she needs."

"So now, I guess, all we can do is wait, right?" Curtis said, mostly for Matthew's benefit.

"Pretty much. But before I go, are there any questions?"

Curtis looked at Anise, Monica, and Aunt Emma, but they shook their heads no.

"I don't think so," Curtis told him.

"Well, if you do, be sure to let us know. And it was good meeting all of you."

"Thank you, doctor," the adults spoke together.

"Thank you," Matthew added.

Dr. Rivers turned back around. "You're quite welcome, Matthew. And don't you worry about your mom, we're going to take very good care of her."

Matthew's face lit up, and Curtis was glad to see it.

They all sat and talked distractedly until Charlotte's parents walked in. They'd phoned Curtis about twenty minutes before, saying they'd made it to town.

"Noreen, Joe," Curtis said, standing up to greet them.

"Have you heard anything else?" Noreen asked.

"No, not since you called me for the directions. I know you're worried, but she really is going to be fine. The doctor seemed to be sure of it."

"I hope so," Noreen said sadly.

"She will."

"So how is everyone else?" Noreen said.

"We're fine, Aunt Noreen," Anise said, hugging her. Then she hugged Charlotte's father.

"How are you, Emma?" Noreen asked her sister.

"I'm fine, Noreen. You?"

"I'm okay."

Curtis listened and realized that there was still tension between his wife's mother and her aunt. He'd known about Noreen sleeping with Aunt Emma's future husband, but after all these years, he was shocked that they still weren't past it. Aunt Emma was a wonderfully kind and gentle woman, but she still hadn't forgiven her sister—or at least it didn't seem like it to him. But who was he to criticize anyone?

"And you, Joe?" Aunt Emma said.

"I'm well, Emma, and it's good to see you."

"This is my best friend, Monica," Anise told them.

"It's nice to meet you, Monica," they said.

"It's nice to meet both of you."

Noreen and Joe sat down and looked over at Matthew. His head was lying across Aunt Emma's lap, and he was sound asleep. Curtis could tell that Noreen wasn't all that happy about it, but she didn't say anything. Joe smiled at his grandson and didn't seem to mind whose lap he was lying on. It was obvious that Joe didn't have one problem with his sister-in-law.

Curtis glanced at Anise; she caught him doing it, and they both looked away from each other very quickly. Noreen and Aunt Emma weren't the only two with a lot of stress between them. He wondered if this attraction between Anise and him would ever settle, especially since it was incredibly strong. It was so strong, he almost couldn't stand it. He felt bad, though, when he thought about Charlotte and what she was going through. He knew, instead, that his mind should have been on her and her recovery. But once again, he couldn't help it. He didn't want to have these thoughts or feelings, but he didn't know how to stop them.

A short, sort of stocky woman walked out to the waiting area.

"Are you the Black family?"

"Yes, we are," Curtis said.

"Well, we're about to take Charlotte up to the room she'll be admitted to, and Dr. Rivers wanted me to come see if the rest of the family would like to see her for a few minutes. You'll be able to stay with her in her room overnight if you want, but he would really like everyone else to come back in the morning. He wants her to get as much sleep as she can."

"Sure."

"We usually allow two at a time in the examination room, so whoever wants to go first can come with me."

"Joe and Noreen, you go ahead," Curtis said.

"Are you sure?" Noreen asked.

"Yes, go, because I'll be with her all night."

"Well, maybe Matthew should come with us."

"That's fine."

Noreen went over and rubbed her grandson's face and called out to him. He struggled to open his eyes and then stretched his arms. Then he realized who was standing in front of him.

"Grandma. Grandpa."

"How's my baby doing?" Noreen asked.

"Good."

"You want to go see your mom?" Joe said.

"Yep."

"Then let's go."

The three of them followed the nurse and stayed with Charlotte for five or six minutes. Anise and Aunt Emma went next, and Monica stayed behind. Curtis had wondered whether Anise was going to go in or not, but he knew Charlotte would be glad to see her.

"So how was Mom doing?" Curtis asked Matthew.

"There were a lot of machines in there with some numbers on the screen, and she had something sticking in her arm, too. It looked like a needle."

"Is that right. But did she talk to you?"

"Yep, but she was real sleepy."

"Did you tell her you love her?"

"Yep, and she told me, too."

"Well, that's good."

"Can I stay here with you?"

"No, you'd better go home with Aunt Emma, and she can bring you back in the morning."

"But I want to stay here with you and Mom."

"I know you do, but I want you to go get some sleep so that you can stay here most of the day tomorrow."

Matthew frowned but didn't say anything else.

"I was thinking that Matthew could come stay at the hotel with Joe and me," Noreen offered.

"That's fine with me, but his clothes are over at Aunt Emma's."

"Oh, I didn't realize that. Then, Matthew, we'll just see you in the morning."

"Okay," he said, and his grandmother kissed him good-bye. His grandfather patted him on the back.

Right after they'd left, Anise and Aunt Emma came back out and also prepared to leave.

"Dad, why can't I stay?" Matthew started up again.

"I already explained that to you. Now you go with Aunt Emma, and I'll see you in the morning. You can call me when you wake up."

"All right," he said in a whining tone.

"Well, I guess we'll go, but you call us if you need to," Aunt Emma told Curtis.

He embraced her. "I will. And thanks for everything."

"We'll see you later, Curtis," Anise said, hugging him.

"Thanks for coming."

Curtis hugged Matthew, and then Matthew joined the others over near the exit. He turned back around and looked at Curtis.

"Bye, Dad. I love you."

"I love you, too, Matthew."

Curtis watched them leave and felt his knees weaken. He and Charlotte could never let anyone, especially Anise's ex-husband, find out about that paternity test. Curtis would never let anyone take *his* son away from him. He would die before he ever allowed it.

Chapter 29

CURTIS OPENED HIS EYES, LOOKED OVER AT THE NURSE, AND WATCHED her checking his wife's blood pressure. It was already seven in the morning, but Curtis hadn't slept more than what seemed like a couple of hours. Which was just the opposite of Charlotte, who had awakened only a couple of times, and even then, it had been for maybe a minute. Noreen had called to check on her around three and then again just an hour ago, but Curtis still hadn't heard from Matthew. Curtis had known how tired he was, which was the reason he'd told him to go home with Aunt Emma.

The nurse smiled at Curtis and left the room, and Curtis thought about the fire. He thought about Aaron and wondered why he'd done the things he'd done—although it was quite obvious to Curtis now that Aaron had flipped out completely. He definitely had a mental condition and was a threat to every human being. Curtis wondered what ludicrous story Aaron had told the police, and Curtis was surprised that no one from the MPD had come to question him. But if he had to guess, they were probably waiting on a report from the fire department. If

Curtis didn't hear from them by late morning, though, he would contact them.

He sat another hour, almost dosing off, when he heard Charlotte calling him.

"Are you okay?" he asked, leaning toward the bed.

"I'm fine. I feel a little weak, but that's about it."

"Are you in any pain?"

"My side hurts a little bit."

"The nurse said it's from the fall you took when you passed out."

"What happened? I mean, how did the house catch on fire?"

"Aaron did it. I didn't see him do it, but I know for a fact that he did."

Charlotte cried silently.

"There's definitely something wrong with him," Curtis continued. "And I'm just glad you weren't killed. And thank God Matthew wasn't at home with you."

"Curtis, I am so sorry. I mean, I know it doesn't change anything, but I don't know what else to say."

"It's all unfortunate, but what we have to do now is move forward."

"Do you know how much damage was done?"

"No, but as soon as your mom and dad get here, I'm leaving to go check on it."

"Can you raise my bed up for me?"

Curtis pressed the remote, and Charlotte told him when she was comfortable.

"Are you hungry?" he asked.

"Not really. Where's Matthew?"

"He went home with Aunt Emma."

"And Mom was okay with that?"

"I don't think she was, but that's where his clothes were, so she didn't argue about it."

"I can't believe she and Aunt Emma still don't have much to do with each other."

"It's too bad, but sometimes people hold grudges forever when they've been hurt."

Charlotte looked at him and he knew why.

"Curtis, I really hate to bring this up, but I can't think about anything else."

"What is it?"

"I need to know if you're still planning to divorce me."

"I've thought about that all night. When you were unconscious and we were riding to the hospital, I knew for sure that I couldn't leave you and Matthew. But then throughout last night I kept wondering if you and I would ever get back to where we used to be."

"Curtis, I'm begging you—"

"Wait," he interrupted. "Just let me finish."

"Sorry."

"I decided that we've both made mistakes and that I am willing to try to make this work. But I want you to know that my main reason for staying is because of Matthew. I love him too much to be without him, and I would never do anything to hurt him."

"I know I don't deserve you, but thank you for not leaving me. Thank you for not leaving our son," she said, grabbing his hand. "And even if it kills me, I'll make everything great between us again."

Curtis didn't know if that was possible or not, but he hoped she was right. He hoped that they could go on and that he would learn to love her the way he once had. But there were definitely no guarantees.

Dr. Rivers walked in.

"So how's my wonderful patient this morning?"

"Tired," Charlotte said. "But I guess I'm fine otherwise."

"Well, I will say this, it's a good thing your husband found you when he did. Otherwise, that smoke would have filled your lungs completely."

"I know, and I'm very thankful."

"Plus, we wouldn't have wanted to lose both you and the little one all at the same time."

Curtis squinted his eyes.

He looked at Charlotte, who wouldn't look back at him, and then he looked at the doctor.

"Little one?" Curtis said.

"Oh, you two didn't know? You're pregnant."

Curtis cracked up laughing. Not because it was funny but because he didn't want to believe that Charlotte was pregnant and that *this* child might not be his either. He wondered if God was playing some sort of joke on him. And if He was, why was He trying Curtis's faith to such an extreme? It was almost as if He was trying to force him out of the ministry and back to his old ways again. Maybe God just didn't realize how little Curtis could take. If He did, He wouldn't be allowing any of this.

"How far along is she?" Curtis finally asked.

"Give or take a few days, maybe about eight weeks."

"But the baby is okay?" Charlotte wanted to know.

"I'm sure it is, but you should make an appointment to see an ob-gyn as soon as possible."

"I will."

"Well, I'm pretty sure your family doctor will be coming in before the morning is over, so I'm going to get out of here."

"When do I get to go home?"

"Well, with the way you're going, I would say sometime tomorrow."

"Thanks, Dr. Rivers."

"No problem. Both of you take care."

Curtis got up and closed the door and then stood at the foot of the bed. "Did you know?"

Charlotte swallowed hard. "I was afraid to tell you."

"You knew about this, and you still decided to keep it from me? Why?"

"Because we were already having all these problems, and I knew this was going to make things worse."

"You are really something else. And to think I was prepared to stay with you. You are such a liar."

"But, Curtis, this baby might bring us closer together."

"How?" he yelled.

"Curtis, please. We're in a hospital."

"I don't care where the hell we are. How in the world did you think a baby that probably isn't mine would bring us closer together?"

"But what if it is yours? What if this baby belongs to you, Curtis?"

"No, the question is, what if it belongs to crazy-ass Aaron? Then what?"

"I'll do what I was planning to do before you found out."

"Which is what?"

"I'll have an abortion."

"You are really going to make me hate you, you know that?"

"We can find out if you're the father before the baby is even born."

"Whatever, Charlotte," Curtis said, slipping on his shoes.

"No, really. When we were at the DNA clinic, I read that a paternity test can be done before a child is even born."

"I don't care what you read," Curtis said, grabbing his keys.

"Then what do you want me to do?"

"I really don't care, but what I do know is that no more babies are coming into my household—especially babies that don't belong to me."

"But—"

"But nothing," he shouted and stormed past his in-laws who were standing outside the doorway. He wondered how long they'd been standing there, but it really didn't matter.

As for Charlotte, she was lucky he hadn't snatched her out of that bed, beating her down to the ground. She was lucky that he just might consider allowing her to have that prenatal test. He might consider it because every man deserved to have a son—a biological son, no less.

Of course, he would never love Matthew any differently, but this new child might actually be his own flesh and blood. It was a possibility that he couldn't ignore even if he wanted to. He had to find out what the truth was.

"What was that all about?" Joe asked Charlotte and closed the door behind them.

"Daddy, Mom, please sit down."

"Are you okay?" Noreen asked.

"I'm fine. But I need to tell you a few things."

"Like what?" Joe asked. "And what was Curtis talking about when he said that no more babies were coming into his household if they didn't belong to him?"

At that very moment, Charlotte knew she had to tell her parents everything. Curtis had insisted that she not tell anyone about Matthew, but they'd already heard too much of his conversation. There was no way she could lie to her father and mother, and she didn't want to. If nothing else, they deserved to know the truth about their grandson. Not to mention, she was tired of all the lying.

"Matthew is not Curtis's son."

"What do you mean he's not Curtis's son?" Joe raised his voice.

"He's not. Curtis wasn't the only man I was with when Matthew was conceived."

"Lord Jesus," Noreen said.

"Then who is his father?" Joe asked.

"David is."

"David who?"

"Anise's husband."

"This just can't be," he said.

"Well, it is, Daddy. I slept with David more than once, and we had a DNA test done on Matthew this past week."

"Does he know?" Noreen asked.

"No, and Curtis doesn't want us to ever tell him."

"Do you think that's the right thing to do?" Noreen asked.

"Hell, yeah, it's the right thing to do," Joe said. "Do you want Matthew's life to be ruined? You know how much that boy loves his father, so this needs to stay between all of us and us only."

"Oh God, Charlotte," Noreen said. "Honey, why?"

"Just stop it, Noreen," Joe demanded. "And stop questioning Charlotte about something she probably got from you in the first place."

"Joe!" she said.

"Daddy, please don't do this."

"Well, it's true. If your mother hadn't slept with your aunt Emma's fiancé, maybe you wouldn't have thought it was okay to sleep with your own cousin's husband. I begged your mother not to tell you about that, *but no*, she wanted her only child to know the truth about her. And this is what the result is."

"Daddy, it's not Mom's fault. This was something I did on my own."

"Maybe, but it's not like you had a good example to follow when it comes to women sleeping around with more than one man."

"Joe, why are you talking like this?" Noreen asked.

"Because I've been wanting to talk about this for years. You always told Charlotte way too much of your business when she was a child. You were so busy trying to be her friend that you forgot to be her mother."

Charlotte screamed out in tears. "Daddy, stop it."

"Joe, this isn't the time or the place for this."

"It is if I say it is. And don't stop me again. I'll talk until I'm finished. And don't get me started on the time you were messing around with that asshole, Raymond, and you had the audacity to take Charlotte around him. She was only six, Noreen, and that child came home asking me who that strange man was. I remember feeling like such a fool and that's why I went off on you. But even after that, you wouldn't stop seeing him. You slept with him whenever you wanted to until finally, he just up and died. And that took five years."

Noreen sniffled and sat down in the chair.

"Daddy, I said stop it," Charlotte ordered. "I did what I did, and this has nothing to do with Mom."

Joe folded his arms and glared at his wife.

Charlotte couldn't believe what she was hearing. She'd heard them argue about this very thing before, but it had been years since her father had brought any of it up. Charlotte had been sure that her parents had gotten past those terrible times and that they were a very happy couple. They always seemed happy in front of her and everyone else, so she was stunned by what she'd just witnessed. It was so unlike him, but her father seemed angry enough to hurt her mother. He looked at her the way Curtis had looked at Charlotte only minutes before.

"The news about Matthew isn't the whole story," she said. "I'm pregnant again, and I don't know if this child is Curtis's either."

"Oh God, no," Noreen said. "Charlotte, baby."

"You're just full of surprises, aren't you?" Joe said.

"I made some mistakes, Daddy. I'm not perfect."

"You know some of this is my fault, too. I spoiled you rotten, and I should have never done that."

"Baby, what are you going to do?" Noreen asked.

"There's a DNA test that I can have before the baby is born, so all I can do is pray for the best. And if it's not Curtis's, then I don't know what's going to happen."

"Charlotte, I'm so sorry. I'm sorry for any influence I may have had on you when you were growing up. Your father is right, I shouldn't have exposed you to some of the things I did."

"Mom, it's okay."

"No, it's not."

Charlotte didn't argue with her any further.

Her father sat down in the other chair and didn't say anything.

Charlotte wondered where Curtis was and what he was thinking. If only she could guarantee that the baby she was carrying was actually his. There just had to be a way. She didn't want to lie and scheme again, but she would do anything to stay married to him. She needed him to be there for Matthew, and God help her, she needed the lifestyle that Curtis was now in a position to give her. She wasn't sure what she had to do to keep her family together, but she had to think quickly.

She thought long and hard, trying to figure out her next move. Her family physician had come in, and shortly after, her aunt Emma and Matthew had arrived. But now they'd left with her parents to get lunch. Well, actually, Matthew had gone with her parents, but Aunt Emma had made up some excuse about having to run a few errands.

Charlotte's mind raced back and forth until, finally, she realized just who could help her. She couldn't believe she hadn't thought of her before, especially since she'd told Charlotte to call her anytime.

The law firm was strict on its policy about not disturbing their clients on a Saturday, but then, this particular call had absolutely nothing to do with business. It was as personal as personal could be, so the fact that this wasn't a weekday was irrelevant.

Charlotte lifted the phone and dialed Meredith Connolly Christiansen, the richest woman in town.

Chapter 30

As soon as Curtis had left the hospital, he had gone to the police station to see what the deal was with the investigation. When he arrived, two detectives were preparing to drive over to the hospital to obtain a statement from him and Charlotte. Curtis went ahead and answered their questions right there in the office. He told them everything they wanted to know, including the fact that Charlotte was having an affair with Aaron and how he'd been stalking and harassing them ever since she'd stopped seeing him. He told them how Aaron had come into the church, disrupting service, and that any of the members would be happy to testify about it. He even told them how he'd considered Aaron his best friend and how Aaron had changed so suddenly and then started making some very strange statements.

But none of what Curtis had said was a shock to the detectives, because they'd already learned a ton about Aaron's true identity. The man Curtis had known as Aaron Malone had been born as Donovan Wainright. Donovan had been in and out of mental institutions for most of his life and apparently had convinced a psychiatrist in Michigan that he was no longer insane and the institution had released him. As early as eighteen, he'd been diagnosed with paranoid schizophrenia, but whenever he took his prescribed medication, he was as normal as the next person. He was able to function and interact the same as any other human being, and he was clever at it. The fact that he'd successfully taken on a whole new identity was enough to verify his intelligence.

The detectives had also explained how Donovan had set the house on fire. He'd poured gasoline on the side of it and then dropped a match on top. The police assumed he must have phoned Curtis as soon as he'd done it. Curtis was in shock at what they were telling him, but it was still hard to believe that he'd allowed someone like Donovan to endanger his family. He couldn't believe Charlotte was so caught up in him that she, too, couldn't see how sick he was. Donovan had manipulated both of them, and they hadn't even realized it.

He was still being held in custody, but from the way it sounded, he had lost his mind almost completely. The detectives were sure that the public defender would plead not guilty on his behalf by reason of insanity and that Donovan would soon be shipped back to Michigan or to some other long-term facility. Curtis hoped it was sooner rather than later.

When he'd left the station, he'd thought about Charlotte, the baby she was carrying, and the chance that it might belong to Donovan. If it did, there was no telling what kind of nutcase it might turn out to be when it grew up. But there was also the chance that the baby was Curtis's, and if it was, he wanted to know about it. He definitely wanted Charlotte to schedule the test she'd spoken of as soon as possible.

Curtis drove to his house and had to brace himself before he could look at the horrible mess. The structure wasn't burned to the ground the way Matthew had been thinking, but anyone could tell that there had been a fire. He stared at it for a few minutes and then walked up the sidewalk. He stood in one spot for a while and then went inside. The offensive odor was unbearable, and chalky black soot veiled each piece of furniture.

He walked around downstairs and then went up to the master bedroom. In there, not much had been destroyed physically, but the smell was the same or worse than it was on the lower level. Curtis doubted that the smell could ever be removed from their clothing, and he was sure that all of it would have to be replaced. In all honesty, he wasn't sure what they would have to do to make the house livable again. Maybe it was possible, but since he'd never experienced a fire before, he didn't know how the cleaning up and remodeling procedure would be handled. He would call his insurance agent's answering service to start the claim process. In the meantime, he would reserve a hotel suite and later look for more permanent temporary housing.

When he left the house, he went to the mall and purchased new clothing for himself and Matthew. He hadn't wanted to, but he'd also bought a summer jogging suit for Charlotte so that she would have something to leave the hospital in. This whole idea of not having a place to live and not having anything to wear was enough to annoy Curtis. It was enough to make him think about Anise and the woman who drove the 500. When he'd been riding in the ambulance with Charlotte, he'd felt guilty about his earlier actions. But now he wished he'd done what he'd wanted to. He needed some sort of outlet, and for him, sex had always been the answer. It had always been the one thing that satisfied him and made him feel better.

To Curtis, sex was the same as what alcohol must have been to his father. But when Curtis had married Charlotte, he'd worked hard at controlling his obsession and hadn't messed up on her one time. Now, though, things were different. They were far different, and he didn't see any reason why he shouldn't get what he wanted. He saw no reason why he shouldn't be happy. Charlotte had gotten what she'd wanted, and as far as he was concerned, it was his turn. He would take his turn, too, when the time was right.

Epilogue

ONE YEAR LATER.

Charlotte walked into the lavender and green nursery and smiled at her six-month-old daughter, Marissa. Marissa Paulina Black was sleeping peacefully, but Charlotte simply wanted to check on her. She checked on her throughout the entire day, every day, something she'd been doing since the day Marissa was born. Charlotte loved her daughter and everything about her, and she was the reason Charlotte no longer missed her career. Charlotte was now a wealthy stay-at-home mother to both Marissa and Matthew, and she was a soccer mom the same as every other mother in the neighborhood.

She didn't like thinking about it, but the fire had been devastating. It had turned their world upside down, and they'd been forced to rent a much smaller house while they waited for restoration. But as soon as the repairs were finished, they had placed their house on the market. Interestingly enough, it had sold very quickly, and Curtis had finally bought Charlotte her dream home. He'd finally given her five thousand square feet, a brand new Lexus SUV, and a weekly allowance that exceeded what she'd earned when she was working. His column had gone international, and the royalties from his book were coming in every few months. They now had more money than Curtis had ever planned on having, and Charlotte was thrilled about it. She finally had everything she could possibly want—the lifestyle that she had always hoped for.

But it was only because she'd taken matters into her own hands. It was only because Meredith Connolly Christiansen had found the right kind of doctor to perform the right kind of DNA test for the right kind of money. Dr. Middleton had been the kind of doctor who would do whatever he was told as long as he was compensated in the right manner. In this case, he hadn't even tested the fetus because Charlotte purposely hadn't wanted to know the outcome. And once Meredith had paid his price, he'd quickly told Charlotte and Curtis that the baby girl Charlotte was carrying was 99.9 percent Curtis's and that the two of them should start planning for her arrival. Charlotte could still remember the joy on Curtis's face when he'd heard the news. She remembered how that very same day, he'd rushed over to the mall and bought Marissa her first stuffed animal. He'd purchased one item after another until the day she was born, and even now, when he was out of town, doing speaking engagements, he shipped her and Matthew more packages than they could keep up with.

As far as the church was concerned, Curtis and Charlotte were still recognized as founders of Deliverance Outreach, but Curtis had recruited a new senior pastor to take his place. They still attended service on Sundays, although Curtis hadn't been home on a weekend for more than six weeks. He hadn't been home much at all ever since the book had been released, but

Charlotte didn't complain. She missed him a lot, but she knew his traveling was necessary. His agent had told him from the very beginning what his publisher would expect, so neither Charlotte nor Curtis was surprised about it.

Matthew missed him terribly though, so Curtis had promised to take him on the road with him the next time he went out, and Matthew couldn't wait. Curtis had promised to take all of them as soon as Marissa was old enough to fly.

Charlotte peeked at her daughter one last time and then left the nursery. She walked down the hall, down the winding wrought-iron and wooden staircase, and strolled across the black and white marble flooring. When she entered the living room, she looked across the backyard and down at the swimming pool.

She stood there admiring all that she and Curtis had accomplished and realized that life could never be better than it was. She realized how wrong Meredith had been the day she'd told Charlotte that money didn't necessarily make a person happy.

Because even if it didn't, money got you just about everything else you wanted.

Curtis stacked three pillows against the headboard and tried to find something interesting to watch on television. He'd been on the road for a few weeks now, and he was starting to feel a bit exhausted. And he missed his family, too. Not Charlotte, of course, but he definitely missed his children. He missed his handsome little son, his beautiful teenage daughter, and his gorgeous new baby girl—the child who had forced him to stay with Charlotte after all. He hadn't wanted to leave Matthew, but if for some reason Marissa had turned out to be Donovan's daughter, he hadn't seen how he could live with that, how he could stand waking up next to a woman who had deceived him as many times as Char-

lotte had. He'd even planned on fighting her for custody of
Matthew if it had come down to it, but as it had turned out,
Marissa was his baby. She was the light of his life these days, and
he looked forward to the day when he could spend more time
with her. He looked forward to spending time with all three of
his children together.

But in the meantime, while he was out on the road, he did
what he had to do to keep himself occupied. He did what he had
to do to stay satisfied and happy. He spent time with Tabitha, the
woman who owned the 500. He'd purchased for them a little
hideaway, halfway between Mitchell and Chicago, and she'd
been touring with him ever since his book was released. She was
more than Charlotte could ever be to him in a million years. He
couldn't say that he loved Tabitha, but he definitely cared about
her a lot. He cared about her because they were good together in
every way.

But he would never divorce Charlotte, at least not while his
children were growing up, and he was always honest with
Tabitha about that. He was glad that she didn't seem to mind,
but it might have been because she was married herself. Although, as of six months ago, she'd separated from her husband
and filed for a divorce, and the final court date was in two weeks.
The most Curtis could hope for was that she wouldn't start pres-
suring him the way Adrienne had. He could never deal with another high-maintenance relationship and wouldn't.

Then there was his ministry and how he'd given it up once
again. Not to the same extent as the other two times, but this
time he'd given up his position voluntarily. He was still a minister, but he no longer preached in pulpits on Sunday mornings.
Instead, he appeared at churches as a guest speaker and signed
copies of his book right after. It seemed that he had finally

found his true calling. He'd learned that a ministry didn't necessarily mean that God had called you to the pulpit. He'd learned that a ministry could be anywhere, and Curtis was finally content with the work he was doing.

He flipped the channel again, Tabitha nestled closer to him, and Curtis wrapped his arm around her. He loved the way she made him feel, and he appreciated her. They appreciated each other.

From where Curtis was sitting, life for him was the best ever.

And according to Charlotte, she had everything, too.

She had everything except him and didn't even know it.

Acknowledgments

I thank God for guiding my life and for the many blessings You have given me.

Will, for always being in my corner and for making my life so complete. What a loving husband and blessing you continue to be. I love you from the bottom of my heart.

Mom, for teaching me such strong Christian and family values and for instilling great confidence in me. There is not a day that goes by that I don't think about your beautiful smile, your kindness to everyone, and the closeness we shared as mother and daughter. I miss you tremendously.

My brothers, Willie Stapleton, Jr., Michael Stapleton, Dennis Lawson, and the rest of my family members for all of your love and support.

My girls of girls, Lori Whitaker Thurman, Kelli Tunson Bullard, Janell Green, Tammy Roby, and Victoria Christopher Murray for more reasons than I could ever list here. Your many years of friendship have been genuine and it has proven to be the best kind—unconditional.

My author friends whom I proudly share this journey in

publishing with, Patricia Haley (my cousin who I love and grew up with), E. Lynn Harris, Eric Jerome Dickey, Jacquelin Thomas, Trisha R. Thomas, Eric E. Pete, Travis Hunter, Monique Jewell Anderson, C. Kelly Robinson, Vincent Alexandria, and so many others.

My agent, Elaine Koster (for everything); my editor, Carolyn Marino (for the same reason); Jennifer Civiletto (for your patience and pleasantness); my in-house publicist, Diana Harrington Tynan (for your diligence and compassion); and all of the other wonderful people at HarperCollins/William Morrow who I am blessed to work with throughout the year.

My Web site designer, Pamela Walker Williams, at Pageturner.net for your genuine dedication to all of your clients; and to my freelance publicist, Tara Brown, for working so hard to get the word out about my books.

All of the bookstores nationally who sell my work, every person in the media who publicizes it (newspaper, magazine, radio, television, and on-line), and all of the book clubs and individual readers who read my stories. This is my seventh time out, and I thank each of you for helping to make my career what it is today. I will never forget you.

At Avon Books, we know your passion for romance—once you finish one of our novels, you find yourself wanting more.

May we tempt you with . . .

- **Excerpts** from our upcoming releases.

- Entertaining **extras**, including authors' personal photo albums and book lists.

- Behind-the-scenes **scoop** on your favorite characters and series.

- **Sweepstakes** for the chance to win free books, romantic getaways, and other fun prizes.

- Writing **tips** from our authors and editors.

- **Blog** with our authors and find out why they love to write romance.

- **Exclusive content** that's not contained within the pages of our novels.

Join us at
www.avonbooks.com

AVON

An Imprint of HarperCollins*Publishers*
www.avonromance.com

Available wherever books are sold or please call 1-800-331-3761 to order.

*G*ive in to your Impulses!

These unforgettable stories only take a second to buy and give you hours of reading pleasure!

Go to *www.AvonImpulse.com* and see what we have to offer.

Available wherever e-books are sold.

AVONIMPULSE

IMP 0811